BENEATH THE BROKEN

SEASON ONE

SARAH MÄKELÄ

KISSA PRESS LLC

BENEATH THE BROKEN MOON

SEASON ONE

Werewolf relationships are all about influence and offspring, especially as they are becoming extinct. But Carmela Santiago resents that type of life. She dreams of falling in love, not following the example her parents have set.

When sensual vampire Derek Ashmore rescues her from dangerous hunters, she tumbles head over heels for him. Not a wise decision since werewolves and vampires are mortal enemies.

Meeting her caring mate-to-be Brendan Kelly has her further questioning the future. Regardless, her life has forever changed now that she's met not one, but two men who pull at her heartstrings...

This is a why choose paranormal romance where the FMC gets both men. Please read CWs on author's website before reading.

Sign up for Sarah's newsletter for her latest news, giveaways, excerpts, and much more!

http://bit.ly/SarahMakelaVIPList

Editor: Word Vagabond

Cover Artist: Yocla Designs

ISBN-13: 978-1-942873-70-9

PART I

CARMELA

*B*ullets peppered the big screen of the *Teatro de la Noche.* Screams rang out around me, and I dropped to the floor, pulling my cousin Chandra down with me. Tension ached in my shoulders, and my heart pounded in my chest like a trapped animal, desperate to escape.

Gunpowder stung my sensitive nose, but through the overpowering scent, I caught a whiff of a hunter heading our way. "Chandra, we have to move."

If Chandra and I didn't get out of here we'd end up dead —or worse, test subjects for the *Cazador*—human hunters ordered to scour the land of nocturnes by the plutocratic government.

"How? They're all around us." Chandra peeked over the seats before dropping back down beside me. "A few of them are chasing down those who ran from the first assault, but two more are heading straight for us." She ran a manicured hand through her honey-brown hair, which was only a shade darker than my own. "Come on. I have a plan. Let's try to sneak out the side door." She crawled in the opposite direction, down the row of seats.

The sight of my cousin's butt cheeks hanging out of her short skirt filled my vision. Some things were better left unseen. I lowered my gaze, particularly since Chandra had forgone panties. She almost always held herself with an air of power and purpose. Perhaps that's what it took to get attention from other werewolves. Chandra got it in heaps, but her lower social status stopped a lot of relationships.

While it was a horrible time to second-guess my modest fashion sense, I couldn't help wonder if I should take a lesson from my cousin. My own blouse and dark blue jeans had much less pizzazz. But I doubted my father would allow me to dress like Chandra. We had a privileged image to uphold.

I bit my lip, struggling to turn my thoughts back to the problem at hand. This was all too much. How could we get out of here unscathed when the roar of gunfire continued to close in?

We reached the end of the aisle. Chandra moved to glance over the seat, when a shout came from the opposite end, startling us both.

"Run, Chandra!" I barely kept my voice to a whisper.

She sprinted toward the bright red exit sign at the front of the theater, and I chased after her, trying to keep my pace natural though Chandra's long legs made it challenging. Maybe if they suspected we weren't nocturnes, they'd leave us alone.

The stomping of heavy boots on the theater's plush carpets said otherwise. Then again, they weren't opposed to taking their fellow humans down too. The very rich in power thrived on oppressing those less fortunate. What better way to keep the populace down than to have their thugs strike whenever possible.

"We should split up." Chandra shoved a heavy trashcan in front of the door, but that wouldn't be much of an obstacle to the pseudo-military bastards.

"What?" I couldn't believe my ears. "No way. If we do that, we'll—" The trashcan scraped the cement as the hunters tried to open the door. Maybe she was right. If we were together, there was a better chance of them catching us both. Alone, we might survive the night.

I nodded to her, and we took off in opposite directions down the alleyway behind the *Teatro*. The door slammed open, smacking the wall hard, as I turned the corner and headed toward the main street. I had to find somewhere to hide out before the hunters spotted me again.

In front of me, another group of *Cazador* chased a few werewolves down the main road. I slowed to keep my distance from them, but if I didn't get somewhere fast, they were going to catch me. Ugh. As much as I loved getting out of the house and going to the movies, I wished I'd listened to my instincts tonight and stayed home.

Two sets of feet pounded the sidewalk behind me. Perhaps they'd spotted me before I reached the corner.

I picked up speed a little, pumping my arms as I struggled to keep to a human speed while staying out of range. The temptation to race through the streets nearly drove me to action, but I glanced back, seeing my pursuers for the first time.

One of the men had greying hair and a rounded belly, which explained the slower, heavier footfalls, while the other guy appeared younger and super-athletic. No wonder I was having trouble getting away. If he hadn't been so scary, he might've been attractive. Pure masculine aggression raged through him, tensing his shoulders as his gaze focused solely on me, his prize. Each man carried a large-caliber handgun. I was just glad they were too busy running to try to shoot me...for now, at least.

My sandal hit an uneven patch of concrete in the sidewalk. My body lurched forward, but I caught myself before I could go down. I should've been paying more attention to the street. Up ahead on the opposite side of the road, I spotted a dark alleyway running alongside a row house. If I cut through, I could safely turn up the speed without exposing myself and lose them.

The older hunter slowed. His breathing had become increasingly labored. He cocked his revolver's hammer, and I darted across the empty road, making a beeline for the alley. The last thing I wanted tonight was to see Dr. Matthews.

Just a little bit farther.

A bullet smacked the ground at my feet, hitting me with fragments of pavement. I bit back a yelp, not wanting to give them the satisfaction of knowing my fear.

"I got this one, old kook," the younger hunter grumbled, and his footsteps slowed too.

Another gunshot pierced the hazy night air. White-hot pain rocked my shoulder, nearly toppling me to the ground. I screamed, unable to hold it in, and picked up speed, no longer caring if I appeared human or not. The faint creak of a door barely registered before a pair of arms wrapped around my waist, jerking me inside the dark row house.

My rescuer softly shut the door, careful not to make a sound, and shoved a hand over my mouth. "Sshhh," he whispered. "I won't hurt you. You're safe." His voice was deep, with an English accent. He pulled me away from the door and hunched down in the darkened room, holding me close, waiting and listening.

Agony clouded my thoughts, but I couldn't let myself lose focus.

Footsteps thundered through the side alley. I stiffened at the sound. The hunters' harsh voices and the clanking of metal were the only differences between them and a herd of cattle. They made no attempt to disguise themselves, taking delight in the fear they provoked. The *Cazador* weren't true predators, but they held power over their fellow humans and the weaker of the nocturnes.

I stayed silent in my mysterious savior's arms. Thoughts of my cousin Chandra sparked inside my mind. She was still out there. What if the *Cazador* found her and killed her as they'd tried to kill me?

This man had saved my life. I needed to do the same for my kin.

His large hand flexed slightly, crushing my mouth. I placed my hand against his wrist, hoping he'd release me, since I no longer heard the disgusting *Cazador* who hunted me like an animal. How had I gotten myself into this mess?

Shifting my weight, I groaned as my shoulder brushed against his smooth chest, my arm hanging limply by my side. The bullet must be impairing my movement. I doubted even shifting into wolf form would fix this right now. What was I supposed to do? Not even my people were immune to blood loss.

The scent of death crept into my nostrils, which could only mean one thing: my savior was a vampire. In this weakened state, he could easily end my life, and I wouldn't be able to stop him.

But why would he save me? Maybe he required his next meal. An icy shiver slithered down the length of my spine. For the first time, I felt real fear.

If only I'd insisted on returning home from the *Teatro* sooner instead of catching the night's second movie, we wouldn't have been there for the raid. Already my energy waned due to the rocky power of the three raging moons. The added exertion of running from the *Cazador* and getting shot strained my body even more.

Somehow, the *Cazador* had known nocturnes frequented the *Teatro*. Who would give that kind of information away?

Wolves wanted the same pleasures in life that humans desired.

My savior readjusted his grip on me, brushing against my upper back. I swallowed a scream, unwilling to alert anyone who might be listening outside this man's home. This *vampire's* home. Clenching my teeth, I pulled at the vampire's wrist. I would not be his victim.

He remained steadfast, proving my weakness. "Don't scream. Don't run. Don't do anything that would force me to hurt you, because I've had a lot of practice." His crisp voice caressed my ear, and his breath moved tendrils of light brown hair, tickling the flesh on my neck. "Do you understand?"

While he meant the words as a threat, I couldn't help the way my body responded to his intensity. I nodded, forcing my thoughts back into place. If he attacked, I needed to remember my Militia training.

The vampire released me, but he stayed still, as if waiting for my next move.

Slowly and carefully, I scooted away and turned to face him. My eyes had gradually adjusted to the darkness, allowing me to see more clearly in the dimly lit room than a human would. What a sight he was. I brushed my fingertips over my sore lips.

Crouching in the shadows, he wore a navy-blue dress shirt with the buttons undone to show off his pale, sculpted chest, and dark jeans that snugly fit his long legs. I'd only seen a few vampires, and none of them had looked this exquisite.

My eyes widened as he ran a hand through his shoulder-length black hair. His gaze had dropped to my lips, and I lowered my hand. Hunger burned in his deep blue eyes; I prayed it wasn't bloodlust.

What was I thinking? Our species didn't see eye to eye on

anything except survival. The Feud between vampires and werewolves had raged on for centuries now, since well before bickering humans shot the moon with a nuke after a resource dispute and nearly killed the world's population. Little did my ancestors know just how much and how fast the world would change. Instead of bridging the gap, vamps and wolves had grown even further apart. No one remembered what or whom first started the divide, but neither race spent any effort on diplomatic relations.

Kill or be killed.

I took a deep breath and sat a little straighter. With space between us, my fear lessened. The Militia had taught me to defend myself against hunters and other nocturnes. They made sure I wouldn't be easy prey for the enemy. Of course —they preferred to have my womb protected, since it ensured our race would live on.

Bitterness soured my taste buds, and the urge to spit overwhelmed me.

Admittedly, vampires were the hardest foes to defeat, and I couldn't practice my skills much these days. Not with Father keeping me almost literally a prisoner in my own home.

But if I had to fight this vampire, I would go out having inflicted a lot of pain.

"Why did you help me?" I asked, keeping my gaze on the wall near his head. No way would I look into his eyes. While I was strong, I wasn't stupid. His kind could easily manipulate, and I had no idea what he had in mind.

"I think it was your caramel-brown eyes, love." He leaned into my line of sight, but I looked away. Instead, he closed the space between us in a heartbeat and gently stroked his index finger along my jaw.

The sudden intrusion on my personal space had me jerking away, but with my back so close to the wall, I had nowhere to run. "How could it have been my eyes?" I crossed my good arm under my breasts, but that drew his attention down to my chest. Not what I'd intended. "I'm sure you couldn't have seen them while I was running from the hunters."

With a sensual swipe of his tongue, he licked his lips. His gaze lifted to meet mine, but I quickly averted my eyes. "You caught me."

The cool, sensual touch of his fingers trailed toward my neck, then my shoulder. My breath hitched in my throat as his hand skirted the edge of the wound. Everything in me demanded I move away, but I refused to show weakness.

The vampire sucked in a deep breath, and he let it out in a slow lustful shudder. "You're hurt." He raked his gaze over my body, taking in all of me. "Those eyes must have captivated me again." From what I could see, I doubted my eyes were the only thing he liked.

"Right." His playful answers surprised me We were supposed to be enemies. If he wanted to drink my blood, he should just say so. But if that were the case, wouldn't he have attacked already? "I should be going. The *Cazador* are long gone by now, so I won't waste any more of your time." I tucked a leg beneath me to climb to my feet, but the vampire grabbed my wrist, holding me still.

Instinct kicked in, and a low growl of warning rumbled from my throat. My teeth sharpened, and the skin on my arms rippled, ready to welcome my beast. But I shut down the change.

He released me and lifted his arms in surrender. "Where are my manners? My name is Derek. I'm afraid I can't let you leave. You're injured, and the hunters could still capture you. Besides, you might tell your wolves where I live." He smiled without flashing any fangs. Others of his kind wouldn't be able to pull that off. He had to be an ancient. "Let me help you. I was once a doctor."

My eyebrows rose in surprise. Such irony. A man who once pledged himself to healing people now drained them of their life's blood. "All I need to do is shapeshift a few times. That'll fix this."

He rose to his feet as if pulled up by strings, then folded his arms. "Shapeshifting isn't going to solve that." Taking in a deep breath, he shook his head. "Not with a wound so severe. If I wanted to hurt you, I would have done so by now. Besides, I just saved you from the *Cazador*."

I hated that he was right. He'd made no move to harm me, and he'd helped when he didn't have to. Sighing, I leaned my head back, wincing as my shoulder touched the wall. "Why did you save me? If the hunters knew, they'd punish you severely."

"More severely than death?" Derek chuckled. "I'd like to see them try."

I stared up at him, a frown tugging at my lips. No one could argue with his logic. He was a vampire. The worst they could do would be to bring him true death. "I'm Carmela. Thanks for the help. Not many would've done that."

"People are afraid of the 'mighty' hunters." He shrugged his broad shoulders, then held out his hand to me. "They're pathetic compared to us."

While I agreed with what he said, I couldn't suppress my wariness at his help. But I didn't have a choice. I was too badly injured to survive the night without treatment. I reluctantly accepted his hand. He lifted me to my feet as if I weighed nothing, then led the way into his living room.

The luxurious room showcased a large velveteen couch with handsome oak inlay in the shape of a creeping rose vine along the back. I leaned down to brush my hand along the forest-green cushion, amazed at the ornate décor, but a trail of my blood slid toward my wrist.

Pulling away, I wrapped my arm around my waist and took in the rest of the room. No way would I ruin his furniture. "This place looks like a museum. It's breathtaking."

"Hardly. It's my home. I have a room upstairs better suited for tending to you." Derek walked toward the banister of the swooping staircase, but he kept his gaze fixed on me as if I'd run at a moment's notice. That should've been closer to the truth. However, I couldn't help my fascination at the way this vampire lived. I'd never seen such nice things before. How many lifetimes had he spent cultivating his collection? "Coming, Carmela?" He waved for me to follow him.

The sound of my name on his lips pulled me forward. I walked to the steps, but weakness weighed down my limbs. How could I make it home by myself if the thought of climbing the stairs drained me? If he'd been a doctor, I might be okay in his care. Doctors followed a code of ethics. My mother used to be a nurse, and she liked to talk about those days when we were alone.

I took a deep breath, and I only smelled the two of us. Not that I thought I might be walking into a trap, but I couldn't be too careful. My gaze swept back to the living room. I wasn't materialistic, but the blatant show of wealth struck the wishful part of me that hoped for more out of life. I bumped into him as he stopped suddenly on the steps.

"Look, I'm not going to harm you." He cocked an eyebrow at me. "Okay?" Worry tightened his lips for a second, but he flashed a smile.

"Fine. If you say so." The world spun a little, and I clenched the railing in my fist, focusing all of my energy on staying upright. My desire to help Chandra would have to wait. Besides, she'd be okay. She was strong and street-smart.

As far as I knew, the *Cazador* had followed me, not her, and I'd be useless searching for her right now.

However, a small part of me whispered that family didn't abandon one another. *Betrayer*, my thoughts hissed, but I shoved them aside.

My legs shook as I reached the top step. Derek watched me carefully but didn't offer his assistance. He probably knew I wouldn't have accepted it. I wouldn't let my weakness get the better of me in front of him, a possible threat. "You'll stay in my spare room. It's a comfortable space to relax while I care for you." I followed him down the hallway, each step harder than the last, and he opened the door for me. "Here you are."

I stayed put and stood up straighter, hoping he'd get the message and go in first, but he didn't. *Right.*

A red paisley bedspread adorned a heavy oak bed with an abundance of matching pillows, befitting royalty. The bedroom was as polished and pristine as the living room. How could I possibly be comfortable with bleeding all over it? If this was how he decked out his spare room, I could only imagine what his room looked like.

I glanced back at the doorway, where he remained. Our eyes met for the first time from across the room, even though I knew the risks. "Where do you want me?" I asked, wincing at how intimate that sounded. "Here?" Dizziness swayed me, and my knees buckled. Strong arms wrapped around my waist before my body could hit the floor.

Derek's concerned face filled my darkening vision. "Yes, here is fine," he murmured, laying me down on the soft bed. "Don't die on me."

2

CARMELA

*C*andlelight bathed the bedroom in a warm glow. Confusion rippled within me. Where was I? I turned to see Derek perched on a stool beside the bed. My heart skipped a beat, and I fisted my hand in the bedspread. His midnight-blue eyes beckoned me closer, urging me to dive into their deep, churning depths. I ripped myself from the connection and focused on the ceiling.

"You're awake. I was worried." His accented voice was smooth and husky, like sex on silk sheets.

What kind of hold did he have on my mind? Fear tickled my senses, warning me to resist his draw. He leaned forward, and I noticed he'd buttoned his shirt—except for the top and bottom few—no longer exposing his chest. However, with his satin sleeves rolled up, his muscular forearms stole my attention as he rested them on his knees. The faint memory of being held by them warmed me. "I patched your shoulder and extracted what I could of the bullet. Seems it was silver shot."

That made sense. America's government-funded laboratories created wicked toys for the *Cazador* and used

BENEATH THE BROKEN

nocturnes as guinea pigs to test their weapons for maximum efficiency. If Derek hadn't taken care of me, I could've died. "Thank you."

Tears burned in my eyes as I struggled against the pain in order to sit up. My injured arm was bound to my torso in a makeshift cotton sling. Had he done that while I'd slept? Dread knotted in my stomach, and I brushed my fingertips over my throat to check for bite marks.

Derek chuckled, igniting molten heat within me. It chased up my neck and nestled into my cheeks. "I haven't bitten you, if that's what you're wondering. I merely worked on your shoulder. As I said, I used to be a doctor when I was alive."

Sighing, I dropped my hand into my lap. Even though he seemed friendly enough, I didn't want to lower my guard too much. Besides, now that I felt better, I needed to return home and check on my cousin. "Guess I'm off then. Thanks again for helping me." I scooted toward the edge of the bed. A cool breeze blew across my face, and Derek pressed his hands into the bed on either side of my hips. His face was less than two inches from mine. Sensations warred within me: part of me felt a seductive pull of energy from him, while the wolf bristled at the intimidation.

"I'm sorry, but that wouldn't be wise. I can't trust that you wouldn't alert your people about me. The risk is too great." His cool breath caressed my lips, adding to the sensual moment.

The scent of peppermint tickled my nose. I grinned in surprise. Now wasn't the time to burst into laughter over minty vampire breath, but it wasn't every day I witnessed something so...unique.

Derek curled his lip back, showing off pointed fangs, and moved in an inch. "You think what I said is funny?"

Shaking my head, I tried forcing the smile off my face, but

15

I couldn't. "Your breath. It smells like mint." The tension between us built, and if I'd wanted to, I could've just leaned in and tasted his kisses. Would they be minty or taste like death? My body sank forward, until our lips were a hairsbreadth apart.

Whoa. Where were these thoughts coming from? My wolf growled, but she wasn't entirely opposed to Derek. She enjoyed the sight of his muscular physique just as much as I did. The wolf demanded a strong mate who could protect our pups. *Stop it!*

Jerking away, he crossed his arms and stalked toward the window, allowing me a good view of his firm butt.

Embarrassment burned in my cheeks. I couldn't believe I'd been so close to kissing him. *No, no, no...* This wasn't happening. It had to be some kind of Stockholm syndrome because of him saving me. If I didn't leave, I might do something stupid.

I crossed my legs, feeling an unfamiliar ache between them. The raw lust I felt for him only made me more confused about what I should do, never mind who I was. Werewolves did not fantasize about vampires. We were mortal enemies.

Anyway, I should've gone back sooner to check on Chandra. My parents were probably concerned, and the more time that passed, the less understanding my father would be. Yet I stayed here, letting myself get swept up by Derek. How could I show my face at home? I'd told my parents we wouldn't be out all night. We gave the show times for the *Teatro*. Father had actually been lenient for once. Nausea spread through my gut.

Keep it together. You've got this.

Focusing on finding a solution helped me feel less overwhelmed. My gaze flicked to the door. If Derek wouldn't allow me to leave, I needed to come up with a way

16

to escape without his cooperation, despite how painful that might be.

Derek shifted his weight from one leg to the other. Tension still radiated in his posture, and I could tell from the humanlike movements that he was warring with himself. Most vampires stayed perfectly still as long as they were in control of themselves or their environment. That restlessness put me on edge. While wolves were supernaturally quick, vampires were somehow faster. With him so alert, I'd never make it without him catching me, unless I surprised him.

Werewolves could muscle our way through conflict using our teeth and claws as weapons, but vampires possessed magical abilities dependent on their bloodlines. Some of those powers were downright scary. I wondered what Derek was capable of. So far, he'd shown no sign of his magic.

Frustration built within me, ready to explode. My wolf grew more and more restless with his domineering behavior. "Are you going to keep me prisoner here forever?"

Derek twisted around to look at me and quirked his lips. "Sounds good to me, love."

I widened my eyes, not expecting that response. Now he was just teasing me. He couldn't have been serious, but the way he held himself proved differently. Grimacing, I scooted out of bed, reluctant to leave the incredibly soft mattress. "I don't think so. You won't hold me here. The Militia trained me to fight your kind. You won't come out unscathed."

"Hmm..." He pointedly glanced at my bandaged arm. "Good luck. Your intimidation isn't working. I've been around for centuries—how old are you, pup?" As if to reinforce his smug certainty, he turned back to the window.

Pup. My blood pressure spiked, and my nails sharpened into claws. I hated being called that, but I had to admit, he'd fixed me up without giving into bloodlust and ripping out my throat, which was particularly impressive given our status as enemies.

Some vampires touted werewolf blood as a divine elixir that held an extra kick, making us more scrumptious than humans. Maybe it came from the power werewolves harnessed, the raw wildness that howled through our veins, or the rigid self-control we exercised during one of the three full moons that occurred within a two-month time span.

Regardless of all that, I needed to keep focused on developing my plan.

"That's none of your business." I glanced at the door and took a quiet step toward it. Derek had been right about one thing. He had centuries on me, and I hadn't been able to properly practice my fighting skills. Given fight or flight, my odds were better with flight. He intimidated me, but despite that, my body ached in ways I'd never experienced before. "What do you care?" Perhaps if I made conversation, he wouldn't notice me trying to escape. Unlikely, though.

He didn't answer, just kept his back to me. Anger boiled up inside me, but I pushed it down. He wasn't worth the possibility of losing control of my beast. My nails returned to normal, and any sign of the nail polish I'd put on that evening disappeared with the change.

Darting to the door, I came up short at the sight of him glowering at me. Only the cool breeze I'd felt seconds before proved he hadn't teleported.

I moved away, taking one step at a time until my legs hit the oak bed. Even if I wanted to change forms, I'd have to get the splint off first. Shifting with it on would be unbearable. I might even further injure myself. "What do you want? What guarantee will you accept that I won't tell my kind about you?" My tone softened, and I stared at my splint. With the way he moved, I wouldn't be able to get it off before he was on top of me. *Back to the plan, Carmela. Don't get sidetracked.*

Talk. "The only reason they want me is for my womb, to bear the next generation of werewolves." The words fell out of my mouth before I could stop them. "They don't really care about *my* safety."

Grinding my teeth, I lifted my gaze to his face, which had become as hard and neutral as alabaster. That topic stung, and I couldn't believe I'd opened up to him, a vampire of all beings. But it wasn't as if he cared.

"That's an important role." He leaned against the doorframe, barring the exit but keeping his distance. "Your kind is near extinction."

I balled my hand into a fist. How could he side with them so easily? My womb belonged to me, and I resented being used as a tool for breeding. "Sure, you try living with the pressure to appease your people when all you want is a life with love and tenderness, instead of an arranged relationship with someone you barely know." I turned my back on him, unable to believe I'd just spoken my true feelings for the first time. My future saddened me, but I'd never revealed that sentiment to anyone else.

Vampires had it easier. They turned humans through multiple bites. They didn't have to worry about dying off like werewolves. He had no idea about my 'important role.'

But pity wasn't what I wanted from him or anyone else. I would do what was required, but that didn't mean I had to like it. Suddenly the thought of returning home didn't feel as enticing as it had moments ago.

"You'd be an Alpha Queen, a sacred title amongst your people, with a mate to protect you and your pups. What more could you want?" On second thought, I could really do without Derek's pep talk. "That's prestigious. Surely you weren't out to get yourself killed by the *Cazador* for that reason alone?" Humor warmed his voice.

3

DEREK

"Of course not!" Carmela whirled on me. "I'm *not* like you. Fancy titles and positions of authority might be what you aspire to, but not me!" A snarl trickled from her throat and her skin rippled as fur spread over her arms before disappearing again. Her beast fought hard to take over.

If I didn't calm her soon, I'd have one pissed-off werewolf on my hands. I wasn't afraid of what she might do to me—she was injured. She wouldn't be able to attack as she wanted, and that meant she'd end up hurting herself more, if not forcing me to end her life. I couldn't have a werewolf rampaging through my home. It would draw too much attention. The flow of her anger wound through the room, a sign of her staunch control quickly unraveling.

"You're wrong. I don't have delusions of grandeur." I didn't dare say more. The High Council would rip me apart over mingling with her kind, let alone telling her about my position among them. However, the apocalypse had changed me. My attendance at meetings had suffered for the first time since becoming part of the upper echelon in Victorian London so many lifetimes ago.

She shook her head but took several deep breaths. "Right."

However, I couldn't understand why, if she were in such a privileged position, she wouldn't want that life? Werewolf society was different from the vampires'. We had centuries to horde wealth, and we weren't in as much danger of extinction as they were. Besides, she'd have a sacred title amongst her people, and a man who would protect her and the pups she bore him.

It had to be better than being one of the Protectors, women who didn't have a noble birthright. From what I'd read, Protectors also bore children and helped continue the race, but an Alpha Queen was special.

Maybe pairing up and bearing children didn't suit her ideals. "What were you doing out so late then?" I ran my gaze down her petite frame. "It isn't wise to roam the city at night. Your people must know the suspicion the *Cazador* has for those active after dark. Don't they?" I remained still, trying not to come across as a threat. That was the last thing she needed right now.

"Of course we do. I was out with my cousin." Tears welled in her eyes but didn't spill over. Her hands trembled, and she acted as if the walls were closing in on her. "Just move, okay?" Her voice rasped the words. "You saved my life, and I'd prefer not to hurt you."

My lips tightened in concern, but I wiped away the emotion. I cocked an eyebrow and looked her over again. If she'd look into my eyes this would all be much easier, but Carmela was too smart for that. "I won't move, and you're too injured to fight me."

"That doesn't stop me from leaving." She twisted around, and before I could figure out what she meant, glass shattered as she dove out the window. A solid thump sounded a few seconds later.

Cursing, I ran to the broken window. She picked herself off the ground and glared up at me for a second before running off in a flurry of motion. I squeezed my hands into fists, knowing I should run after her, but that might put me at risk. I needed to trust that she wouldn't do anything to bring her people or the *Cazador* to my door.

Not that I had any reason to. We were sworn enemies, after all.

If only my heart agreed.

4

CHANDRA

I crossed my legs, then smoothed the wrinkles from my skirt as I stared silently at Uncle William's red, angry face from across the massive oak desk. Aunt Katarina sat in the chair next to me, wringing her thin hands in her lap.

What would he and Katarina say if Carmela was gone for good? My cousin had always been the shining star, even if she didn't realize it. I worked hard for the attention I received. There were no mates in my immediate future, no prized position amongst my people, and yet she complained about it all.

I wiped a tear from my cheek. Even if I had my issues with Carmela, I didn't want her dead. She'd been my only friend when I'd come in off the street.

William leaned forward, his thick hands flat on the surface of the desk. His dark brown eyes scanned mine, and he drew in a deep breath as if searching for signs of deceit. "Get on with it. What happened this evening?" His voice reminded me of a drill sergeant from the Militia, pitched barely lower than a shout. A thick vein protruded from his forehead.

I tugged at the hem of my skirt again. "We were at the *Teatro*." Sniffling, I met his gaze, knowing it was a thin line between challenge and standing up for myself. Most of the time, I wondered where the chips would fall. "Someone started yelling at the back of the theater during the movie, then bullets started flying and everyone ran. The *Cazador* knew a group of nocturnes would be there. We escaped out the exit door and split up in hopes of losing the hunters." I dipped my head, unwilling to tell the whole story. If they knew I'd had reservations during the intermission, I would be blamed for Carmela's death. "Several nocturnes were killed. I don't think they were trying to capture us." The *Cazador* had shouted for us to remain in place. As if. Nocturnes, especially lycanthropes, weren't stupid.

After I made sure I wasn't being followed, I tracked Carmela and saw the hunter shoot her. If my cousin wasn't here now, she had to be dead. However, I'd looked for her all over, covering several city blocks. But she'd vanished as if by magic.

Something was off.

Katarina rubbed her hand over my back in soothing strokes, but it did little to settle my confused emotions. "Oh, dear, we're glad you're safe. Can I make you a cup of hot chocolate?" she asked, her voice gentle and calming.

I glanced her way and nodded. "Thank you, Auntie."

Katarina stood up straight, keeping her shoulders back, which only emphasized her thin, frail-looking frame. "Maybe we should send out a search team to find our daughter. She could be—" She stopped herself and sighed. "Forgive me."

"Just go make your niece some hot chocolate, woman." Uncle William rose to his feet and circled the desk. He was tall and stocky, making him formidable both as a human and a werewolf. He leaned against the edge and stared over my shoulder as if waiting for my aunt to leave. Once satisfied she was gone, he knelt before me and brushed his knuckles across my cheek in a firm, almost painful, gesture. "If you're lying," he said, brushing his lips against my ear, "I'll make you wish you hadn't. Do you understand me, girl?" He bit my earlobe hard enough to hurt but not bleed.

I winced, but a sensual shiver chased down my spine all the same.

After a few moments, soft footsteps signaled Aunt Katarina's return. William pushed off from the desk, then crossed to the large fireplace, resting his hand on the mantle. His gaze met mine before darting away. He wouldn't let slip to Katarina what went on between us. If she told anyone, he'd be punished. Granted, he had ways of convincing those under him to obey.

Fear mixed with forbidden lust. I didn't want to be this messed up, but sometimes...it felt so good. My shoulders hunched, and I grudgingly accepted the mug, keeping my gaze fixed on the warm cocoa—with a spoonful of whipped cream, just the way I liked it.

My aunt was too good to me, and I didn't always feel deserving of her care.

5

CARMELA

*a*fter traveling almost a block, I slowed my pace and glanced over my shoulder to see if Derek had followed me. Kind of silly, since he could've caught me before I made it out of the alley. Crashing through the window wasn't as painless as the movies made it look. Feline shifters had it so much easier. Then again, the blood loss had made me weak. Whatever the method, I still freed myself from him.

Although not every part of me was happy about that.

My vampiric savior had a strange allure about him, one I hesitated to admit even to myself. Not that it mattered— Father had chosen my mate. Soon enough, I'd be in his possession.

Would forever in the vampire's care have been so bad?

Shit! What am I thinking? I needed to get a grip. We were enemies. Mortal enemies. Even if we had some kind of fling, our people would hunt us to the ends of the Earth, hell-bent on our deaths.

Father would kill me. Literally.

Rubbing a hand down my hip, I limped along the cracked

sidewalk, scanning the row houses that lined the street with their peeling paint and dusty windows. Other people strolled along the pavement, but they averted their gazes from me, obviously uncomfortable. I couldn't blame them. Derek might have cleaned the wound, but blood stained my blouse and dressy jeans.

I groaned.

Shiny new clothes weren't easy to come by. Not in this day and age. People of my class tended to have fine things, but not me. Father was so controlling. He never allowed me to look 'too nice.' Chandra, on the other hand... *Don't even go there, Carmela. It's not worth it.*

Even though I was twenty, he didn't treat me like an adult. He treated me like a possession, always wanting to show me off at Alpha meetings, but never spending time with me. How would I tell him I didn't want to be with someone who only wanted a female to bear his pups?

If anyone really looked at *traditional* werewolf society, they'd know how much it favored the female sex rather than their male counterparts. Yet men these days liked the prestige and power of being in charge. No one considered how change might improve our existence. Equality? Not in this lifetime.

My home came into view, and a sigh of relief shuddered through me. Finally. I'd be able to calm my parents and check if Chandra made it. If not, I'd go search for her myself. I didn't care how long it took.

Chandra's life was worse than mine. Her parents had tossed her on the streets to fend for herself when she was little. Only when my mother heard about her sister and brother-in-law's death did we find out what happened to her, and I'd hate myself if she'd perished while I was safe and tended to at Derek's house.

I glanced over my shoulder at the now-deserted street

before heading up the front steps. I didn't want anyone to know where I was going. Yes, I was paranoid, but people *were* out to get me. Whoever had alerted the *Cazador* to the nocturnes at the *Teatro* didn't care if my people lived or died.

Steeling my shoulders, I pushed my hand into my jacket pocket and withdrew my keys. Before I could slide them into the door, it swung open. A scowl curled my father's thin lips. It was enough to bring any pup to tears.

I gulped and stepped inside after him. "Hi, Dad."

"Where have you been?" His nostrils flared, and he narrowed his dark eyes at me. My heart raced. He ran a fingertip over the arm splint and brought it to his nose. "What is this scent?" He inhaled deeply but shook his head. "You were out getting in trouble? Do you have any idea how worried your mother was about you? We were about to send out a search team." He placed his hand on my uninjured shoulder and drew me to his side. "Wouldn't want anything to happen to my girl."

Even as he said those words, his tone was flat. Maybe he didn't want anything to happen to me, but he wanted that so I could be mated to some influential Alpha's son. I knew he wasn't concerned for my well-being, and he never bothered to deny it.

While I was growing up, I witnessed many arguments between my parents. Particularly he liked to snarl that his only offspring hadn't been a boy. That Mom was at fault for not bearing more children.

When my mother gave birth to me, something in her body gave out. Her womb couldn't handle having a pup within it. Mom liked to say my birth was a miracle, but I didn't agree, not when Father made me feel otherwise.

Grimacing, I glanced up at him.

He shoved me toward his office on the ground floor.

"Come now. I'll call Dr. Matthews. Your mother is waiting to see you. Go show her you're okay."

I walked through the French doors into the large bookshelf-filled room with its grand oak desk, positioned facing the door. The sting of being sent here when I was younger never went away, regardless of the many times I'd been in the room since.

My mother leapt from a chair angled toward the large stone hearth. "Oh, my dear! Come. Let me look at you. What trouble did you get yourself into?" She crossed the room to me, her light brown eyes wide with concern.

"They raided the *Teatro*. Chandra and I ran, but they caught up to me and shot me." My gaze landed on the other chair as my cousin stood.

"Carmela, you're alive," she said. "I hope you're okay." She smiled, but there was something off about her tone of voice, as if she knew something I didn't. "We were so worried." She didn't give away anything more. Could she be trying to warn me? If only I could decipher what she was hinting at.

Father's voice came from the other room, most likely using his treasured analog phone. He was a business owner, which gave him a certain level of influence. Probably one of the factors that contributed to my family not being lower class like other werewolves. With that influence, he sometimes had the ability to go outside the norm of what others could or couldn't get. The phone had been a gift from one of his loyal clients. They were fairly rare and expensive these days, unlike before the disaster when almost everyone had a cell phone.

"You should sit down, sweetheart. You look pale." Mother guided me to the chair Chandra had vacated. Leaning my head back against the chair's plush upholstered fabric, I closed my eyes and brushed my fingertips over the cottony splint holding my arm in place. My shoulder still burned in

29

agony, and whatever sleep I'd gotten at the vampire's didn't seem to help the drowsiness weighing me down now.

If the bullet had been lead, I might've been able to shrug the injury off, but that wasn't the case. The *Cazador* had known what I was. They'd shot me with silver. Fear chilled me to the bone.

"Are you cold? Here, I'll fetch a blanket," Mother said from nearby, but I didn't pay her much attention. Goosebumps rose up over my skin, and pain gnawed at my shoulder like a dog with a bone.

Weight descended upon me, and I blinked my eyes open. Mother smiled as she tucked a large wool blanket around my shivering body. "Does that help any? Should I have your father light a fire?"

"She does *not* need a fire, Katarina. She needs the doctor to examine her." Father walked around from the back of the chair to tower over us. "Who fixed you up?" He tugged the blanket down, his gaze dropping to the arm secured to my side.

"I don't know, Father. I passed out." I couldn't tell him it had been a vampire. For some reason, they weren't able to smell Derek. It probably had to do with the blood and fear that coated me.

"You don't know?" He straightened his spine, and ferocity creased his forehead. "What do you mean you don't know?"

Mother placed a hand on his thick arm. "Honey, maybe she doesn't—"

Father snapped his attention toward Mother and snarled at her. His gaze was so intense it would have made anyone else spill their guts at his feet. He turned his head back to me, his eyes narrowing. Now I knew why Chandra had acted oddly. Father was in a seriously bad mood. "What about when you woke up?"

"When I woke up, I found my way home." I took a deep

breath, trying to calm myself enough that he wouldn't downright accuse me of lying. But with the way he was acting, it was hard. I didn't want him to strike Mother or anyone else.

Leaning in closely, he growled, "You better not be lying. Do you understand?" I quickly nodded. "Good. You know I'm fully capable of disciplining you, right?"

Fear choked me. He wouldn't think twice about hurting me. He called it 'disciplining,' but that didn't cover what he did. What he seemed to enjoy doing. "Yes, Father." My voice broke slightly, and I wanted to avert my eyes, lean away from him, do anything to gain distance between us, but that wasn't the way to handle him. Not as a werewolf. He'd believe me to be guilty, which I was if truth be told, but he couldn't know that. He'd kill me if he thought a vampire had *tainted* me.

"Doctor Matthews will be here shortly. Go up to your room. Don't make things difficult for him. He's coming all this way because you couldn't stay out of trouble." His lips curled back in disgust, and he straightened to his full height.

I pulled away the cozy blanket and tried to stand, but my muscles weren't cooperating. Dizziness swept through me, and I bit my lip against the wave of nausea roiling my gut. "I don't feel well."

Father grabbed me by the front of my blouse, popping a few buttons in the process, and hauled me from the chair. The tips of my toes barely touched the ground as he lifted. Breathing became difficult, and the gnawing pain in my shoulder grew almost unbearable as my shirt pressed into it. Sheer hostility filled his eyes, and he watched for signs of my pain.

I groaned and wriggled, trying to take some of the pressure off my shoulder by holding myself up, but he hefted me higher.

"Dear, I'll help her to her room. She's hurting. Please

don't cause her more pain." Mother stood a few steps behind my father. Fear was evident in her widening eyes. She didn't want to get involved, didn't want to upset Father, but she loved me. Loved me enough to risk Father's wrath.

Father's grip fell away, and I plummeted to the ground. A loud smack of flesh sounded simultaneously with me thudding against the floor. I lay on my uninjured side and blinked my eyes to see Mother on the office rug with a big red handprint on her cheek. Blood trickled from her lower lip.

"Don't tell me what to do. She's my daughter. I can discipline her how and when I see fit. She left us to worry over her whereabouts. And look at this." He whirled, waving his hand at me. "She comes back injured and 'not knowing' what happened. The little bitch knows how important she is, especially when she'll be meeting her mate tomorrow." He crossed his arms over his chest, and he slid his gaze over my body. "Damn. With the condition she's in, I'll probably need to reschedule." He paced across the room and back, retracing his steps in a circular track. "I don't want the boy thinking he's in for more trouble than she's worth."

I stayed on the ground, unsure if standing would provoke him further. Instead, I tried to lie as still as I could. My shoulder didn't like this position, but I remained quiet.

Mother climbed to her feet slowly, regaining her prim posture. She glanced between her husband and me. It was apparent she wanted to do something, but she was afraid of enraging him further. So she stood there, waiting like a servant.

"Fine, go to her," Father said after a long stretch of silence.

Mother knelt beside me, carefully pulling me into her arms. Her smile held regret and sadness, and I didn't have to wonder why. She hated the way Father acted toward me. At least one of my parents cared. I loathed that once I left, she'd have to continue to deal with how he treated her. Werewolf society didn't allow for divorce. We mated for life.

Mother carried me upstairs, then nestled me into bed. She brushed my hair back from my face and sighed. "How did you get hurt, my dear?"

"Honestly, the *Cazador* shot me with their silver bullets. I managed to lose them. My wound was bleeding heavily, and I passed out." That was pretty close to the truth, too. I covered my mouth with a hand, stifling a yawn. "I'm not sure what happened after I fainted." Also true.

Mother shook her head sadly. "That story doesn't please your father. I find it hard to believe myself. Are you certain you don't know who helped you? If anything, tell me so I can thank them. I'm glad someone took care of you."

I smiled but refused to answer.

"You should have stuck closer to your cousin. You're there to protect one another. Soon you'll have a new home and a great privilege amongst your people. Your father doesn't want you to mess up that opportunity." Mother shrugged her shoulders in a dainty bounce. "You get some rest, and I'll be back once the doctor arrives." She stood and walked out of my bedroom, shutting the door behind her.

The smile slid from my face, and I leaned my head back. Why was everyone going on about how wonderful being an Alpha Queen would be? I didn't want the chore of shooting out babies in a loveless relationship. I'd seen the horrors of arranged relationships in the example my parents provided. Male werewolves were known for their atrocious tempers. Who said I wouldn't be paired with someone like my Father? I didn't want that kind of life.

I wanted love and respect. Was that too much to ask?

6

CHANDRA

I bit my lip hard and stayed as still as I could in the high-back chair Aunt Katarina had occupied moments before. Uncle William's temper was on a very short fuse, and I didn't want to risk his wrath, especially not when it was overblown like this.

I wished I hadn't been left downstairs alone with him. Fear tickled the back of my throat. Sometimes he excited me when he got all Alpha-male, but other times he held such violence inside him that it was better to stay out of his way. Right now was the latter.

He normally didn't hit Aunt Katarina, much less do what he did to Carmela, in front of everyone. We all knew he abused behind closed doors. Now his rage was out in the open. This could set a horrible precedent.

His gaze swung in my direction, and I couldn't breathe. Heat burned my skin, and I fidgeted with the hem of my skirt. He narrowed his eyes as he stalked toward me, his arms crossed. He stared me down as he had Carmela.

"I guess you were telling the truth, but I know you're hiding something."

My eyes widened before I could control my reaction. "I don't know what you're talking about. I told you everything," I said, my voice breathy even to my own ears.

He fisted his meaty hand around my upper arm, yanking me from the chair. "Don't play coy with me, little girl. I brought you into this household. If you don't want to go back to the streets where Katarina's sister left you, you'll do as I say."

Adrenaline pumped through my veins. Those words ripped through me, leaving me raw. Pain radiated from my arm, but it was nothing compared to the hurt in my heart. He stomped toward the stairs up to my bedroom, dragging me along with him.

I'd taken his rough treatment, but only because I yearned for something better. However, the thrill of Uncle William had diminished. I couldn't believe he was taking this out on me. Why not aim it at its rightful target, Carmela? But he wouldn't sully his *little girl*—she was far too important.

He shoved me toward the bed, then pulled a set of keys out of his pocket.

Panic sent my pulse into overdrive. If I could have, I would've run, but I knew I'd never be safe. Not from the *Cazador*, as the *Teatro* incident proved, and not from him.

Uncle William was powerful. He'd made me feel safer than anywhere I'd been before coming into the Santiago household. But right now, he was wrong. Dead wrong.

The key turned in the lock with an ominous click.

7

DEREK

I cracked my knuckles. The broken shards of glass had lain on my spare room's floor long enough. If I didn't want wind and red dust blowing through my house, I needed to cover the window and sweep up. I turned my attention to the jagged hole, still unable to believe I'd let her escape.

I nailed a large piece of cardboard and secured a sheet of plastic over the hole. If I didn't fix this within the next day or two, I'd get a notice from the community. Guess I'd be going to the local hardware store. The *Cazador* hadn't circled back since last night. They appeared to have moved on.

It wasn't as if the city's other residents demonstrated much upkeep of their areas, but everyone liked to believe things hadn't changed from before the moon rained down to Earth. That meant keeping up with ridiculous regulations. When I took a deep breath, I could still smell her floral shampoo, still see her caramel-colored eyes, petite frame, and supple curves. Beyond her physical beauty, I appreciated her fire. She didn't cower from me, regardless of her injuries.

I shifted my weight and glass crunched under my boot. My fist clenched on the broom, making the wooden handle groan under the pressure. *Damn...* I'd gotten caught up in daydreams again.

The glass from the alleyway should be swept up too. I might be fined if someone were stupid enough to walk down the path and step on it, most likely some homeless person who might make a lovely snack.

I didn't like going out of my way to deal with silly mortal rules. If I could have, I would've left city life behind, but food was scarce elsewhere. Humans felt safer in cities these days.

My thoughts drifted back to Carmela, and my blood warmed. I rubbed a hand through my hair. Her expression when she first smelled my breath had surprised me, but that interaction stuck like a note from a lover: the smile on her face, the way her eyes lit up when she giggled.

Shaking my head, I pushed the memory away. For all I knew, she might be out telling her people about me, ensuring the werewolves or even the *Cazador* would pursue me. I needed to be on alert. No reason to chance an attack. I'd lived this long. It would be a pity to die by a hunter's bullet...or a werewolf's claws.

Carmela's face danced through my thoughts even as I swept up the broken glass. She was a werewolf. There was no reason I should be this taken with her. Swirls of blood marred the pavement, and I'd crouched to examine them when a breeze blew across my cheek.

Fellow High Council member Elliot Quinn stared down at me, his full lips quirked in a mischievous smile. "Looks like you're busy dealing with a mess, mate." Humor warmed his aristocratic features as he knelt, and his blue eyes showed too much curiosity.

"There was an incident. My window was broken, and

someone must have stepped in the glass," I said, keeping my tone flat. "What are you doing here?" I stood, holding the full dustpan in one hand.

"Just reminding you about the upcoming meeting. Lord Prescott showed much displeasure over you missing the last one." His crisp British accent thickened, underscoring his worry. "I'd recommend you make this one a priority." Elliot crossed his arms.

"Guess I need to check my calendar more often." High Council meetings were the last thing on my mind. I'd hoped my absence would signal that, but Lord Prescott was too stubborn to let go of his members.

I walked up the alley toward the back door, Elliot perfectly matching my stride. I knew Elliot was only looking out for me by passing on the message. We'd known each other a long time—in fact, he was the closest thing I had to a friend.

"I know you've begun to dislike politics, but you don't have a choice. This is who you are: you're a High Council member. You've known Prescott a long time, so you have a better idea than most how he can be when someone displeases him. You don't want to put yourself in that position." Elliot grabbed the door and held it open.

In the darkened kitchen, I emptied the bloody glass and dirt into the trash, then tossed the dustpan in the corner. Elliot was right. Prescott didn't take kindly to insubordination. He'd been patient so far, but it wouldn't last forever. I leaned against the counter and sighed. "Fine. I'll be there." Turning to Elliot, I added, "Don't expect me to like it."

"Wouldn't dream of it." He grinned, showing sharp, pointed fangs.

A breeze spread through the kitchen, and Elliot was gone. I only saw him leave because, as an older vampire, I could track his movements. I wished he'd be more careful about

"Could I use the other one?" I didn't want to raise suspicion, but having something with me that Derek had touched felt right.

Dr. Matthews frowned, deepening the lines around his mouth.

"I was starting to get used to it." I forced a bright smile. Or as bright as I could manage with my arm hurting this much. It wasn't like I'd ever see Derek again, but at least I could keep his memory.

"Yes, of course." Dr. Matthews nodded and placed the new splint back into his bag.

Mother helped me into a sitting position and held me as Dr. Matthews wrapped my shoulder, then slid my arm back into the sling.

He angled his body away, and I wondered what he was doing. Then he turned to me with a needle, which he tapped lightly before reaching for my arm.

I scooted away. Pain was one thing, but I hated needles. I crawled to the other side of the bed, but before I could flee, Mother pressed a hand against my chest to hold me down.

Dr. Matthews gripped my arm, hard enough to hurt, but that didn't matter. I writhed and bucked, trying to get away.

"Please, don't." My voice came out weak and helpless. "Please. I'm okay."

"Carmela, don't be silly," he said.

My mind flashed to the hazing I'd been through in the Militia. The other wolves had held me down and jabbed sharp needles into my skin, thinking they could break me of the fear. It only made things worse. My time in the Militia had been hell on Earth.

"Mother, please. Let me go. I'm fine, seriously." I stared up at her. A sharp jab stung my arm, and I bit my lip hard as tears streamed over my cheeks.

"It'll be okay, Carmela. We know you don't like needles.

We've gone over this before—it's for your own good. You're in pain, and you need your rest. We're just trying to help your body heal. Calm down, dear." Mother's face blurred. "I'll be here when you wake up."

I blinked, trying to fight the drugs. "Don't...like needles." Lightheadedness kept me in bed, even though I wanted to run.

Dr. Matthews's face came into view. "This is for your own good, doll. If you don't rest, your body won't be able to focus on healing that shoulder. Your father wants you to be in good shape for your mate. You don't want to give the wrong impression." He smiled and brushed a strand of hair from my forehead. "I'll check on you tomorrow."

Now the truth was out. This wasn't about my pain. It was about Father's plans being executed the way he saw fit. He didn't want anything to mess up the first encounter I had with my mate, not even me. I was in my birthing prime. He wanted me to have the sons he'd wanted for himself, sons my mother had denied him, instead of the daughter he barely held back spite for. He only thought about himself. Who cared how Mother felt? He was the center of his universe.

I groaned, surrendering to the drugs.

DEREK

*N*ight descended, allowing me to once more travel about the city. I pushed open the hardware store's door, and a bell chimed over my head. The people inside were crowded along aisles filled with everything from hammers to screwdrivers to ladders. Several of the customers stopped and stared, as if expecting an attack.

Charles, the older man who owned the place, stood behind an old-time cash register at the checkout counter and waved, a big smile on his wrinkled face. "Come on in, Derek. It's been a while. What can I get you?"

Tension left the store in a rush, and everyone returned to browsing the aisles again.

"Someone broke one of my windows last night. Need to get it fixed before the community finds out." I slid Charles a piece of scratch paper with the measurements on it.

"Sorry to hear about that. You sure do need that window fixed. They're real sticklers about things like that. Don't worry, though. I'll get you taken care of like usual." Charles looked at the paper and flipped through a catalogue, stopping at a window that would work for the spare room.

"Thanks for this."

"You're always welcome. We'll have this to you tomorrow afternoon. How does three o'clock sound?" Charles scribbled on a receipt, then tucked the pen in his shirt pocket.

I wouldn't be awake at three o'clock. It didn't matter how old I was, I wasn't immune to sunlight. "I have an appointment already scheduled at that time. I won't be home until later. How about tomorrow evening at six or seven? That'll give me a project for the weekend." I slid a few bills across the counter to Charles, hoping he wouldn't question the timing, then tucked away my copy of the receipt.

The idea I might be something other than human didn't even seem to occur to Charles. He just nodded. "Yeah, you're right. Keep an eye on your place so no one breaks in between now and then." He frowned, concern tightening his eyes. "You're a good man. I wouldn't want anything bad to happen to you."

"Thanks." The only people who were likely to break into my second-story window were those who could fly. Or someone brave enough to use a ladder, but that would cause a commotion. His words still sunk in, though.

I didn't need yet another reason to feel paranoid, but it was too late. Would someone dare break into my home while I wasn't around? Or worse...when I was asleep and helpless?

A foreboding feeling urged me back home. I walked quickly at first, but my nagging intuition screamed at me, 'run.' As I stepped into the alley, I saw a hole where the cardboard and plastic were supposed to be.

My fears were proving to be justified.

With a curse, I jogged inside using supernatural speed and stealth. Though the blackness would hamper any human, I could see every detail of my home like it was daytime. Yet something lurked, just out of sight. I could sense an unspoken threat. Someone wanted me dead.

"Come out. Stop wasting my time," I yelled into the darkness. What use would cowardice be?

A shadow moved in the kitchen, and another darted across the balcony overlooking the living room.

My fangs lengthened into sharp points with a quiet snap. I stepped out of the den, but kept my back to the wall. These beings were professionals. I wouldn't allow them an opportunity to surprise me from behind.

Someone whirled toward me from the kitchen. I slammed my fist into the man's chest, causing a loud crunch as he stumbled back and hit the floor.

The black-clad figure from the loft flung itself over the railing and soared down to the ground, landing with an arrogant flair.

This didn't make sense. The man in the kitchen wasn't a vampire, but there was something about this one. The rapid tap of footsteps drew my attention toward the kitchen. Maybe I'd been wrong about him.

Before I could do anything, a solid weight barreled into me, slamming me into the wall. Fingers dug into my arms, and magic thrummed through the air. The magic held a dark, powerful taint almost like that of the necromancers of old. If I didn't stop him, I'd die a true death.

I shoved him, and the man flew away from me, smacking into the opposite wall. A loud *pop* resounded from where the man in the kitchen had been. I leapt out of the way and wound up on my hands and knees in the living room.

Another wave of magic slammed into me, and I dropped to the floor, pain eating at me. I wouldn't let this happen. I'd never give in to these men. I was a vampire, a superior being.

Pop.

I jerked to the side, knowing they weren't trying to kill me. What they *were* trying to do was much worse than death —they wanted to capture me. I reached out my hand toward them, drawing on the telekinetic magic of my bloodline. I clenched my fist and jerked it toward me. The deathly pain immediately stopped, but my head swam from the after-effects of the necromancer's magic.

The man from the kitchen lay beside me, his stunned hazel eyes staring at the ceiling. The tranquilizer pistol shook in his hands. I dragged him toward me by the neck. A thick leather collar circled his throat, so they must have suspected what I was. The necromancer's presence confirmed that.

I sank my fangs into his wrist, keeping my crushing grip on his neck. His hot coppery blood slid down my throat, revitalizing each cell in my body. With my energy this low after the fight, the need to feed overwhelmed my desire for answers. When the man stopped fighting, his heartbeat a small, fragile bird fluttering slowly in his chest, I closed the wound with my tongue.

The necromancer must have fled, leaving his less powerful friend to die.

I swiped a hand over my bloody lips, staring at the darkly clad intruder. Why were these people trying to capture me, and how had they known I was a vampire? Maybe I should've fought my needs and questioned him while he was conscious. I might still have a chance. He wasn't dead yet.

Slumping into a chair, I sighed. My life had been simpler before meeting that werewolf. People hadn't been after me for mysterious reasons, and I hadn't had to deal with the tendrils of desire that stirred within me when I thought of her.

The smile on her lips, and the way she giggled. *Damn.* I wanted to see her again, but we weren't meant to be. We could *not* be.

CARMELA

linking my eyes open, I stared up at the ceiling. The soft, plush bed relaxed me immediately. Dreams of Derek toyed with my heart. The way he'd smirked and threatened to keep me by his side forever. How did I feel about that?

Werewolves mate for life, and I'd never wanted an arranged marriage like my parents. The abuse my mother suffered, and the misery that radiated from her, made my urge to break the mold clear. But Derek wasn't a werewolf. Would that make a relationship with him different? I had no idea.

Shifting in bed, I tried to turn on my side, but I couldn't move. Ropes dug into my limbs. Someone had tied me to the bed. Only my injured arm escaped the bindings. No one else was in the room. I'd wanted to cling to the unrealistic dreams of Derek, but I never expected to wake up to this.

Agony still pulsed through my arm, but it wasn't as overwhelming as what I'd felt last night. Looking out my bedroom window, I saw I'd slept the day away.

Wasn't Dr. Matthews supposed to check on me?

A grimace curled my lips, and I tugged at the ropes again. Part of me wanted to scream, but I knew Father had tied these, because they didn't budge. If anything, they were too tight. My hand and feet were asleep. I needed to move my limbs better than this. If they wanted to give me more medicine, then fine, but this was crazy.

"Mother?" I whispered, hoping she was somewhere nearby. I waited a moment, but heard nothing. A thud sounded from the other side of the wall near my head, followed by the sounds of crying and my parents' headboard slamming against the wall. I'd heard those noises before, for years.

"What did I tell you?" Father yelled, and the banging continued.

The idea of sex repulsed me. How could anyone find the act enjoyable? I remembered the romance novels I used to sneak from my mother's hidden bookshelf. The characters within those pages enjoyed lovemaking. It didn't have the violence I heard from behind my parents' bedroom door and had cried myself to sleep to so many nights. But those pages were lies.

The sobs quieted, and I squeezed my eyes closed, wishing I could be away from there. Father pretended to be a respectable man, but it was all for show. Hopefully, I could deal with the mate Father intended for me. Perhaps he wouldn't be as horrible. *Or he could be worse.*

My bedroom door slammed open, and my heart pounded in my chest. I closed my eyes, focusing on keeping my breathing slow and even. Father's loud footsteps approached the bed, and I shoved down my fear. Maybe if he thought I was asleep, he'd leave.

If not, I wouldn't be able to fight off his attack, not with my limbs firmly bound. Who was I kidding? When was I ever able to fight off his attacks? He scared me too much to even try most times.

His hot hand descended on my stomach, burning my skin through the blanket. He slid his hand over my belly button and toward my hips.

"William!" Mother shrieked. "Stop it!"

I opened my eyes, unable to keep them closed any longer.

Father darted a glance toward Mother and growled. "Get out of here, Katarina! Now!" He pulled away from me and stomped toward my mother.

"She's your daughter. Don't put your hands on your daughter like that. You already treat her poorly–"

A wrenching slap sent my mother careening out of the room. Father strode out, then slammed the door behind him. Screams sounded beyond the door, and I was helpless to do anything. The echoes of pummeling punches reverberated through my ears.

Tears streamed my cheeks. In a way, I wished I could've taken the brunt of Father's wrath so she wouldn't have to fall prey to it yet again.

The door opened again, and my eyes widened.

Chandra walked in and stared at me with hollow eyes. Bruises marred her complexion, and her lower lip was split open. Sighing, she shut the door after her. Her features twisted in pain as she limped across the floor of my bedroom. My cousin raised her arm back, then slapped me across the cheek.

"This is your fault." Her voice matched her eyes. Empty. "I don't know why Uncle William even tolerates you, you selfish bitch." Pain contorted her face. "Don't screw up the meeting with your mate. I doubt you deserve him, whoever he is. Aunt Katarina shouldn't have stopped him. You're the one he should target, not us. But maybe that's for the best.

No one would want you if you were ruined too." She spun on her heel and left the room.

I couldn't hold back my astonishment. How could she say that? *She's angry and not thinking straight.* Maybe I did deserve the harsh words. No... I came home as soon as I could from Derek's, regardless of the consequences, but my effort meant nothing. I was never good enough for them.

I bit my lip hard, holding back a scream. Tears cascaded down my cheeks. If I hadn't been tied down, I might've left and never returned. The only person who cared about me was my mother. But how could she continue to love me when I caused her so much pain, even if it was through Father?

Sobs shook my chest. The pain in my shoulder felt like a mosquito bite compared to what filled my heart. I had outsmarted a vampire and jumped from his window while injured to come back to these people, and yet Chandra and my father would be just as happy if I had died. At least if that were the case, maybe my mother wouldn't be abused like this. Maybe Father wouldn't feel like he needed to beat her for truly loving me.

But what did Chandra mean about him ruining her? An ugly bruise stained her face, but surely there wasn't anything more serious than that. Even as I tried to deny that Father could stoop to such a wicked level with Chandra, I wasn't surprised. He beat Mother regularly, what stopped him from raping Chandra? If Mother hadn't stopped him, he would've done the same to me, regardless of trying to find me a mate.

I wriggled against the ropes, trying to slacken them. If I were at my full strength, I could've broken through, but I'd only draw more attention to myself. Even if Father's senses were dulling from age, he'd be able to hear that much commotion.

Instead, I stayed quiet and hoped Mother would loosen

the bindings. Surely Dr. Matthews would be around soon. They wouldn't keep me like this with the doctor set to arrive, would they?

I frowned and looked out the bedroom window again. At least Derek had been kind to me, even if being in his presence was hazardous to my health.

Father was just as dangerous to my sanity, after all.

CARMELA

I opened my eyes to see Mother standing over me. Sunlight peeked through the window. Faint bruises still marred the skin of her face, neck, and arms. She worked a knife through the ropes that bound my wrist.

"I'm so sorry, dear. Your father is just stressed. Since you weren't feeling well yesterday, he moved the visit with your mate to today. He'll be here in a few hours. I'll be helping you get ready."

"What about Dr. Matthews? He said he'd check in on me." I frowned and stared down at my hand, which had become red and slightly cool from constriction. Rubbing it against my leg, I watched her cut the bindings on my feet, relieved it was a new day.

"He came yesterday afternoon. Before...this." She pointed to the ropes and sighed. "He said you seemed to be well enough, considering the circumstances. Dr. Matthews realizes how important it is for you to meet your mate. He'll be back in a week to recheck your shoulder." Mother attempted a smile but looked defeated. "There you go, sweetie." She lifted me into her arms and slid me to the edge of the bed, then rubbed her hands over my feet and ankles.

Pinpricks of pain flowed through my hand and feet from the blood returning to them. "How are you?" I traced my fingers over the splint Derek had fitted me with.

"Oh, I'm fine, sweetie. Don't worry about me. Today is your day to shine." Mother hugged me gently and put a little more effort into her smile. If it weren't for the bruises, she might have been convincing. However, hurt tightened the corners of her eyes, and I hated that.

I opened my mouth to argue with her, but what good would it do? Instead, I pushed my legs off the bed and stood, hoping I wouldn't collapse to the floor. My legs shook, but at least I stayed upright. "Do you know who he is? My soon-to-be mate?"

"Yes, he's a nice young man named Brendan Kelly. Comes from a *very* good family. You two will be happy together." She nodded, a little too quickly. "Now, enough with the questions. We need to get you ready." Mother took a hairbrush from my vanity and went to work on the tangles caused by being in bed for an extended length of time. Next, she set out a washing bowl with a washcloth in it. It wasn't often we took actual baths.

Water was rationed, and only the very wealthy could afford to use the amount it took to fill a bath or, heaven forbid, take a shower. Instead, society had reverted to times when people merely sponged off. Didn't make for excellent hygiene, but it was better than nothing.

I sat up and cooperated with Mother, getting ready for the big meeting everyone except me was excited for. I wanted to get away from Father. Did it matter who the mate was?

Not really. Whoever it was wouldn't care for me. He'd be

someone who wanted to mate for lineage and political purposes. I hung my head, staring at the sling. It was crazy, and possibly Stockholm syndrome, but my feelings for the vampire were more than I'd had for anyone else.

I wondered if I was broken for feeling the way I did about Derek.

12

DEREK

I stretched out on the spare bed Carmela had occupied while she'd been here. I could still smell her, still taste her in my mouth. I'd ended up having to lick her wound to stop it from bleeding so heavily after most of the fragments were removed. A vampire's saliva coagulated blood so our prey wouldn't bleed out completely. It'd been hard to stop at just a few swipes of my tongue, but I'd managed.

Unfortunately, the same couldn't be said about the weaker of the two attackers. He hadn't survived, so I was left with plenty of questions about who was behind the assault. I'd dumped the body before the sun came up, in one of the unguarded open graves where the poorest of the poor were discarded.

Tonight, I would repair the damage Carmela had done to my window, once the new one arrived. The High Council meeting was also this evening. Part of me wasn't terribly excited about going, but after the attempted kidnapping, my curiosity was piqued.

Had other council members been targeted, too? If this

wasn't about council members, then it had to be an assault due to the werewolf. But if she'd said something to someone, werewolves would be attacking me, not a necromancer and a human. The *Cazador*? Hmm... They didn't work with people gifted by the supernatural.

Nothing made sense.

I rubbed my hand over the stubble on my chin. If I knew the cause, I could handle whatever was going on. Ever since Carmela appeared, my life had been turned upside down and shaken like a snow globe.

I let out a sharp breath and held up my watch to read the time. Nearly six o'clock. I should be receiving the window any time now.

Grimacing, I slid off the bed. I needed to stop thinking about her.

13

CARMELA

I stared at myself in the mirror. The sleek black dress hugged my curves, and the make-up on my lips and eyes presented a nice polished appeal to my features. Mother put my hair into a high ponytail, styling it to finish off the look. I didn't know what I would do without her.

Male voices drifted up from downstairs. One was obviously Father, but the other must be my soon-to-be mate. My heart pounded in my chest, and I took a deep breath.

Mother held my hand and walked with me to the top of the stairs. She cast me a small smile and nodded. "Go now, dear. You two have a lovely time."

I averted my gaze, staring at the floor. It hurt to leave her here alone with that monster. Chandra had holed up in her bedroom, but I didn't blame her. We'd all suffered because of my father.

Mom's fingers caught my chin, and she tugged my head up to look her in the eye. "None of that, now." She pressed her lips against my ear and whispered so low I could barely hear her. "This is for your own good, my precious daughter.

Your safety." Pulling back, she placed a small peck on my cheek. "Go on. He's waiting for you."

I forced a neutral expression and turned away. Mom was right. It wouldn't be proper for me to look upset. I had to face this like a woman. Walking down the steps in the new heels she'd given me, I wobbled a little from being in bed so long. I gripped the stair rail tightly and kept my gaze in front of me.

"Well, here comes my girl. It's about time. Shall we?" Father's voice sounded from his office.

My spine stiffened. Fear and disgust battled in my chest while nausea knifed through my stomach. I fought to keep my feelings under control, to wear the neutral look I so needed to have, especially in Father's presence.

"Sure," a deep, masculine voice responded.

Two sets of footsteps closed in on the bottom of the stairs, and I spotted a pair of shiny black shoes and nice dress slacks. My gaze drifted up the long legs as I kept walking down the stairs, until it landed on a very attractive face. Clear blue eyes stared at me, watching my every move. The man had sandy blond hair, which he'd brushed back from his face.

My foot slipped, and I stumbled forward. Before I could tumble down, strong arms circled my waist and steadied me. I stared into those blue eyes from just inches away. How could I be such a klutz? A smirk tugged at his lip, and he moved back to offer me his arm. Embarrassment burned my cheeks as I placed my hand on the crook of his elbow, allowing him to help me down the rest of the steps.

My father's face was bright red with anger, but he smiled in time as Brendan glanced his way. My heartbeat quickened, and not because I'd nearly fallen face-first down the stairs. What would Father do to me once I got home from my date with this seriously attractive werewolf?

"I'll have her back before curfew, sir," Brendan's husky voice announced, and he turned his gaze my way. "Shall we?"

I nodded before cutting my eyes to Father. "Bye, Dad."

"Goodbye." He came behind us and shut the door as we descended the front steps.

"Carmela, you have a lovely name. Where would you like to go?" He turned to the left, leading me toward the shopping district.

"I don't know. I'm good with anywhere." *Anywhere but here.*

He chuckled. "I see. That makes things easy. I'll throw out some suggestions, and you can pick your favorite."

"Okay."

"Do you like seafood? Steaks? Sandwiches? I'd like to take you out for dinner, but before that, I have two tickets to a play I've wanted to see. Haven't had anyone to go with me."

"I like steak." Smiling, I lowered my gaze. It had been so long since I'd eaten a steak. Not because I didn't want it, but because Father never went to the expense to take us out, nor did he let Mother buy any from the store to cook. The sound of a delicious steak for dinner whetted my appetite. "I liked seeing movies at the *Teatro.* Where is the play we're going to being held?"

"Ah, the *Teatro.* Weren't they raided the other night? I've heard some nocturnes were killed. That's horrible. Where we're going isn't far from there, but if you like the *Teatro*, I'm sure you'll enjoy this place."

"That sounds lovely," I said. I looked up to see him staring at me intensely.

He nodded to the sling. "What happened to your arm?"

My lips parted, and I frowned, instinctually pulling away, but his grip on me tightened. "Let me go. Please."

He released my arm, and I stumbled a step away from him. "Are you okay?"

My mouth went dry, but I nodded. "Yes." Panic coated my insides, and I swept my tongue over my lower lip. "I'm fine, thanks. What's your favorite steakhouse?"

His nostrils flared, and my heart skipped a beat. Could he smell Derek on me? Brendan sighed before extending his arm to me again. "It's a place near the theater."

Placing my arm back on his, I stayed quiet, but now the silence was awkward. For a moment, I'd felt a semblance of comfort with him. Now that was gone, and I wasn't sure how to feel.

After several blocks, I caught sight of Derek's home. My heart pounded in my chest. I didn't worry about him taking me away or hurting me. The only thought floating through my head was the almost-kiss.

I caught sight of Derek heading through the side alley toward the back of his home. His shoulders stiffened, and he turned in my direction. Our gazes met, and he blinked in surprise. He looked like he'd seen a ghost.

"What's wrong?" Brendan asked, pulling my attention back to him. He glanced between Derek and me, sucking in a deep breath. His lips curled back in a snarl. "Let's go."

I opened my mouth to explain. But what could I say that wouldn't incriminate me? Besides, I didn't know Brendan very well. What if he found out what Derek had done for me? He might have him killed. "What are you going to do?" I asked. "He's minding his own business." I glanced back at Derek before he faded into the shadows.

Brendan stared at me, pressing his lips together in thought. "What would you like me to do, Carmela?"

I shrugged my good shoulder. "Nothing? Just take me out to dinner and a play. We don't need this incident to ruin our evening." I forced a smile, knowing I looked at my future in his eyes. Derek was someone I wanted, but he wouldn't be the one I got.

"That's against our laws, you know." He cocked an eyebrow. "What if he tells his kind about us?"

"We'll be gone by then, but if you're worried, maybe we should ask him not to?"

Brendan chuckled, and amusement brightened his eyes. "You've lost your mind." He quirked his lips in a half-smile. "Come on. Let's get to the theatre."

14

DEREK

*F*ire burned in my chest, and I had to force myself to remain where I was. Carmela was with another man. From what she'd said previously, I doubted she was in a consummated relationship. Was this guy her chosen mate? Grimacing, I watched the male werewolf escort her down the street. Would the werewolf report my presence even though she'd asked him not to? I shook my head, turning toward the back of the house.

Elliot stood before me and grinned. "Caught skulking about by some werewolves? Speed and stealth, mate. The two joys of what we are."

"Caught? No, I wasn't caught. Just walking around outside of my home. I have repairs to do." I jerked open the back door and walked inside. After dealing with the necromancer and his helper, I'd gone back to the hardware store to add to my order. Seemed I'd be doing remodeling instead of relaxing before the High Council meeting tonight.

That was probably why Elliot was here. He likely wanted to make sure I would be attending. How thoughtful of him...

I started toward the spare bedroom, but stopped myself.

If Elliot followed me, he'd smell Carmela, and that was the last thing I needed.

I glanced back to find him sniffing around my den and living room. Elliot knelt in his nice suit and slacks and placed his nose just above the tile where the necromancer's helper had perished. "What's this? Someone died here." Elliot looked to me with his now-black eyes.

"I was attacked yesterday. I'm not sure by whom, or why they were here. He didn't leave me much choice but to drain him before he...killed me. I tried to question him, but he succumbed to his injuries." I leaned against the wall by the back door, not sure how much I should tell him. If I mentioned the necromancer and the kidnapping, Elliot might talk to Lord Prescott, and I didn't want that. He might discover that I'd helped Carmela.

Elliot's lips pulled away from his fangs. If it had been anyone else, I might've felt threatened, but with Elliot, it was just a sign of frustration.

"There's more to what you're saying. I smell something else here. This man wasn't working alone." He bent by the area where the necromancer had knocked me against the wall. "There's something familiar about this lingering energy. Afraid I can't place it though." Casting a glance at me, he added, "Sorry."

I shrugged. The less Elliot knew the better, at least for the moment. I'd figure out who tried to kidnap me. Necromancers were rare these days, and not many roamed this city. "Guess we'll see who doesn't arrive at the meeting tonight."

"Just because I recognized the scent doesn't mean they're connected to the High Council. This doesn't feel vampiric." Elliot took another sniff before standing to his feet. "No, they might play a smaller role. As impressed as I am with your formidable skills, I don't think you would last long if two

High Council members ambushed you. Besides, they wouldn't want to risk their necks. Perhaps it was done by minions."

"Since when do you hang out with minions of other High Council members?" I raised an eyebrow at Elliot, glad he wasn't paying any more attention to the scents around my place.

Elliot groaned. "It's not what you think. Some of us have a libido." A grin cracked his lips. "Or do you have one? Does fur fulfill your tastes better?"

A hiss escaped my lips before I could catch myself. "I don't know what you're talking about."

"I see. Why the visceral reaction? Maybe because it's true." He leaned in and winked. "Don't worry. I won't go against our friendship. Even if it forces me to compromise my duty as a responsible vampiric denizen." His smile widened, flashing a lot of fang.

"I'm not attracted to her." I gritted my teeth.

"That's good. Then you won't mind if I tattle on her to the *Cazador*, or worse, our fellow High Council members." Elliot's eyes narrowed, and I felt wholly discomforted by this exchange.

"Fine, I am. Don't mention *anything* about her to *anyone*. It's not like there's any chance for us. Besides, she's with someone else, and even if we were together, I'd have to protect her from our kind's wrath."

Elliot chuckled and shook his head. "Well, it seems like you're more screwed up than I am. That's a first."

PART II

1

DEREK

The headcount began, signaling the start of the High Council meeting. I reclined in a plush red velvet chair next to Elliot, already wanting it to be over. Many years ago, the meetings had appealed to me, and I'd listened to the drawn-out political babbling as if it all mattered. Now I forced myself to attend.

Sadly, my disdain of being here wasn't the only thing on my mind. Someone was after me, and I didn't know who or why. What did they know? If someone had discovered I helped Carmela... I locked the thought away. Some vampires were telepathic, and thinking of her could be treacherous.

The other council members were from all walks of life, and ranged in appearance from young adult to elder. Some smelled as if they'd walked in from a shantytown, while others were well-groomed and polished.

A few kept their minor nocturne minions seated at their feet in what the council believed was a manner appropriate to their class. I didn't subscribe to that school of thought. Who was becoming extinct? Nocturnes. Who was the threat? The humans striving to build up their numbers again.

The progress humans and nocturnes alike had made over the centuries had mostly been lost, secreted away by the human government in their laboratories and military bases. They thought their wealth could protect them from the horrors of this new post-apocalyptic life, but history had proven time and again that the average person wouldn't be suppressed forever.

Lord Prescott entered from his private chambers at the front of the room. He appeared young and lanky, as if he was in his late teens or early twenties, but he'd been the High Council's chairman for centuries before I was even born. The power emanating from him swept through the chamber, flooding everyone with its intensity.

Goosebumps pricked my flesh, and I clenched the arms of my chair. Elliot stiffened beside me. One would think we'd get used to this after a while, but Prescott made sure his vampires obeyed him. No one would dare to threaten his position.

"Most of you know why we've gathered here." Prescott stood next to his throne. He fixed his gaze on me. "Why don't you remind us, Derek Ashmoore. I'm sure you know, yes?"

My lips pulled away from my fangs, but I forced my expression to remain neutral. Giving him a piece of my mind wouldn't be best. "As the chairman, I assumed you would tell everyone why we're here."

Prescott narrowed his grey eyes at me, then turned to another vampire. "Giles Cleaver, what's the main item on our agenda?"

Giles, a crooked old vampire, cast a haughty glance my way before addressing Prescott and everyone else. "We are here to acknowledge the death of Tom Turner, a senior High Council member. You shall pick the newest senior member, my lord." He bowed at the waist before sitting back down.

"You received the memo. Good." Prescott seated himself

on the throne. "As Giles said, one of our own has been murdered. This doesn't even speak to the fact that the kindred beneath us are murdered every day by those human creatures. The *Cazador*... what a dreadful name." He entwined his fingers over his flat stomach and observed the council members.

"Who is worthy of fulfilling the role of senior member? Who has earned his place among us and will act in our best interests?" He narrowed his gaze on me, and the muscles in my shoulders tensed. Prescott swiped his tongue across his slightly yellowed fangs, enjoying the sight of watching me squirm, then he twisted his attention to my right.

"Elliot Quinn. How long have you been among us? Since the reign of Queen Victoria, yes?"

Elliot stood with his head bowed. "No, my lord, I became a vampire during King Edward VII's reign." His knuckles were white from clenching his hands together.

"Yes, that's right. Still, you have a few centuries under your belt, and continue to prove yourself useful." Prescott scanned the room, drawing out the spectacle.

Elliot retook his seat after a few moments. He nearly vibrated with nervous energy, which wasn't like him at all. This was a big deal for him, since he still believed we could make a difference through politics.

I leaned forward in my chair, resting my hands on my knees. Prescott needed to pick someone already, and end this verbose meeting. One of our kind had been killed, and that led me to wonder if the attacks on me were related.

What reason would a necromancer have for putting his life on the line to kidnap vampires, though? Maybe Tom's death wasn't connected.

"Head in the clouds today, Derek?" Prescott steepled his fingers under his chin. He shot a tidal wave of power at me, hitting me in the chest. My body jerked back into the chair at the impact, and air rushed from my lungs. Agony burned inside me like a blazing torch. I clenched my hands into fists to keep from reacting. "See me after the meeting. Now, focus on our business here."

I flinched, wanting to get out of here. Elliot bumped my foot. No, this wasn't the way to get on Prescott's good side after my absence.

"At any rate, I will promote Elliot Quinn as the newest senior High Council member. As far as Tom Turner's death, I *will* find who committed this crime. If I find anyone to be less than honest and forthright with information, I will rid this forsaken planet of you and your underlings. Obey our laws, and don't bring harm upon our kindred. We need to remain strong. Understood?"

A low rumbling of agreement filled the air.

"Good. If no one has any further concerns, we will adjourn."

The room remained silent.

Council members very rarely offered up their fears to Prescott in the public forum. Most tried to stay out of the spotlight.

"Adjourned." Prescott rose from his chair with a flourish, brushing aside his platinum blond hair, and waited there.

"What was that about?" Elliot whispered as we walked down the stairs of the large lecture hall. A couple of vampires shook their heads at me as they filed toward the exit.

"Derek, come. Let's go to my office." Prescott waved his hand toward the door of the private chambers near his throne. "Elliot, you may join us if you wish."

I cut my gaze to Elliot. He should go home instead of getting wrapped up in this.

Something was wrong. I could sense it the closer I was to Prescott. He masked how he truly felt in public behind a façade, but I'd spent enough time with him over the centuries to pick up on his mannerisms.

We followed him into his grand office. Many Renaissance paintings lined the walls, and a colossal crystal chandelier hung overhead. I kept my arms at my sides, focusing on remaining calm and neutral, especially after my misbehavior during the meeting. Besides, Elliot had warned me about Prescott being on edge due to my recent lapse in attendance.

Our chairman sat in a massive brown leather chair behind his ornate mahogany desk, and waved to the crimson seats facing it.

Elliot took the one on the right, and I sat in the other.

"Congratulations on your promotion, Elliot. You are witness to this discussion." My friend nodded, and Prescott turned his gaze on me. "What distracted you in the chamber? You don't like politics, but there is an air of unease about you. You *will* tell me the truth."

Thankfully, Prescott wasn't a telepath, but he was excellent at deciphering lies.

I lowered my head. "I'm wary after hearing about Tom Turner, my lord. An attack was made on my life yesterday." It took all my strength not to shift in my chair, especially under Prescott's watchful eyes.

He nodded. "I see. You clearly fought off your assailants. Did you know either of them?"

I shook my head. "I did not."

"If I may, my lord..." Elliot stood and bowed at the waist.

Prescott waved his hand in dismissal. "Save the formalities for the council's chamber."

"I visited Derek at his home and noticed a familiar scent, presumably belonging to one of the attackers."

"And who would that be? Do you have more than that? A name, perhaps?" Prescott turned the full weight of his gaze on Elliot.

"Sadly, I don't recall where I know the scent from." Elliot didn't shrink back.

"Disappointing." Prescott examined a few papers on his desk. "I'd need more information before I can say if the attacks are connected." He leaned back in his chair, glancing between us. "I have the initial information on Tom's death here. If you agree not to speak of this matter with anyone else, I will share it with you."

"I won't say anything." If my attempted kidnapping was connected, I might figure out who was after me. I doubted whoever it was would give up so easily.

2

CARMELA

*B*rendan intrigued me. There had to be more to him than what I knew. I mean, our box seats at the theater had an excellent view, with the added bonus of someone catering to our every need. The play itself had enthralled me from the moment the curtains lifted.

The steakhouse we were at now was a five-star restaurant, and unlike any I'd ever been to. The menu hadn't even listed prices, so I imagined our meal was costing Brendan a pretty penny.

He smiled at me from across the table, the expression warming his ocean-blue eyes. The more time we spent together, the more I wondered about him and our potential future. Could I trust him?

Maybe my wariness was due to my experiences with other werewolf males. Mother sometimes talked about how things were with my father before they mated. He wooed her and treated her well, until she conceived a female child. Would Brendan be the same way? Did he value a male werewolf for an heir so much that he would shun me or the female offspring I might bear?

I stabbed a juicy piece of rare steak and plopped it into my mouth, trying to use the manners my mom had drilled into me. As I took in the classy surroundings, I realized now was certainly one of those times when I needed them. When he'd offered to take me out for steaks, I should've known it wouldn't be to a diner, but I hadn't expected all of *this*.

I savored the steak's taste and texture, not knowing when —or if—I would ever have something so delicious again. Maybe if I mated with Brendan, I wouldn't be under the strict constraints Father placed on our family. I might be able to make my own choices, if the face Brendan showed now was any indication of who he really was. What other werewolf would brush off a vampire encounter because I'd asked him to? I couldn't think of a reason for him to do that, unless this union meant something to him other than fulfilling an obligation or making a power play.

I hoped what he portrayed wasn't a lie meant to lure me in. If he sunk his claws into me and then expected to treat me the way Father treated Mom, I would run away to the Outskirts. Life was a lot more dangerous there, but I wouldn't submit to more abuse. I refused.

Brendan placed his hand on mine. "Is everything okay?" He glanced down at my plate to see the meat almost gone, and smiled again. "If you'd like another steak, we can get more."

My eyebrows rose. Another steak would be divine. But thinking of Father and the fact that I'd be returning home soon made me nauseated. I couldn't handle more food even if I wanted to. "Everything's great. The food is wonderful, but I'll have to pass on another steak. Thank you, though."

"I know what you're holding out for. Dessert, right?" He held up a hand for the leggy blonde waitress, who hurried over to us. "A dessert menu, please." Brendan kept his gaze on me instead of on the waitress, showing that his interest was in me, the woman he'd be mated with.

A sigh of uncertainty escaped my lungs. He seemed almost too good to be true. Why was he doing this? My father had arranged our mating, so pretense wasn't required. *Except on my part.*

The waitress returned with the dessert menu and placed it in front of us. She looked to Brendan, as if desperate for his attention. "Would you like a little time to look over the menu? Or do you know what you'd like?"

"I'll defer to the lady," he said, smiling at me. "Do you know what you'd like, Carmela?"

I glanced at the menu, feeling the pressure of his gaze on me. The thought of having more food didn't sit well with my stomach, but I didn't want to ruin the evening by telling him what really bothered me. "Hmm... How about the molten hot fudge brownie?"

Brendan nodded. "That's my favorite too."

"I'll have that right out." The waitress took the menu and retreated from the table, her shoulders slumped.

"Are you sure everything's okay?" he asked once the waitress was out of earshot. "I want you to enjoy yourself. If there's anything I can do to make this better, tell me." Concern crinkled the corners of his eyes, and his lips tightened into a slim pink line.

Acting so downtrodden wasn't fair to him. He'd gone through the effort to plan this evening for me. I shouldn't be giving off negative energy when he obviously wanted our first date to be special. "I'm sorry." I let out a breath I hadn't realized I'd been holding. "I guess I don't want our evening to end." *Truth.* Going back home would mean dealing with my father.

"Do you mind if I ask a personal question?" His piercing gaze made me feel naked.

"That would depend on the question." I lowered my gaze, not wanting the conversation to descend into anything uncomfortable, but then again, maybe I owed him for such a wonderful evening.

"Does your father hurt you? Be truthful with me. This is important."

My mouth dropped open. I should've expected he would ask something like that, considering how standoffish I'd been with him, but I couldn't help the keyed-up nervousness that betrayed my baggage. Father had acted rather confrontational at the house, too. Maybe he'd noticed that. I moved my mouth, but no words came out. I just stared at him, speechless.

"Please, answer the question. I don't want to force the issue." He pointed at my shoulder splint. "Did he do that to you?"

I shook my head. "No." If only he knew... My chest clenched, and I wondered what he'd do if he found out my father did hurt me sometimes. *Calm down. Don't panic. It'll all be okay.*

Brendan's brows drew together and he leaned in. "Fine. If you want to tell me, I can make sure he doesn't hurt you anymore. You don't have to protect him. He's not worthy of a wonderful daughter like you."

I blinked at him, relieved that he seemed concerned about my safety, but also scared. Maybe he thought he could protect me, but I doubted that was possible, given my father's prestige. How could he beat a man like that? He'd only get himself hurt.

The scent of hot fudge filled my nose as the waitress headed toward our table. *Saved by a brownie.* I wrung the napkin in my lap as she placed a hot fudge brownie delight on the table with two spoons sticking out of it.

"Would you like anything else this evening?" she asked, looking between the two of us.

"No," Brendan said.

"I'll leave the check here. Feel free to pay when you're ready."

"Thank you." Brendan grabbed a spoon from the dessert and ate a couple of small bites with whipped cream and hot fudge. He didn't look at me or say another word.

Sighing, I picked up the other spoon and kept to my side of the brownie. Heaven forbid he thought I didn't want any. That might upset him even more.

We shared the blame for the evening falling to ruin. If he hadn't insisted on bringing up my father, then I wouldn't have refused to give him a proper answer, let alone the truth. But what could I do? Say my father was a cruel bastard who seemed closer to diving off the deep end than ever, and then deal with the consequences of my actions? Brendan couldn't do anything about my father. Only the Alpha of Alphas' opinion would carry any weight, and a werewolf like that wouldn't care for a random girl like me.

I needed to leave the restaurant and get away for a while. Just take a walk and be on my own. I set my spoon down on the edge of the plate, not willing to eat anymore. If I left Brendan, I could be throwing away my future. He'd been kind, if a little pushy. Besides, Father would be furious if I arrived home by myself, and if the *Cazador* showed up...I'd be *screwed*.

The idea only having one arm to defend myself—and of risking further injury if I shifted—made me that much more desperate to shed my human skin and run free. Life had become far too stressful. Maybe the Outskirts *would* be better than this.

The people around us all seemed happy, regardless of the

apocalypse the world had faced. Their smiles and lingering touches hurt my heart. I wanted those things so much. A true, loving relationship...could that ever happen for me?

The harsh bang of a gun firing sounded somewhere outside, and I nearly jumped out of my seat. Panic thrummed in my chest. Another bang followed the first, and loud scrambling noises ensued. The *Cazador* were after more nocturnes. I glanced at Brendan, and our eyes met.

He appeared stoic, but the energy around him spiked, giving me a sensation like ants marching across my skin. His gaze shifted to the door, as if willing someone to come through so he could kill them.

The shouts and gunshots grew louder. But we should be safe here. The hunters wouldn't dare rampage through such a fancy restaurant, not when the people who frequented places like this funded them. Though that might not stop them if they were in pursuit.

My shoulders tensed, and I placed my hand on his. "Don't. You can't risk yourself."

Brendan looked at me for a moment, then pulled away. He dug through his wallet, leaving more money on the table than I typically saw in a year. "You're right. Let's get out of here. I don't want you to be this close to danger, especially while defenseless." He stood and held out his hand for me.

"I'm not defenseless." Frowning, I stared up at him. "I could protect myself if I had to." I'd handled myself with Derek, after all. Getting one up on a vampire wasn't an easy task.

Narrowing his eyes, he extended his hand farther. "Right now, you're *my* responsibility. I'm in charge of your safety. Don't make me cause a scene, because I will." Anger darkened his eyes.

I drew in a shaky breath, not comfortable with this side of

him, but I accepted his offered hand. The last thing we needed was attention drawn to us.

The large windows at the front of the restaurant shattered, and glass rained inward. Several guests screamed and ducked under tables. Having the *Cazador* interrupt an evening wasn't uncommon, but they usually kept to the streets unless they were in pursuit of nocturnes.

Brendan crouched beside me, his hand squeezing mine a little tighter.

Fear pumped through my veins as three *Cazador* filed through the front door.

Near the shattered glass crouched a man. No, it was a nocturne, with blood trickling over the pale skin of his face and arms. He watched the *Cazador,* wrinkling his nose with utter disgust. The nocturne flashed long fangs and darted toward the back of the restaurant, past our table. He sucked in a deep breath and paused to hiss at us before continuing.

At the restaurant's entrance, the hostess held her hand over her mouth, swaying on her feet as if she was moments from fainting. One of the hunters poked her in the chest, causing her to collapse to the floor, while the others darted after the vampire. Satisfied by intimidating the woman, the third man barreled through the restaurant to catch up with his pals. My heart skipped a beat. He was the younger hunter from the *Teatro* the other night.

Oh no. I dropped my purse and ducked my head, hoping he wouldn't notice me. Brendan pulled me closer to his hard torso and kept my panic at bay.

Thankfully, the hunter ran by without even a glance in our direction. Once the commotion died down, I strode toward the door, with Brendan close behind in the small crowd anxious to leave their ruined dinners behind. Once we were outside, he grabbed my arm, pulling me aside.

"What happened in there?" He tilted my chin up, forcing my gaze to meet his. "You hid from the last guy."

"He was..." My voice broke a little and I cleared my throat. "He was at the *Teatro*..." I scanned the street around us, making sure no one was nearby, then glanced back. "He shot me." I pointed at the shoulder splint, grimacing at the constant throb of pain.

Brendan's spine stiffened. "He hurt you." The muscles in his jaw tightened, and he clenched his hands into fists. "He could've killed you. I can't stand by and let him get away with that."

I grabbed him by the arm as he turned away. "Stop. Please." I tried to pull him in the direction of my home. We needed to get out of there before the hunters came back. But he stayed rooted in place like a large tree. I tugged harder, using my supernatural strength, but he still didn't move. "Brendan, we should go home."

Footsteps and more gunshots sounded nearby. Probably the *Cazador* continuing their vampire hunt. With how rowdy they were, it was curious that they actually found nocturnes in the first place. People ran on the sidewalk behind us, and before I could turn, the vampire from the restaurant barreled past, shoving me into Brendan, who stumbled against the wall.

The three *Cazador* rushed past as I tried to regain my composure. One of them rammed his elbow into my shoulder as he went. I bit my lower lip, holding in a scream. Tears slid over my cheeks, and I buried my face in the hard planes of Brendan's chest.

He carefully wrapped his arms around me and rubbed my back in soothing circles. His touch comforted me, but we couldn't do this here. It was too dangerous. I pulled away as the hurried footfalls faded into the distance.

"We need to get out of here. We're lucky the hunters

didn't spot me." I glanced up at him. "Besides, I do need your protection, and I don't want you to die trying to get revenge."

Warmth glowed in his eyes, and he nodded. "You're right. Let's get you safe."

I brushed my fingers along his jaw line and smiled. Maybe not all men were like my father.

3

DEREK

"*A* vampire killed Tom. It's disgusting to see our kind turn on each other. We aren't humans. We should be above trivial civil wars." Prescott glanced between us. "Reports from a surviving member of his entourage, a wizard, said there were three unfamiliar vampires. Tom's people killed one. By the time the wizard escaped, his master was dead, and he had no clue who'd murdered Tom.

"I suspected the wizard had a part in it. After all, how best to escape one's master than by one's own hand? However, you had a similar experience. Now I fear something more menacing is going on. I'd appreciate you telling me if you notice anything else out of the ordinary. We can't afford to lose another member of the High Council." The concern wasn't lost on me, even though he pretended it was for my role in the council. Prescott leveled his gaze at Elliot. "You need to be careful as well. You'd be no good to us dead. I don't want your promotion to be in vain. Now go."

I lowered my head, glad the meeting was over, even if it hadn't given me any clarity. Perhaps Tom's entourage had killed him. There were rumors that he hadn't been the nicest master. But I didn't keep pets—life was simpler on my own—so that wouldn't explain why the necromancer and his friend came after me.

Elliot swept into an elaborate bow. "I will do my best, my lord."

Prescott waved his hand at my friend. "I told you to do away with formalities."

Once Elliot and I were outside the High Council's building, I released a premature breath of relief.

Gunshots and the thundering of boots revealed the *Cazador* were already roaming the streets. I needed to return home. I didn't want to risk dealing with the annoying hunters.

I clapped Elliot on the back, urging him along. After one attempt on my life, I didn't want to stay still. Fate need not be tempted again, and I had limits to how much drama I could handle in one evening.

"When will you take Lord Prescott's hint and act more casually during private meetings? Sometimes you allow your manners to get in the way of business." I glanced at the century-younger vampire and smirked.

Rolling his eyes, Elliot brushed my hand from his shoulder. "It's not my fault. I have some humanity left in me, unlike some who will remain unnamed."

"You do? Then why do you enjoy the politics of the council? Since when does that relate to anything humane?" I shook my head. "No, I don't understand those who enjoy it. Not in this day and age. When the world was still whole and politics didn't bring us to this level of depravity, sure, even I didn't mind the game, but now...it disgusts me."

I leaned closer to Elliot and spoke so softly I could barely hear myself. "Especially since some place themselves on moral high horses when really, what difference is there among the nocturnes when we're all in the process of being exterminated like insects? No one looks at the threat humans pose. No one thinks to quit fighting amongst ourselves and work together."

Elliot's expression turned grim, and he shook his head. "How can you think that would be the answer? Not harming lesser nocturnes wouldn't solve the problem. It would only make us appear weaker. We wouldn't have our position of authority with the races we are at peace with."

I balled my hands into fists. Elliot's opinion was the popular one amongst vampires. They believed it was better to be powerful alone than to ally with the other races, but my interaction with Carmela showed the potential for peace.

Not everyone was of the same mindset. We were the hunted, not the hunters, these days. Being centuries old and knowing how our ancestors had thrived frustrated me. We'd always had easy prey living amongst humans, but those days were firmly in the past. I lamented them because I had witnessed that paradise for myself. Those days weren't a fantasy to me as they were for some of my younger kin.

"You don't understand the brainwashing you've been subjected to, Elliot. That's all."

Before I could react, he slammed me into the building next to us. Elliot's face hovered before mine. His upper lip trembled with the effort to keep his fangs hidden as a light shade of pink flooded his cheeks. "*You* don't understand. I know what's going on with you—why you want change. I smelled *her* on your spare bed. No, don't give me that look. I snooped because you made me suspicious. You should be ashamed of yourself." He drew in a breath. "I, as your friend, gave my word that I wouldn't tell anyone about your tryst with the lycanthrope. Maybe the reason you're interested in becoming friends with everyone else is that you don't want to hide your relationship with her. Maybe you don't care about what it could do to our people."

"And what would that be?" I glanced around the street, making sure no one was around to witness our discussion. "Having more unity, less pissing around with others, not holding firm to a Feud that no one knows the purpose of? How many years has it been going on? Not even Lord Prescott has said why the Feud continues. Perhaps even he doesn't know, and he's been around longer than you and I combined." I shoved Elliot away from me, tired of him being in my face.

He stumbled back a few steps. Frustration drew his eyebrows together. "Fine. I have my doubts about it, but *I'm* not willing to throw away my people's security for a wolf who might have been sent to eradicate us. But as your friend, I'll let you make your own decision. Make sure it doesn't drive all sense from you and get you killed." He looked up into the cloudy night. "Don't make me act on behalf of the High Council, especially now, with my promotion. You saved my life by turning me, and I don't want to betray you. But I can't be disloyal to Lord Prescott. He'd sense it."

Frowning, I smoothed out the wrinkles from my shirt. "I don't want to put you in that position. I'm not having relations with the w..." I scanned the darkness around us again, uneasy about having this conversation in public. There was no way of telling who could hear us. "Woman. However, I don't think singling each other out is the best way to stay alive. We should try to do something about the situation we're in instead of blaming others, especially since we know nothing about why the Feud is happening."

"But if our elders saw fit..." Elliot raised his clasped fists toward me as if begging me to understand. But he let his hands slowly fall to his sides and shook his head. "You're right. Perhaps we should figure out why our people are dying before bringing something like this to Lord Prescott. I wouldn't know how to explain it. He has such a strict view on things."

"You don't have to be the one to tell him. Once we find out why Tom was killed, I can explain the reasoning behind my ideas. Hopefully he'll listen, but if not, I won't have to feel bad about getting you involved. Besides, Lord Prescott and I have an agreement letting me freely communicate my concerns to him." Granted, that was before I started skipping High Council meetings left and right, but I didn't think he would have me killed for speaking my mind. If that were the case, I would've been dead long ago. The only way Prescott might be convinced to kill me would be for disobedience. Actions like not showing up for meetings...or worse, helping an injured werewolf and developing feelings for her.

If Elliot remained true to his word about not telling the council, then I had no reason to fear. But what if Prescott discovered my deceit and ordered Elliot to talk? Elliot would sing like a bird about my relationship with Carmela. Maybe I did have reason for concern after all.

Pounding footsteps thumped against the sidewalk ahead, and I turned toward the noise. I didn't want to deal with the *Cazador,* tonight of all nights.

Elliot froze in place, and his gaze searched the area.

A grinning vampire jogged toward us, flashing his fangs. Behind the vampire were three *Cazador,* huffing and puffing as they ran.

I rolled my eyes. This wasn't what our kind needed, someone acting stupid just to show off.

One of the *Cazador* looked familiar. Anger darkened his eyes, and he removed his pistol from its holster. Digging into his pocket, he pulled out a glowing bullet that looked like it had sunlight radiating from it.

I jerked my head to the side, trying to get the vampire's attention. If only I possessed telepathy instead of telekinesis, right now would've been an opportune time to use it. The young vampire ignored me, not heeding my silent warning.

"Die, bloodsucker," the hunter said.

The gunshot exploded through the night air, and I had a moment to see the vampire's eyes widen before he exploded into dust. The bullet flew through his ashy remains, straight toward us.

I pulled Elliot toward the building and pressed myself against the wall, not wanting the bullet to touch us. I had no idea what was in it, but whatever it was, it was lethal.

Elliot and I crossed the street to put space between ourselves and the *Cazador*. We could've died from the strange bullet. The hunters were still humans, but they grew more dangerous with each passing day.

4

BRENDAN

*T*he tender feeling of Carmela's hands on my skin brought my beast closer to the surface. I couldn't wait to undergo the official ceremony and take her as my mate. She made me feel so many emotions that I'd never felt for anyone else.

I drew her in for another hug before letting go. We stared into each other's eyes, neither of us moving to leave. While I knew she was right and that we should get her home, I didn't want the night to be over.

The bang of a single gunshot sent shivers down my spine. It sounded so final, so definite. A growl rumbled in my chest before I caught myself. "Let's go. That hunter could come back. I don't want you to be spotted." She would be my mate. It was my job to keep her safe, regardless of her Militia training.

"Yes, you're right." Her voice trembled, and she looked physically shaken.

I rested my hand on her uninjured shoulder. "Are you okay? They hit you hard. If you need to see Dr. Matthews, I can send for him once we reach your home."

She smiled, but it looked more like a wince. I should've thought about getting her seen sooner. Her shoulders were bunched up, and pain tightened the corners of her lips and eyes. She seemed to consider my offer for a moment, but shook her head. "No, thank you."

"Let me know if you change your mind." I offered her my arm, and she placed her hand on the crook of my elbow.

"Thank you." She walked with me, jumping at each bump in the night. It made me increasingly on edge. Then a feeling of being watched crept over me.

Across the street, the dark-haired vampire we'd seen earlier strolled along with another vampire. The other one turned his gaze to us. A smirk tugged at his lips, but he kept his fangs hidden. Carmela's fingers bit into my arm, and I placed my hand on hers, trying to comfort her.

She looked up at me, loosening her grip as if remembering I was there too. Looking ahead, I saw the *Cazador* who had shot her walking toward us, seeming pleased about something. His gaze rose and Carmela gasped. A second passed before recognition lit up his eyes and he reached for his gun.

I swirled around, pushing Carmela ahead of me, and we darted back toward the restaurant where we'd eaten dinner.

She ran, but it was plain to see the pain weighing down her movements. She tried holding her arm in place so it wouldn't jerk around too much. The idea of tossing her over my shoulder and taking off crossed my mind, but that would take a moment away from the chase, a moment that might cost us dearly. Besides, I didn't want to injure her further. But her life was more important than momentary pain. Once we were out of sight, I'd sweep her off her feet and get her to safety.

"Just go without me," she said, pain clear in her voice. "I'm slowing you down."

"No. I'm not leaving you to fend for yourself."

More voices shouted behind us, making all kinds of excited yells. The hunter's buddies had come along for the party after all.

She turned a corner at full speed. The high heel she wore snapped, sending her crashing to the ground. I yanked her to her feet without stopping. She kicked off the other heel toward a pile of trash. There was the crunch of broken glass underfoot, and she cried out.

I scooped her into my arms and continued running.

Two dark figures blocked the exit of the alleyway. How could the hunters have gotten there so quickly? That didn't make sense. Heavy clomping footfalls echoed from behind us.

As I ran closer, the scent of death filled my nose. Vampires.

"Hurry. Follow us," the vampire from earlier said in a harsh whisper.

"Why should we trust you?" I hissed.

A loud bang echoed in the alleyway, and I jerked to the side as a bullet narrowly missed us. "Fine, but don't give me a reason to tear your heads from your shoulders."

"This is a waste of time," the second vampire said. He ran off, his steps swift and light as he headed south, to the area of town where werewolves frequently resided.

"We'll follow you," I said, looking down at Carmela. A shard of glass stuck out from her foot, and she bit her lower lip to keep from making any more sounds.

I easily kept pace with the two vampires as we nearly flew through the night, much faster than what the *Cazador* could manage. Filthy humans. They hadn't been able to assault us. We'd been lucky this time.

The loud bang of gunfire startled me. Carmela looked over my shoulder with wide eyes. The bullet whipped through the air, and I yelled as my knees gave way and Carmela spilled from my arms. I reached for her, desperate to keep her safe.

The vampire from earlier grabbed Carmela, while the other one pulled me into his arms and kept moving. My hackles rose at being touched by him, but there was nothing I could do. For some reason they'd decided to help us.

"Lycanthropes. You're just not as quick as we are," the vamp carrying me said.

5

DEREK

*P*ain tightened Carmela's face. Something about her made me want to cradle her close and not let go. What was I doing? I'd gotten Elliot involved in all of this, and he was a senior High Council member now.

I could detach from my feelings and tell myself that advising Lord Prescott and the High Council about uniting the nocturnal community was a matter of politics and smart thinking. But holding Carmela close and breathing in her scent, I knew this was more personal than I'd convinced myself.

Perhaps Elliot was right. Was I doing this for a chance at being with Carmela? I didn't know.

Elliot stood beside me with the werewolf flung over his shoulder. He held the male like a sack of potatoes rather than a vicious beast in human form. Then again, there wasn't any difference between the person Elliot carried and the one I held. After all, if I fought for equality among the races, and for the community to come together, how could I act untoward to her future mate?

I saw how close they were earlier, how he'd positioned his

hand on Carmela's shoulder possessively. But I didn't have any right to think I could stake a claim. Our people would kill us if we were found out. Besides, she seemed pretty content with him.

My heart didn't feel the same way, however. For the first time in a long time, I wanted to do something utterly senseless.

We lost the *Cazador* as Elliot and I ran at our true speeds. The hunters probably weren't used to dealing with vampires as old as we were. Humans didn't have the ability to detect the dark blur of shadow that vampires encased ourselves in. Precision shooting wasn't their strong point, either. The young vamp had ended up dead only due to his own stupidity and apparent desire to show off.

Prescott wouldn't like that news, especially after his speech tonight. Poor Elliot. He'd have to report what he'd seen.

I hated the idiocy our younger kin showed when they fooled around with the *Cazador*. What the vampire had done during that chase decreased our population at a time when we needed our numbers.

We slowed down when we were far enough away. An older warehouse loomed above us, looking like a good place to rest. The building probably hadn't seen use in several years. Elliot and I laid our werewolves on the concrete floor.

I knelt beside Carmela, staring at the blood as it dripped from her foot. I lifted her ankle slightly, noting the way her dress shifted. Her white, lacy panties caught my eye, and lust warmed my veins, sending blood to my groin. Clearing my throat, I refocused my gaze on the glass embedded in her foot.

"What are you doing, vampire?" the male werewolf spoke up. His gaze locked on mine without fear, even though I had more power here.

"I have medical expertise. I used to be a doctor as a human. I can help her, and you, if you'll let me." My voice was low and calm. The last thing I needed was to pick a fight with an injured werewolf. That would not only cause him more anger and stress, but he might feel obligated to protect his soon-to-be mate and push his body beyond the restraints of pain. That would do neither of us any good.

"Just chill out, please. Brendan, they probably wouldn't have saved us from the hunters to make us into a snack," Carmela kept her gaze on me before shifting it to her foot.

Grinning, Elliot circled us, keeping just out of Brendan's reach. "A snack... Now that's a tempting offer. Sadly, I've already eaten for the night. Maybe we'll have to reschedule for some other time." For someone who didn't favor the nocturnal community coming together, Elliot certainly seemed to be taking this situation in stride.

Brendan watched Elliot, a feral snarl rumbling in his chest. "Don't even *think* about it, vampire." At least it took his attention off Carmela and me for a moment.

"I need something to stem the blood flow after I pull the shard of glass from your foot." I looked around the room, unsurprisingly not finding a first aid kit, or even anything clean. I stood, ready to rip off a section of my shirt.

Carmela opened her mouth to respond, but Brendan answered first. "Here. Use this." He pulled a handkerchief from his pocket. It was stark white, soft, and made from fine linen. It had a golden B.K. embroidered on it. It was obviously expensive, and yet he was so eager to give it up for her.

"Thank you." I accepted the handkerchief and tucked it in my pocket to keep it from touching the dirty floor. My fingertips brushed the edges of the glass, and Carmela pulled her foot away from me. "Stop moving around, C..." I cursed myself. If I used her name, I'd strike up suspicion with her mate and Elliot. "Keep still. If I don't get this glass out, you won't heal properly."

"It hurts," she said. Apparently, no one had caught my near-slip. Carmela closed her eyes and bit her lip, holding in the pain.

Elliot knelt beside me and grabbed her shin, holding her leg firmly.

Her eyes snapped open. She flailed her arm, and this made me happy I'd ended up binding the other one to her torso so well. Her panic spread through the room, and Brendan growled, crawling closer to her. He caught her free arm, entwining his fingers with hers. The intimate act spurred jealousy in me. It took all I had not to pry their hands apart. "Just relax and let them take out the glass." Brendan slid his other hand through her caramel-colored hair. "Everything's going to be fine. I'm here."

I tugged the glass free—maybe a little harder than I needed to—and placed it in my back pocket. She yelped, and the wolf grunted, presumably from her white-knuckled grip on his hand. I barely restrained my smile.

With the shard out, I tied the handkerchief around her foot to help stanch the bleeding. It wouldn't do much, but it'd be enough to help her get home and be seen by a doctor. I moved away from her, uncomfortable with the way she held Brendan's hand but kept her gaze on me. "There, you should be fine soon."

"I'm not so sure about that." Brendan sat up a little more, clenching his teeth against the agony of his wounds. "She was shot the other day, I presume with silver. That might explain why her skin didn't heal around the glass. Her body may be too overloaded to heal with ease." As soon as the words left his mouth, he smacked his fist against his forehead.

Carmela raised her eyebrows at Brendan but stroked his arm, trying to soothe him. "It's okay."

"No, it's not. I shouldn't have given that information to them. They're our enemy."

She jerked away from him. "Enemy? They just helped us."

I glanced over at Elliot, who was perched on an old crate. "Fun evening, huh?" He shrugged his shoulders, looking amused by the bickering wolves.

Pushing aside their arguing, I studied Carmela's body. I'd removed the bullet from her shoulder a few days ago, and while she'd been shot with silver, I did find it odd that she still wore the brace. Hadn't she shifted yet? What was her doctor thinking, allowing her to stay in human form instead of forcing her to shift?

But what did I know? Her doctor had studied their physiology and healing rates, unlike me, who only knew about them from books and gossip.

After waiting for a few moments, I cleared my throat. "If you two would stop for a moment," I said, ready for the night to be over. Trying to pretend like I didn't know her, and being with her almost-mate, set me on edge. "I'm sure she'll heal when she shifts."

I glanced between the two wolves. Since I'd helped Carmela, I needed to offer the same courtesy to Brendan. "Would you like me to check your wounds?" The pool of blood around him grew, and I hated to think about him getting delayed treatment. "I don't have my tools with me, but I might be able to stem the bleeding and see what they shot you with."

6

BRENDAN

I stared up at the vamp doctor, not excited about having him near me, especially while I was vulnerable. However, I felt my strength ebbing, and if I didn't have his help then I would grow weaker, until I wasn't able to protect Carmela at all.

I finally nodded and rolled to my stomach, giving him access to the wound on the back of my leg. This evening was already tense from the *Cazador* attack, and now I was dealing with vampires. Huffing, I rested my chin on my palms and stared at the far wall, but I kept my ears alert to any whisper of movement. If I needed to defend us, I would. Injuries be damned.

"Calm down," Carmela said, placing her hand on my shoulder. As soon as she did, the bulk of tension drained from my body, and I let out a deep breath. I couldn't believe the impact she had on me already. This relationship was so much more than I'd anticipated could happen between mates.

The vampire doctor knelt near my leg, and I glanced over

my shoulder. He frowned, a spark of concern lighting his eyes. I followed his gaze to the bloody mess covering the back of my pant leg. I placed my hand over Carmela's and focused on breathing. "I'll need to rip your pants at least to the knee for a better look."

Stay calm. If you shift now, you'll do more harm than good. If I accidentally hurt Carmela or even killed the vampires who'd helped us, I'd regret it. Something about those two was different from what I'd heard about the majority of their people.

"That's fine," I said, surprised at how calm I sounded.

The other vampire began pacing back and forth near the door as if afraid Carmela and I would bounce up and run away. Not likely.

From what I could see in the dim light, the vampire's black eyes burned with hunger. He paused as he looked at me, then continued pacing.

"Don't worry about Elliot. The blood is calling to him. He'll be fine." The vamp doctor still looked composed, but his movements were jerkier than they'd been with Carmela, as if he had to restrain himself more now.

"Fine. Just do what you have to do." I only hoped I didn't regret saying that. "It hurts like hell." I ground my teeth, feeling my body tense up again as he placed his hands on the bloody fabric. He shredded the pant leg all the way up to my thigh with one yank. I jerked, ready to fly at him and attack.

A growl bubbled up from my throat, but Carmela kept her hand firmly on my shoulder. The only way I could get up was by brushing her aside and potentially hurting her, and I refused to do that. Instead, I continued growling.

"The bullet struck and tore through the muscles. Hmm... I'm not sure what they shot you with. I can't tell without the proper equipment. However, the wound is filled with a mixture of silver and something else." He tore the shredded pant leg off as if to make them into fancy cutoffs, then tied it around the gunshot wound. "I'm sorry I can't be of more help. You'll need to see someone with the proper tools, and quickly, given the severity of your wound."

Elliot stopped pacing and stared between the doctor, Carmela, and me. With the wound bound, he appeared more like the vampire who'd helped me than one who wanted to feast on my blood. Good to know he hadn't changed his mind about making us into snacks.

"Where's your home? Your doctor needs to treat this immediately. This is like nothing I've ever seen." He hesitantly wiped his bloody hands on his black jeans, and I wondered for a moment if he'd wanted to lick them clean.

That thought set me on edge, so I pushed it away.

"Why should I tell you where I live?" I rolled—albeit a little awkwardly—onto my back. Intense pain from my leg left me staring up at the ceiling. *Breathe in, breathe out.* "How do I know you won't attack me or send your people after my family?" If he did, I knew where he lived, so I could easily retaliate. But if he was right, and I suspected he was, then I needed to trust them.

"For the same reason you won't attack me after having discovered where I reside." He narrowed his eyes at me, but his attention wandered over, for the briefest of moments, to Carmela before looking back at me.

The need to protect her rose in my chest, but I couldn't help wondering if there was something here that I didn't know about. Why else would he have helped us so selflessly? "Fine. I'll keep quiet."

He nodded to Carmela. "What about her? She'll need treatment too."

I forced myself into a sitting position, regardless of the

pain. "She'll go with me." Wrapping my arm around Carmela's waist, I pulled her closer. Maybe I was being territorial or whatever, but she was promised to me. *Mine.* I told them where to take us.

7

CARMELA

*B*rendan's hand on my waist both soothed and unnerved me. Maybe he'd caught the way Derek looked at me, or perhaps it was just his way of being a macho male werewolf. I didn't know.

Elliot walked a few feet closer to us. "We don't have much time. Let's get them home."

Frowning, I looked between the two vampires. What did he mean about not having much time? The realization struck me like a hammer to the chest. The sun. An overwhelming dread squeezed my throat until breathing became a struggle.

Father was probably furious with me. Fear and nausea roiled my stomach. *Don't give in. Keep calm.* I needed to focus on my breathing with Brendan and Derek so near. When Derek touched my foot, I'd felt something beyond pain, something that made me wonder if my feelings for him weren't just wistful dreams after all. And his curious gaze...would it have been so bad to stay with him instead of running home?

I shoved the thought away.

Derek watched me as if he could see inside my head, but I

knew that wasn't the case. I never would've escaped in the first place if that were true. Oddly enough, I wasn't scared of him. He'd had plenty of chances to use his power on me, to take my mind or drink my life's blood. But he hadn't.

I trusted him.

Brendan's grip fell away, and Derek lifted me into his arms as if I weighed nothing. The vampire stole my breath, and I averted my gaze, trying to keep some semblance of distance. What I felt for Brendan was real. He was kind and caring. If he truly was the man he portrayed himself to be, then he'd be the mate I'd hoped existed. However, what I felt for him was different from what Derek stirred inside me. Brendan watched me from the floor with concern, and I couldn't help but feel conflicted.

Glancing up at Derek, I wondered what the future I desired with him could hold. Most likely death, pain, and suffering. Neither werewolves nor vampires would ever allow us to be together. However, the relationship I'd soon be in with Brendan was arranged, and I refused to have my life dictated to me. It wasn't rebellion, just my objection to not being given the chance to fall head over heels for someone.

Elliot hefted Brendan over his shoulder again. This time he appeared a little more careful, but Brendan went with it, even if I could hear soft growling coming from him. Elliot zipped to the door in a blur, and Derek followed. Dizziness overwhelmed my senses as wind blew my hair into my face. I could barely make out the alleyway we darted through.

Squeezing my eyes closed, I focused my thoughts on the play I'd seen with Brendan. They'd performed *Romeo and Juliet*. It had been breathtakingly beautiful, though entirely tragic. Taking a few breaths, I felt the nausea at the feeling of flying through the air slowly dissipate. While my kind were strong, I wasn't used to this excessive speed, and the idea of puking on Derek was embarrassing.

Without much thought, I wrapped my arms around Derek's neck, burying my face into his chest. He stiffened at my touch before relaxing. Maybe my feelings weren't one-sided. He and Elliot had helped us with the *Cazador,* after all.

After a few moments, Derek slowed before coming to a stop. I withdrew my face from his chest and stared up at the palatial house before us. It was much larger than the one my parents owned. It also wasn't a row house but a standalone.

Surprise widened my eyes, and I glanced at Brendan in amazement. No wonder he'd been able to take me out to such a fancy restaurant and the play. His family was apparently very wealthy.

With that kind of money, one wouldn't have to worry about purchasing simple things like a new pair of shoes or good food for the table. My father was stingy. Although he always used the word 'frugal,' I saw through his act. I knew the difference between what he said and what was true.

Elliot walked up the stairs and knocked on the door. Derek followed, closing the distance between me and Brendan. I remembered too late about my arms circling Derek's neck.

Brendan lifted his gaze to me. The muscles in his jaw tightened as he ground his teeth, but he didn't say a word. That startled me more than him snarling or showing his anger.

I pulled away from Derek and averted my gaze from the men. Instead, I stared straight at the lit upper window of the house.

Noises sounded inside the house, and Derek gently lowered me to the ground. Brendan didn't get the same treatment. He grunted as his ass smacked the concrete porch. He narrowed his gaze at Elliot and snarled.

The vampire hissed back at him, then nodded at Derek. "See you around, friend."

"You as well. Stay safe." Derek swept his gaze over me one last time, then a cool breeze caressed my cheek. I looked around, but they were gone, as if they'd never been there at all.

The front door opened, and a middle-aged woman with blonde hair and light blue eyes stared at us. She pressed a hand over her mouth.

"Who is it, Beatrice?" a concerned male voice asked behind her. A tall, ruddy man hovered behind the petite woman. His eyebrows drew together. "Son? What's going on?"

Brendan cast a glance in my direction, brushing a hand through his blond hair. "Meet Carmela, my future mate. On the way back to her place, hunters attacked us. I didn't think it'd be safe to drop her off at home, so I brought her here." He struggled to a standing position and leaned heavily against the railing before reaching for me.

I accepted his hand, and he pulled me into the warmth of his arms.

Beatrice nudged her husband aside and waved us in. "Let's get you two comfortable and call the good doctor." She led the way, but she kept her gaze on us. "Do you want your father's help, Brendan? Your leg doesn't look good at all. The scent of blood is so strong, dear."

Brendan hobbled inside, barely keeping himself upright. I tightened my grip on his waist, and he smiled at me, giving me a little more of his weight. We could do this together. "I'm fine, Mother."

The den was down a long hallway, and I limped along, trying to help him even though my own balance wasn't the greatest. The home was very nice, but unlike Derek's, which looked more like a museum, Brendan's was obviously somewhere lived-in—albeit in rich abundance. We collapsed on a plump leather couch together. He kept his arm around my shoulders, but was careful not to hurt me.

I couldn't help feeling awkward, wondering what he was thinking right now. Had he seen my moment of weakness with Derek for what it was? When his gaze met mine, I saw fear, and my heart leapt into my throat. What was he afraid of? Did he know? Had I given my feelings for Derek away? I didn't want to hurt Brendan, especially since my life would be with him. Was he afraid I didn't return his feelings?

I shoved my building emotions down and rested my head against his shoulder. Brendan's father sat in a chair on the other side of him and placed his hands on his knees. He leaned forward, his slightly wrinkled face intense and his gaze probing. "Now, what happened exactly?"

In the corner of the room, Beatrice dialed the elegant old phone. I couldn't help listening in to the conversation. "Greetings to you, Dr. Matthews. Our son Brendan and his soon-to-be mate, Carmela—yes, Carmela Santiago—need your assistance. They were injured tonight." Dr. Matthews replied, but I couldn't make out what he was saying. "Oh, really?" Brendan's mom glanced over at me.

A chill slid down my spine, and I diverted my gaze back to Brendan and his father.

Brendan scratched the back of his neck. Tension tightened in his body, and I couldn't imagine how he must be feeling right now. Although I suspected I'd be in much the same state when I reached my own home.

"We were eating dessert when the *Cazador* chased a vampire through the restaurant. We made it out and started walking back to her house. After they finished off the vampire, they came after us. We ran, but Carmela stepped in glass, and after I scooped her up, I wasn't fast enough to escape their bullets. I considered fighting them, but Carmela was my priority. I needed to make sure she got to safety.

Once we were out of harm's way, we tended each other's wounds."

He kept his word. He didn't mention Derek and Elliot, even though he very easily could've told the truth. The way he spoke, his words sounded like truth. Maybe he had more practice at keeping secrets than I would've thought.

I wanted to scoot away from him, but the warmth of his skin and his steady heartbeat lulled me into a cozy state. Besides, it was better to present a united front than pull away after he'd lied.

"Wise choice, Brendan. I wish the two of you hadn't been harmed, but you'll be in good hands soon enough." His father leveled his gaze at me, then held out his hand. "I'm Neal Kelly. It's been a while since I've seen you. I only wish we could've formally introduced ourselves under happier circumstances."

Smiling, I accepted his hand with my good arm. If only I could remember where I'd met him before...it had to have been at the Pack meetings my father used to parade me around at, but I was drawing a blank.

"Carmela. It's a pleasure to meet you too, sir." I wished I didn't look so unkempt. Meeting Brendan's parents was a special event. I dipped my head, showing the appropriate submission.

"Carmela, that's such a lovely name." Brendan's mother sat next to me. I nearly jumped off the couch. I'd been so focused that I'd lost track of Beatrice. She took my hand in both of hers. "Just relax for a while. You're safe, sweetheart. Dr. Matthews will be here soon. He's calling your parents as well. They called him earlier this evening and were worried about you. How sweet is that? I'm sure they'll be over as well."

My pulse raced. The smile I wore faded at the corners and wasn't genuine anymore.

Brendan dipped his weighty gaze to meet mine, and I caught the unease in his eyes. He sensed my emotions and I wondered if he didn't like that my father would be coming by. However, I liked it even less. Regardless of my feelings for Derek, being with Brendan was safe, especially after what I'd been through recently. I didn't think he would treat me poorly like Father.

"Thank you, Mrs. Kelly. I appreciate your hospitality," I said.

"Is there anything I can get you in the meantime? Tea? Coffee?"

"No thanks, Mom." Brendan rubbed his tired eyes and rested his head against the back of the sofa.

"I'm fine. Thank you." I gently removed my hand from hers, placing it in my lap. I leaned into Brendan's shoulder again to rest for a moment, hoping my parents wouldn't arrive too soon. I didn't want to deal with Father. Not after the way he'd acted.

Neal stood and followed Beatrice out of the room. "We'll leave you two to relax before the doctor arrives." He closed the sliding doors shut and left us alone in silence.

8

BRENDAN

*C*armela's soft body molded perfectly against mine. Her breathing was steady and deep while her limbs were heavy from sleep. I stared at the ceiling and remained still, unwilling to disturb her. The sight of her arms wrapped around the vampire's neck had bothered me. He was the same one she'd asked me not to say anything about earlier in the evening. Plus, I'd never witnessed a vampire helping werewolves. The more I thought about it, the more I had to know what was going on with Carmela.

Should I be the one to broach the subject? I hated lying to my dad. He always had a way of finding out about these things. Frankly, I was surprised that he'd bought all of what I said in the first place. Maybe the pain I was feeling and Carmela's presence had distracted him from the white lies.

Regardless, now wasn't the right time. I'd want to have her somewhere private where I knew no one could overhear us, not with my parents likely sitting in the other room having coffee.

Carmela hid more than she told, that much was certain. If only I had a way to penetrate her walls and get her to open up to me. Her father was another topic I needed to know about. When I'd talked with him, he came across as pompous and condescending even to me, the son of the city's Alpha. I'd seen the hateful looks he'd given her when he thought I wasn't watching, too.

I released a deep breath to keep calm. Soon that man would be in my home, and while I wanted to tell my father about the possible abuse, I didn't want to disturb her as she rested her head against me. Besides, she wasn't even willing to ask for my help.

The more time that passed, the more blood dripped from the scraps of my jeans. Guess it would give Mom another reason to go shopping if she couldn't remove the stains from the rug and furniture.

A loud banging sounded on the front door. Carmela jerked her head up and glanced around the room before settling her gaze on me. I held her a little tighter and looked toward the closed door leading into the hallway. My mother answered the door, while I returned my attention to Carmela.

"You're afraid," I whispered quietly.

She drew in a breath to speak, but no words came from her lips. Finally, she nodded.

"Why didn't you tell me earlier? I saw how you reacted around him. Let me help you. Please." I slid my knuckles over her cheek, relishing her soft skin.

Seeing her like this made my thoughts about the vampire slide away. She was mine. We would work through whatever was going on.

"You wouldn't be able to do anything. Not with him." She glanced back at the door and frowned. "I'm sorry about all of this. I don't want to mess up things between us."

I gripped her chin and forced her to look at me. The front door thumped shut, and I leaned in until our lips almost touched. "Don't pull away from me." The thought of kissing her nearly distracted me from what I needed to say. "I don't want you to suffer. You're special to me." I clenched my teeth as the sound of footsteps echoed on the hardwood floors in the hall.

"Thank you." Her breath caressed my lips, and I couldn't hold back. I kissed her. Her soft moan urged me on, but the harsh words outside the den made me draw back.

Her father's voice set me on edge, and I took a couple of deep breaths, trying to calm myself. But as easy as that seemed, I couldn't. She didn't pay them any attention. Her honey-brown eyes stared up at me in wonder.

9

CARMELA

*W*hile I'd heard everyone in the hall, the kiss from Brendan stole my focus. I didn't want him to stop, but we shouldn't be making out right now.

The den's doors slammed open, and Father stepped into the room, staring between Brendan and me. His lips curled in a sneer. "This is how well you protect my daughter? You're not fit to mate with her." He jerked his gaze toward Mr. and Mrs. Kelly, shaking his head. "Your son hasn't turned out well, unable to prevent an attack like this."

Neal Kelly flared his nostrils. "Be careful. You know who you're dealing with. Don't think for one second that you can enter my home and criticize my son." He pointed a finger at me. "She already has a broken arm. Whose fault is that? Yours. You can't even keep track of your own daughter—never mind keeping her safe."

My eyes widened. If I knew I wouldn't fall over, I would've run away. Tears welled in my eyes. The argument between our fathers made me want to curl into a ball and hide. Everyone glanced at me as if assessing my worth in this mess. Neal had seemed so decent moments ago. Now it appeared he resented me. I hadn't tried to get into trouble.

Brendan drew me closer to him. I loved that he wanted to help, but I couldn't bear the closeness, not when my father was doing his best to ruin my chance of being with Brendan. I had to do something about this. He'd kept me mostly prisoner, hiding me away from the world unless it was convenient for him. I wouldn't let him steal this from me. I pushed to my feet, fighting the pain in my foot.

"I can't believe you, Dad. Stop mistreating Brendan's parents. They took me into their home. They have been kind to me, unlike—" My body sailed backward. Pain burned my cheek, and I smacked into the floor on the other side of the couch. Rough hands flipped me to my back, and my father drew back his fist. Biting back a growl, I threw my arm up to ward off any blows.

Two distinct snarls rose from the room. Brendan loomed over us from the back of the couch, his eyes full of rage and hate. The other man, presumably Mr. Kelly, wasn't in my line of sight.

"Back away from her." Brendan's voice came out gravelly. He held himself stiffly, as if ready to intercede with my father's abuse, regardless of the consequences. We weren't mated yet, and my father still held the most power over me. Brendan couldn't really do much without overstepping his reach.

"My daughter shouldn't disrespect me, especially in front of others. I have a duty to make her obey. I doubt you'd be good at handling her." Father's lips curled back again. He grabbed me by the upper arm and hauled me to my feet. Agony flooded through me, from my face to my shoulder and down to my hip and foot. I could barely remain standing. "We're going home." He jerked me toward the door, and my legs gave way, spilling me to my knees.

"Don't treat an Alpha Queen like that. You're not immune to punishment, even if you are a hotshot businessman." Neal blocked the door. His large frame filled it so Father wouldn't be able to get past unless he muscled his way through. No good would come from that. My father wasn't stupid. He'd back off and try to save face.

Dr. Matthews spoke up from the opposite side of the room, near my mom. Her eyes were wide and her face pale white. "He's right, William." He sounded calm, professional. "She did speak out of turn, but as her physician, I'm concerned about her shoulder wound. You shouldn't handle my patient like this. You hired me to treat her wounds, but it'll do neither of us any good if you're reinjuring her."

Father squeezed my arm. I stayed still, not giving him the pleasure of seeing my pain. If he did anything else in this room, he'd be outnumbered. Grunting, he released me with a slight shove that knocked me off-balance.

My injured shoulder smacked the floor, and I choked on a scream. Pain sank its claws into me, and I rolled to my back. My vision closed in, fading fast.

Silent, hobbling footsteps came to me, and I blinked, doing my best to focus on Brendan. Tears I hadn't known I was crying spilled from my eyes. He knelt on the floor, discomfort tightening his features but concern shining in his eyes. He brushed his thumb across my cheek, wiping away a tear that mixed with blood from my split cheek.

Shame washed through me. If I hadn't provoked my father, he wouldn't have acted out. What did Brendan think? Could he think I wasn't worth the effort? *Nonsense.*

He positioned himself between my father and me, like a guardian. Funny, since my gender was supposed to be the warriors. At least until the Alpha females bore children.

Dr. Matthews knelt on my opposite side and helped align my body into a more comfortable position. His sharp features were strained with pity, something I didn't want. I just wanted freedom from my father's tyranny.

If only the *Cazador* hadn't seen and shot me after escaping the *Teatro*. Winding up with Derek had made things worse. Not only had I been with my people's foe, but my feelings for him were inappropriate, especially after the comforting moments in his arms earlier.

If I'd stayed at his place, life might've been better. However, I wouldn't have met Brendan. That wasn't something I'd want either. He was sweet, considerate and protective.

Why had I returned home? For my family and the responsibility I had to them. Unfortunately, I would remain under their thumb until I mated with Brendan. There wasn't a lot any of them could do, except expedite the ritual, but neither of us were healthy enough for that.

Glancing up, I caught sight of my mother. Sadness filled her eyes, and she had a slight bend to her stance that was uncharacteristic.

What was I going to do? I couldn't leave her alone to suffer in silence from that monster I called 'Dad.' The only way she'd break free from him was death—either his or hers. Divorce didn't happen among wolves.

I averted my gaze before I cried even more.

10

CARMELA

*B*rendan and I lay side by side in his bed, with him on his stomach. The room was warm, inviting, and utterly masculine. His scent lingered in my nose, and I let my eyes remain half-closed. The comfort of being close and safe beside him relaxed me a little.

Dr. Matthews had said he wanted us where he could keep an eye on us both and do his job, but I think there was more to it than that. He cleaned my foot first, making sure all the glass was out, then bandaged it. Once he finished checking my shoulder, he switched to Brendan's side of the bed. *Stupid.* Brendan needed the doctor's help more than me, but I wouldn't say anything. Not after how my words were received earlier. My jaw still ached and the thought of moving it made me cringe.

"This is curious." Dr. Matthews examined Brendan's leg, his lips pursing in confusion.

Brendan grabbed my hand almost hard enough to hurt. Pain etched lines into his face, but he didn't make any noise as Dr. Matthews continued to poke and prod the wound.

"What is?" Neal Kelly said.

I closed my eyes to block the sight of Brendan's father and my mother, who stood beside the doctor as his nurse. Whenever the opportunity struck for her to use her nursing skills, she jumped on it.

My father was still in the den with one of the wolves Neal had called over.

The bed moved from Brendan shifting his weight, and he groaned in pain.

"I'll take a sample from this area of his leg to examine at the lab. This seems like a new creation from the *Cazador*. I haven't seen anything quite like it. It appears to have been a silver bullet—which explains why he's not healing quicker— but these fragments..." He let out a breath. "Let's just say I suspect the bullet was comprised of a lot more than just silver." His voice held calmness and curiosity, as though he was holding in his emotions for the sake of everyone in the room.

I opened my eyes and tried to look at Brendan's leg, but from that angle, I couldn't see much. "Is he going to be okay?" I said, unable to hold back. In the abandoned warehouse, Derek had blocked my view. Besides, my attention hadn't been completely on Brendan. But now the doctor's words made me fear the worst.

Dr. Matthews cleared his throat. "I can't say for certain. I'll need to run some tests, but he'll have to get plenty of rest. I'll bring a crutch by to help him do whatever minimal movements he needs, but he should remain in bed as much as possible."

Neal stared at his son's leg. "Expedite the tests. I want the results as soon as possible." His face appeared stoic, but there was a tightness around his eyes. He glanced my way, and his eyes narrowed on me. While I would've liked to say it wasn't my fault, the *Cazador* had been after me. I was their primary target, not Brendan. He just got in the way of their bullet.

I returned my attention to Brendan, but I still felt his father's cool gaze. He brushed his hand across my cheek. A kind gesture, but it didn't make me feel any less disliked by his dad.

I pressed into his touch, soaking in the comfort he provided. "It's going to be okay, Brendan." My smile didn't reach my eyes. Instead, it felt hollow and sad. While I knew being with him was safe, I couldn't remain here forever. I'd have to return home with my family, at least until we mated, if it was still agreeable to everyone else.

"I know it will," he said, trailing a finger toward my lips. The memory of our kiss swept away some of the building negativity. "Stay strong."

He was right. I couldn't lie down and take it.

I had to make a future for myself. Whether that would include Brendan now, I wasn't sure. His father might forbid him having a relationship with me. After all, my father had publicly wronged his son.

Something very unbefitting of an Alpha Queen's father.

At least they'd stood up for me, but the primary purpose of a werewolf in my position was to breed. Nothing more, nothing less. That would be my role in life, and if I didn't provide children for whomever I mated with, I would be worthless to them, just like my mother was to my father.

Was that how life would be with Brendan? If I didn't provide children for him, would he consider me worthless? My gaze connected with his, and he pulled away, his fist gripping the sheets between us.

Dr. Matthews cleared his throat again. "I'll come by this afternoon, sir. I should have the results and the crutches for your son. Carmela, you and Brendan both need rest."

"Dr. Matthews is right." Mother didn't look happy about it, but we couldn't stay. It wasn't proper. "Let's get you home, sweet daughter," she said, holding her hand out to me.

SARAH MÄKELÄ

"Dad, what if—" Brendan's words were cut off with a stern look.

I gave him a soft smile. He'd stood up for me again. Maybe our relationship meant more to him than I'd previously imagined. Still, my heart sank, and I reluctantly accepted my mom's hand. Like Brendan said, I needed to stay strong.

11

CARMELA

*I*f anyone could've influenced the decision for me to stay at the Kelly household it was Neal, but he'd remained silent. It wasn't really their place to have me over, but I wondered if he no longer wanted me mating with his son. Understandable, I guess, but it also hurt.

Maybe my chance at mating with anyone was gone. Who would want me now, particularly if this whole debacle came out? Werewolves gossiped and talked amongst themselves. Word spread quickly and lives could be shattered.

I sat on my bed, trying not to think about those issues, but a tiny niggling thought plagued me. What if we ended up like Chandra's family, on the streets? If no one supported my father's business, we'd become homeless.

The thought didn't scare me, just made me numb. Here I'd been worried about fulfilling my birthright and having children, and my family might lose it all because of what my father had done.

Rubbing a hand over my face, I kicked off my house shoes and crawled under the covers, more than ready for a renewing sleep. Hopefully when I woke up, life would be better.

Pulling the comforter to my chin, I closed my eyes. Sleep tugged at my mind, and I began to drift off. Footsteps pounded up the stairs, but I lingered on the edge of consciousness. Maybe Father would go to bed and not bother me.

On the way home, he'd cursed a blue streak under his breath, fuming at himself. His aggression had been barely restrained, but the angry power oozing from him concerned me. However, he was known for his mood swings...

No, I wouldn't think that way. He cared for his own reputation, if nothing else, and the ability to say he married me off to a hotshot soon-to-be Alpha like Brendan fit the bill. But that might very well not happen at all.

The footsteps moved toward my parents' bedroom at the end of the hallway, but they paused. I held my breath. Any sleepiness I felt faded away.

The person came back toward my room and stopped at the door.

I watched the door through my eyelashes, continuing to breathe normally as if I were asleep. This person couldn't know how much they frightened me. If it was my father, it would give him the ammunition to blow up at me.

The knob turned, and the door creaked open.

I closed my eyes, feigning sleep, but the eerie feeling of someone stalking toward me while my eyes were shut freaked me out.

The door closed behind the intruder. I desperately wanted to see who it was and tell them to go away. A hand touched my foot over the blanket, slid to my knee, and then my hip. It took all my willpower not to recoil. The desire to grab the hand and toss it away overwhelmed me.

The scent of Father's cologne, mixed with the

overpowering smell of his favorite whiskey, burned my nose. A chill chased through me before I could control myself. Father only drank when he was furious. Fear and anger sparred inside of me like two trapped beasts, causing my pulse to accelerate.

The blankets were ripped from my hand. My eyes snapped open to see him leaning over me. I tried to scream, but he slapped a meaty hand over my lips.

"No, you don't. Not this time. Your mother is asleep. We wouldn't want to wake her, would we?" he said, slurring his words. His tone was a mix of annoyance and disgust. He slid his other hand over my torso, curving across my stomach and up toward my breast. He squeezed it hard enough to bruise.

Could this be what Chandra meant the other night? I didn't want to hurt my father...but I wouldn't let him do this.

He hopped onto the bed in a clumsy drunken leap and nearly fell off in the process. His eyes were full of loathing—maybe even self-loathing. "You were supposed to bring this family out of the hole it's in." His voice cracked a little, as if he'd cry. It broke my heart to see him this way, even though I was terrified. "Instead, what happens? You screwed things up, you stupid girl. Do you know how hard I worked to have Brendan Kelly mate with you? Do you know how prosperous he is? His father is *the* Alpha," he said, his voice a harsh whisper.

Neal Kelly was the Alpha of Alphas? Tears burned my eyes. Now I remembered him. Father had pointed him out at one of the meetings when I was younger.

Neal wouldn't save me from my father, but my desperation didn't want to listen. "No, Dad, I didn't mess up." My voice lacked any emotion, which fit the increasingly numb sensation that sheltered me. "You insulted our Alpha's son and my future mate. Why?"

His lips curled back from his teeth, and he narrowed his eyes at me. "How dare you! You should've kept out of danger and not gone to his home without my permission. You always get into trouble. Our family will be disgraced because of you." He forced his way between my legs.

I slammed my knee into his groin, and he slapped me hard. Pain radiated from my cheek. I snarled, but he pressed his hand over my mouth again. Sinking my teeth into his fingers, I savored the taste of his blood trickling into my mouth. The need to shed my human skin and rip out his throat snapped inside me. That brought back my training.

I punched him in the jaw. His head snapped backward and he lost his balance, collapsing on top of me. I headbutted him in the face. An audible crack broke the silence.

His hand clenched over my breast again, as if to anchor himself and regain his power over me. But I wouldn't fall for that. Not with my confidence crashing back into me.

Stay strong. Brendan's words echoed through my head.

I punched him again, throwing more force behind it. This time he toppled off the bed, but not without ripping my nightgown.

I clutched the pieces together and scrambled off the opposite side of the bed. Father growled behind me. Sprinting to the door with a supernaturally fast limp, I reached for the doorknob. My fingers had barely brushed it when he grabbed the back of my neck and slammed me face-first into the door.

Blood trickled from my forehead, and my legs weakened from the impact.

Father fisted his hand in the nightgown, and I slammed my head back, hitting his nose again. He released me to cover his nose, cursing all the while.

I scrambled for the doorknob again. If I could just wake my mother, I might be safe. She'd fight him with me. If he succeeded, my position as an Alpha Queen would be ruined. *I* would be ruined. That couldn't happen.

The door opened a crack before I could turn the knob, and Chandra peeked inside. Her eyes widened and her jaw dropped open. The door snapped closed behind her, and her footsteps hurried down the hall to her room.

She chose not to help. She'd said it should be me. Now she was getting what she wanted, I guessed.

Tears streamed down my cheeks as he dragged me to the bed. He forced my face into the mattress, muffling my cries. His zipper opening was the only other sound.

No. I refused to let this happen. I pushed up from the bed and spun to face him, ready to fight until one of us was dead. He clocked me in the jaw, and darkness shaded my vision. My body fell back, feeling weightless for a moment before I hit the mattress.

The image of Chandra colliding with my father as he reached for me was the last thing I saw. She was back.

"You bitch," he slurred. "You'll pay the price for her this time, then." Chandra started to scream, but it cut off with a thud. A door rattled in the hallway. That's why Mom hadn't come to help. She was trapped in their room.

Betrayal stabbed me in the heart like a knife.

I couldn't stay here after this. It didn't matter if I lived as a vagrant in the Outskirts for the rest of my life. I'd survive even this.

12

CARMELA

I opened one eye. The other had swollen shut from Father's punches last night. My body wasn't healing as quickly as it should have. Could it be from not shifting? The visit with Dr. Matthews came back to me. No, it had to be the silver bullet.

My limbs refused to budge, but I had to leave now before Father came back. Remembering yesterday brought tears to the surface, but I held them at bay. For now, I needed to focus on the task at hand.

Hefting myself up, I nearly flopped back onto the bed from the agony ripping through my body. I climbed to my feet, then carefully made my way to the closet, easing it open without a sound. No one could hear me leave. They might try to stop me. I pulled a small duffel bag out and unzipped it, cringing at the sound it made. That same noise brought back the near-desecration I'd suffered from the man who was supposed to love and protect me. I knew I'd hear it play back in my mind for a long time to come.

Chandra... I glanced around the bedroom, but she wasn't here. Part of me wanted to check her room to see if she was okay, but fear kept me rooted in place. If my father was home, he could try to finish what he'd started.

I tossed a few outfits into the bag with my good arm, grabbed a couple of essentials like a hairbrush and a picture of my mother and me smiling. After closing the bag, I went to the window and pushed it open to see if anyone was lingering outside. My bedroom faced the street. I had to be extra careful not to get caught.

The sun was just above the horizon. I couldn't count on Father being at work. He could be passed out on the couch for all I knew, especially with all the alcohol he'd consumed. No one would take him seriously smelling like the bottom of a whiskey barrel.

I looked down at the sidewalk below the second-story drop, remembering how badly it'd hurt jumping out of Derek's window. This time I was even more injured, but I wasn't about to stay here and put up with more. Mother might suffer from my actions, but I couldn't remain under that man's power after he almost raped me.

I put on some clothes and shoes, then ran my fingers through my hair. If I looked suspicious, the *Cazador* or police might be curious about me. Neither sounded good. I couldn't tell the police what had happened—it would force my family into plain sight, and the *Cazador* would have even more targets to hunt.

Where could I go? Maybe I should accept my fate and go to the Outskirts. The area was originally a refugee camp for those trying to get into the city, but the people who lived there were poorer than poor and far more dangerous than anyone you'd find here. They were more like animals than people, nocturne or not. I shoved the thought aside. Right now, it didn't matter where I went, as long as I got out.

As I tossed my leg over the windowsill, fear clenched my chest at the drop. *Stop it. You have to leave.* I threw my bag to the ground, then leapt before I could convince myself to stay. My legs buckled beneath me as my weight hit the ground. Pain gnawed at me like a million piranhas, nearly crippling me.

I clawed my way to my feet, snatched up the bag, and hobbled away. For a long time, I just put one foot in front of the other, sticking to the shadows as much as I could. My thoughts were mostly empty. If I didn't think about what had happened, maybe I could pretend it was just a dream. But that didn't calm my fears. I kept an eye out for anyone I knew. At any moment, I expected to hear Father's voice shouting for me to come back.

My feet shuffled along the sidewalk. Dusk settled in around me, and the surrounding streetlamps bathed me with their glow. I lifted my gaze to see Derek's home, and I froze. Should I knock? What if he turned me away after seeing my condition? What if he thought I was too much trouble?

My shoulders sagged, and I sighed. What other option did I have? Brendan? My father would expect me to run there. He might try to negotiate to bring me home again. No way could I run to him. It was too dangerous. Besides, he'd tried to protect me from my father, but it hadn't helped. Maybe I should've told him about the beatings sooner. But what could he have done? We weren't mated yet.

I peeked into the alleyway alongside Derek's house. It was empty. Inching forward, I kept an eye out for anything suspicious. Elliot, his vampire friend, could be with him for all I knew. Maybe this was a bad idea.

What would I be opening myself up to by asking for his help? Did it matter? I didn't have anywhere else to go. I reached the back door and raised my fist to knock.

I tapped on the door twice. If he wanted to invite me in, he'd answer. If not, I would survive without him. One of the werewolves I knew from Militia training lived in the

Outskirts. She'd been friendly, while most of the others looked down on me for being an Alpha Queen. They were jealous, but it was understandable. Life was hard for them.

Besides, I'd been given enough training to not let what happened get the best of me. At least not the physical pain. Hopefully the emotional trauma brewing inside me would disappear with time as well.

PART III

1

DEREK

*T*he weight of the sun's power made my limbs feel heavy and lethargic. It was rare for me to be awake with the sun still in the sky. Today I'd awakened twice. But sunset was nearly upon the world now.

Two soft taps at the back door had me pushing through the haze. No one should be knocking on my door, especially at this time of day. The necromancer and his friend were certainly not that polite.

I walked to the back door, barely managing a human pace, and opened it.

Carmela leaned against the doorframe with her head bowed. When she looked up, she had a bandage on her cheek and a black eye marred her beauty. Bruises littered her soft skin. Her shoulders hunched forward, making her seem so unlike the woman I'd left at Brendan's doorstep last night.

My heart ached for revenge.

Taking a deep breath, I drew her scent into my lungs and almost wished I hadn't. The strong scent of a male werewolf and whiskey wafted through the air around her.

Any ill effects from the sun evaporated as it set,

unleashing the full sting of my power. My blood boiled with the pure rage pounding through my veins.

Carmela winced and drew back a little. "Maybe I shouldn't have come here." She averted her gaze, staring down the alleyway.

I reached for her bag, but she jerked away from me. Her heart raced, and instead of a predator, she looked like prey. Grimacing, I stepped away from the door to allow her entry. "Please, come inside."

She watched me for a moment, then walked past me, clutching the duffle to her chest. Her gaze skimmed my place as if checking for anyone else's presence. Her shoulders trembled with nerves.

"I won't allow anyone to harm you again. I promise." I held out my hand. "May I have your bag?" I nodded toward the staircase. "You can use my spare bedroom. You're already familiar with it. I could put your things there while you rest."

She stared down at the bag. Her lower lip trembled, and she handed it over. "Thank you for your hospitality. I didn't know where else to go."

The werewolf scent on her wasn't Brendan's. Why didn't she turn to her future mate? I didn't understand. What that man did to Carmela was a crime. He'd be punished by her people, yet she turned away from them. "Why didn't you go to Brendan, if you don't mind me asking?"

Her breath hitched, and she shook her head. "I'm sorry. I shouldn't have come." She turned toward the door, but I blocked her way. While I didn't want her to feel trapped, she couldn't run out on the street and put herself into more danger. A protective need reared its head. I'd do anything to help her.

"I apologize. I'm just curious why you chose me. Just give me a chance. Open up to me." I set her bag on the floor carefully and clasped my hands in front of me, when what I most wanted was to take her in my arms and hold her. Instead, I tried to portray a relaxed disposition. But I could barely hold onto that demeanor while I was itching to kill the bastard who'd assaulted her.

"I told you. I didn't know where else to go." She swayed on her feet and looked like she would fall over, but caught herself at the last moment.

"Come, let's sit down. You look like you need some rest." I offered her a smile, but she didn't return it. Instead, she stared at the worn leather chair in my den. "No, let's go to the living room, if you don't mind. It's more comfortable."

Nodding, Carmela took a few hobbling steps toward the living room, but her knees gave out. With a quiet yip, she tumbled forward.

I dove toward her, grabbing her before she could hit the ground and pulling her into my arms. Her wide eyes stared into mine. I considered drawing her in and taking away her pain, but that might end up hurting her more in the long run. Instead, I persuaded her mind to release her from the worst of her fears.

I laid her on the ornate couch, then smoothed my hand over her caramel-colored hair, brushing it from her face. "I don't have anything for you to drink or eat, but if you let me know what you'd want, I can go to the store. Would that be okay?" I knelt beside her and watched her closely, hoping to comfort her in whatever way I could.

Frowning, she tried to sit up, but her muscles didn't seem to work. "I don't need anything now. I'd rather you didn't leave. Please?"

"You can't go without food and drink. Not with your injuries. Lycanthropes need a lot of sustenance to survive, and you shouldn't get too dehydrated." I trailed my fingertips through her hair, unable to help myself. My finger brushed a large bump, and she cried out and pulled away. "Sorry, love." I dropped my hands to my knees.

"You're right." Carmela sighed. "I will need to eat." She shivered and stared up at the ceiling. She was still so skittish. I considered increasing my power over her to calm her, but that was wrong.

"Is there anything specific you enjoy eating? I could make whatever you'd like." I smiled. "Just because I'm a bloodsucking vampire doesn't mean I don't know how to cook. I was once alive too. Granted, my cooking skills might be a little rusty, but I probably won't ruin your meal." I fetched a blanket from the armchair and laid it over her. "Here you are. Make yourself at home."

She drew it up to her chin and gave me a small smile, the first one I'd seen that day. Something inside me relaxed. All was not lost. She'd be okay. "Anything beef. Steak, maybe even hamburgers. Rare, preferably. Potatoes are good too. I also like hot chocolate."

"Good choices." Hundreds of years had passed since I'd last eaten, but I'd do what I could to make sure she regained her strength. Smiling, I gave her an elaborate bow. "Your wish is my command."

A feeling of comfort swept through me. Full darkness had finally descended. I swept my gaze over Carmela. Her eyes fluttered shut. She looked almost peaceful, aside from the pain etched into her face. From the pace of her breathing, she seemed to have drifted off to sleep.

I waited there a moment, watching her. I savored having her back in my home, but the circumstances could've been better. And how long would it be until someone found out? Brendan had seen my home. He could easily track her to me.

Someone knocked on the back door, and I turned my head toward it. Perhaps her mate had already arrived.

Carmela's eyes snapped open, and she struggled into a sitting position.

"It's okay, love. Don't worry. I'll go see who it is."

She slowly lay back on the couch, but her eyes remained open, as if she trusted me, but not enough to fall back asleep. Her heartbeat raced, and her skin was pale. The worry of being here had to be eating at her. But I couldn't save her from that.

I went to the door and opened it a crack.

Elliot stood there with excitement in his eyes. He pushed against the door, trying to brush past me. "You'll never believe what..."

I grabbed Elliot by the collar and pushed him outside, then shut the door behind us. Now wasn't the time for him to intrude. But I couldn't push too hard now that he was Prescott's lapdog.

He narrowed his eyes at me. "What's your problem?" Taking a deep breath, Elliot paled more than a vampire should. "You're kidding me. She's here? What were you thinking—?"

"What do you want? I'm busy right now." A severe frown strained my lips, and my fangs bit into them. I leaned in a little, not wanting to speak the words aloud. "She's been brutalized by her own kin."

Elliot pulled away, disgust curling back his lip. "You're sure? Is that why she came to you?"

"Honestly, I don't know." I crossed my arms and looked up into the hazy night sky. "Something must've happened between us dropping them off and when the sun rose." I met Elliot's blue-eyed gaze again. "I want to keep her safe. Whoever did this could have easily killed her, and will probably try when they find out she ran."

2

CHANDRA

For years I'd yearned for stability with my parents, if not prosperity, and living with Uncle William and Aunt Katarina, I'd finally found that. Plus, I used to have a friend in my cousin. Now my life had shattered like glass. The one person William had never touched was nearly ruined. Things would never be the same again.

Her battered face and the look of fear and defiance in her eyes haunted me. I'd been right there. I could've helped, should've helped before things got so far. Instead, I'd cared more for my own safety than for what was right. But he'd raped me, not her. She was still safe...for now. My words to her the other night were awful, and now I wanted to talk with her more than ever, but I wondered if she hated me for my abandoning her at first.

Katarina busied herself in the kitchen, cleaning like a woman on a mission. A nasty bruise on her face was slathered in make-up, as if that would hide anything. She didn't meet my eyes when I walked in. I had a feeling she knew what had happened the night before. The walls weren't very thick.

"C-can..." I cleared my throat. It still hurt from William wrapping his hands around it. "Can I help?"

She nodded to the plates on the counter. "Could you take Carmela some food? There's some for you as well. I need to finish this up before William comes home."

Dread tightened in my stomach, and suddenly the thought of eating wasn't as appealing. "Sure thing, Auntie."

I grabbed both of the plates, unable to bring myself to return to the kitchen. Not with all of the nervous energy Katarina was displaying.

The closer I got to Carmela's room, the more I felt like something was horribly wrong. With my acute sense of hearing, I'd normally pick up some movement, but I heard nothing. Maybe she was just peculiarly quiet today.

I knocked on the door, but she didn't respond. "Carmela? Can I come in?" Still no response. Then again, I didn't blame her. "I have food." Nothing.

I juggled the plates and opened the door. The bed stood empty and unmade. I set the plates on the dresser, then noticed the closet door was open. She rarely left it open. We'd told too many ghost stories as children. A warm breeze blew into the room, and I dropped to my knees.

No!

The window was opened wide. I blinked at it. My heart hammered in my chest. How could she do this? When William found out that Carmela had escaped, there would be hell to pay. Maybe there was still time. If I found her before he came home, we'd be okay.

I jumped to my feet and sprang down the steps, taking them three to four at a time.

Katarina met me in the hallway. "What's wrong?" Fear paled her face, making the bruises stick out that much more. "Is she—"

"Gone. She ran away."

She looked conflicted, as if unsure whether to be happy or terrified. "We need to find her before he comes home. If he discovers her gone, he'll be furious." Tears welled in her eyes, but they didn't fall. She opened the front door.

I walked outside with her. We searched the darkened street. I focused on the shadows, willing my eyes to adjust to them. I hoped she'd be back, but doubt reined in any positive thinking. What reason would she have to come back? She'd be a fool if she did.

"Should I go search, Auntie?" I glanced over at her, hoping she'd agree to it.

Katarina worried at her lower lip. "I think it's—" Her attention swiveled to the other side of the street, and she straightened her spine. Fear etched itself in the lines of her eyes and her lips, but any tears were gone.

I didn't want to look, but I did.

Uncle William stood across the street. He waved at us as if he wanted us to go back inside. So far he was acting like his normal self. In fact, maybe more pleasant than usual. He didn't suspect anything. How long would it be before he knew?

He walked toward us, crossing the road, and snapped, "Shut the door before too much dust gets in the house. What are you doing outside anyway?" He froze in the street and drew his gaze up to Carmela's open window. The veins in his forehead popped out, and I turned to retreat.

He charged like a bull, grabbing us by the arms before shoving us inside. "Make yourself scarce, Katarina." He shut the door and locked it, keeping his back to me. But the tension and hatred wafting off him choked me as if I were breathing water.

My aunt looked between us and mouthed an apology before darting upstairs. The soft click of the door closing made me cringe in remembrance of the last time William had directed his anger at me.

"Where is she?" he growled. The animalistic words were nothing human vocal chords should've produced.

"I don't know. Neither of us do." I took a seat on the stairs. "We didn't realize she'd taken off."

The phone rang, but he remained in place, ignoring it. However, the caller let it ring and ring. He turned to me, and his eyes were wolf-amber, not their normal brown shade. "Wait right there."

I released a shallow sigh as he left the hallway, and placed my head in my hands. Maybe we all should've escaped while he'd been away. But I couldn't bear the idea of going back to living on the streets. That pain kept me trapped here, blinded by a need to escape poverty.

Pain by William's hand or homelessness. Sooner or later, I'd have to decide which hurt more.

"Brendan Kelly, what a surprise to hear from you." He sounded cordial, which was a complete change from how he'd been seconds ago. "No, she's sleeping at the moment. You should call back later. Yes, you'll talk to her. Right. Bye now." The phone slammed onto the cradle. "Get out on the streets and find her. Now," William bellowed from the office.

I slid on my shoes and bolted out the door, pushing down the throbbing physical pain in my neck and thighs. Searching for Carmela was a fate I much preferred to his wrath.

Maybe I'd already made my decision. If I didn't find Carmela, I'd find my own place in the world. I'd done it before when I was younger. I could do it again.

3

BRENDAN

*a*nger burned in me. My thoughts remained glued on Carmela, even though my parents tried to convince me to rest. Not a lot could be done within the werewolf hierarchy. I couldn't endanger the engagement, and my father had warned me away from speaking up on the issue in front of the others.

I groaned as I moved my leg. I had to talk to her at the very least, and now was the best time for it. My father was attending a business meeting while my mother was out grocery shopping. She'd given me plenty to eat and drink before she left so I'd be taken care of while she was gone. Sweet, but it seemed like sometimes she forgot I was a man, not a boy.

I pushed myself out of the bed and grabbed the crutch, then carefully walked down the stairs to the den where the phone was. I dialed the number, and it rang and rang and rang. My pulse thrummed a quick beat. Should I go there in person? Maybe no one was home? Was everything okay?

The old-fashioned phone's reception crackled a little

140

when the person on the other end picked it up. "Hello. May I speak to Carmela?" I tried to remain civil.

"Brendan Kelly, what a surprise to hear from you." My nerves shattered even more as her father spoke. He sounded pleasant...like nothing had happened last night. Bastard. "No, she's sleeping at the moment. You should call back later."

Part of me demanded that he wake her up. Why would she still be asleep, anyway? It didn't quite make sense, but she'd been injured too. She needed to recover. "Tell her to call me when she wakes up."

"Yes, you'll talk to her."

"Don't bullshit me," I said, my temper unraveling. "Promise you'll relay my message."

"Right. Bye now."

The line disconnected before I could say more, and I balled my hand into a fist. Maybe she didn't want to talk to me. No, I doubted that. There was something going on. He'd sounded much different than before. Perhaps he was scared that my father would change his mind about my future with Carmela. That was something I worried about as well.

Regardless of those fears, I had to remain patient.

I crossed over to the couch. A few drops of blood remained on it as evidence of the encounter. Likely my mother would purchase a new one in the coming days. We had humans over at times due to my father's business, so this would be unacceptable.

However, lying on it and breathing deeply of Carmela's scent created a heaviness in my chest. I'd finally found the woman I wanted for the long-term, and now my life was more complicated than it had ever been. Would she even be within my grasp now? My father might change his mind after what happened last night, but I didn't want anyone else. I wanted her.

However, she'd also showed affection to the vampire, and I couldn't live in someone else's shadow. Could I?

I needed her like a thirsty man needed water.

Sucking in another lungful of air, I closed my eyes, concentrating on her scent. My eyes watered a little, but I forced the emotion down. I *never* should've let her walk out of this house.

4

DEREK

"What are you going to do about it?" Elliot asked, looking from me to the door and back again.

"Take care of her as best I can. I haven't figured out exactly what I should do yet."

"Sooner or later someone is going to find out, if you keep her here." Elliot shifted from side to side, a nervous habit from when he was human.

I hated to admit it, but he was right. "Keep quiet. Word will probably get out soon enough."

He cocked an eyebrow at me. "I'm in this as much as you are. I was there last night saving them at your side. We could both go down."

"I'm sorry I dragged you into this madness." An idea came to me, and while I didn't want to ask him about it, he'd brought up a valid point. If Carmela remained here alone, she could be up against the attackers who had broken into my home. They could kill her in her weakened state, or worse, abduct her.

I glanced at Elliot. "Would you mind staying here? I need to get supplies for her."

His eyes widened slightly, and he stared at the door. "What? She probably won't like me hanging out alone with her."

I narrowed my eyes at him. "Stay out of her way, and if she needs anything, make yourself useful. I don't think she'll do much aside from rest for a while."

He nodded and headed inside. "Don't be gone for long. You owe me."

Really. News to me, especially with how often the other vampire said that. "Lock the door."

Once I heard the lock click behind Elliot, I ventured off. Maybe I'd be able to pick up Carmela's scent to figure out where she'd come from and who had beaten her so badly. But I didn't want to take too long. I wouldn't abandon her in her time of need.

My kind didn't have senses on par with werewolves, so it took a while to get my bearings. I thought back to the direction she'd been walking from with her mate and headed that way. At one of the row houses ahead, I spotted a young woman rush outside, carefully closing the door behind her. Her hair color was almost the same as Carmela's, and there was a strong resemblance. They had to be related.

She looked back up at the house as if it was the last time she'd see it, then she ran toward the nearest alleyway.

The scent near this house was heavy with fear and despair. It smelled of Carmela and the male who'd attacked her, as well as two other females. Her home.

I headed toward the general store nearer to my house.

"Hello, Derek. You must have heard about the *Cazador* killing one of our own. It's good to see you're okay," Prescott said from behind me. I twirled around to face the old vampire. He stood a few feet away, and I couldn't believe I'd been so caught up in my thoughts that I hadn't sensed his presence.

I bowed my head. "Thank you."

"Has there been anything else worthy of my attention?" He watched me closely and tilted his head to the side.

If I said no, he'd know I was lying. My best shot of escaping this meeting without giving the absolute truth was to lie through omission. But what could I say? "Actually, I witnessed the young vampire's death. The *Cazador* have a dangerous new tool in their arsenal." I lowered my voice as two humans walked by. "The bullet glowed as if with sunlight."

"That's intriguing. I'll need to look into this discovery." He nodded as if pleased with the new information. "Good work. Carry on." He walked a few steps away before turning back. "I'm not a fool. You're hiding something. Be careful with that. I wouldn't want any harm coming to you."

"Yes, sire." I bowed my head again. When I looked up, he was gone.

The night couldn't get any worse, could it?

5

CHANDRA

*T*he whole search was beginning to feel rather hopeless. Carmela's scent was potent near where we lived, but she'd done so much aimless walking, looping around alley after alley, that I'd lost her direction. I wanted to scream.

Sitting on someone's front steps, I put my head in my hands and fisted my hands in my hair.

What had I done to deserve this kind of life? Ever since I was born, my life had been a hard slog. I'd been born to parents who were thrown on the streets and didn't care at all about me, then I finally found a home with Uncle William and Aunt Katarina, only to be subjected to his abuse. Now my life and future was based on whether I could find Carmela or not.

The sun had nearly set, and time was running out. I should report back to Uncle William soon—if I decided to go back—but as I continued to search, the sinking feeling that I'd come up empty-handed kept increasing.

Glancing up at the red sky, I felt a warm breeze on my skin. Desperation for some kind of direction and guidance overwhelmed me. The hair on the back of my neck rose at the sensation of being watched, but I caught the faintest scent of Carmela. Hope surged in my chest.

My gaze scanned the gloomy streets, renewed determination lifting my spirits. Sniffing the air again, I caught sight of a darkened alley. Warning bells went off in my head, but it made sense she would go there, especially to keep out of the hunters' view.

Chill out. It'll be over soon.

I slowly walked toward it. A shadow moved further within the darkness. *There.* I picked up my pace, but when I reached the alley, I didn't see anyone. It was as if she'd vanished. Were my eyes playing tricks on me? I rubbed them and stepped deeper into the alleyway to investigate.

I drew in a breath, and a musky male scent lurked among the sour stench of garbage. Alarm ripped through me, and I started to turn around. A solid torso slammed me into a wall, pinning me to it. He pressed a towel over my nose and mouth. A sharp chemical burned my nostrils. I fought to free myself but my limbs weakened.

"Sshhh. Relax into it, girl. Don't fight, and it'll all be okay." His warm breath caressed my neck, and I would've shivered if I could. The only movements I could make were with my eyes. My mouth wouldn't even let me scream. "I know you're seeing the vampire. Cross-species relations are strictly forbidden for a reason."

What was he talking about? I kept my distance from those bloodsucking fiends. My ideal man was a werewolf of high standing. My lower lip quivered, but no words came out.

My captor turned me to face him, pressing my back to the wall. His face was covered in a skull mask, and he wore a hoodie that covered his hair. "You're pretty. It's too bad you made this mistake." He tossed me over his shoulder like a sack of potatoes.

If I'd just run when I had the chance, I might be off starting a new life away from Uncle William and all the trouble associated with him. But I didn't understand why this man thought I had anything to do with vampires. Besides, he didn't smell like a werewolf. He held the faint scent of death, but not because he was a vampire. It was different than that.

Zombie? Nope. Those were rare. They only happened when necromancers summoned them... *Necromancer.*

My gut tightened into a nervous ball of energy. If my people were a dangerous category, then his were legendary, and not to be messed with. But what purpose did he have in policing what the nocturnes did or didn't do?

I had a feeling I'd be learning that firsthand, and soon.

6

CARMELA

I blinked my eyes open, then glanced around at my surroundings. Pain saturated my senses. Where was I? Something felt off. As I sat up, agony gripped my muscles and forced me back onto the velveteen couch. I groaned and did my best to relax. The blanket that had covered me pooled to the floor.

Movement caught my attention from my peripheral vision. Elliot, the vampire from last night, stood in the doorway to the den staring at me.

"Can I help you with anything?" he asked, shuffling his feet. His English accent was crisper than it had been last night.

I shook my head—instantly regretting the motion—then stared at the inlaid rose vine on the back of the couch. Derek's home. Memories barreled back toward me. I dug my nails into my palm, trying to get my emotions back under control.

"I'll be in the den if you need assistance." Light footsteps retreated from the living room.

"Wait." Curiosity tugged at me. I should've let him go, but I wanted to know more about him, especially if Derek trusted him. "You're Derek's friend." My voice croaked, and I cleared my throat.

He froze, his back still to me. "Yes. He's been my best mate for a while now." He faced me but remained in the shadows. "What is your name?"

"Carmela." I pulled the covers back over me. Where was Derek? Oh, right. Food and drink.

Distantly, the sound of rattling keys caught my attention, but I closed my eyes, trying to act uninterested in the noise. Could it be Derek? The back door creaked open, and Elliot spoke quietly to someone.

"How is she?" Derek's voice caressed my ears.

"Woke up moments ago." Elliot sounded carefully neutral.

The crinkling of paper bags and the delicious aroma of food piqued my interest. A cool breeze brushed my cheek, and I looked up to see him watching me. He set the two bags on the coffee table in front of the couch. "How are you?" He gave me a soft smile.

What could I say that wouldn't be a lie?

A rosy glow filled his cheeks. He'd fed. "I'll go cook something for you, okay?"

"Okay."

He reached his hand out to touch me, but I pulled back. A flicker of rejection slid through his eyes but vanished in an instant. "Here's some cold water." He set the bottle on the coffee table, then picked up the bags. "Let me know if there's anything else I can do. Try to drink and replenish yourself."

"Thanks." I didn't move. If I pushed Derek away too hard, I feared I'd be back on the streets. While I'd tried to convince myself that I could survive in the Outskirts, my rationale slowly faded as I faced the brutal reality...I was far too weak.

Maybe when I recovered, but at the moment, I needed Derek. I had no money, no food, and no shelter of my own.

Once again, my supposed enemy had become my savior.

7

DEREK

I pulled a skillet from one of the grocery bags, then removed the steak from another. "It's been centuries since I've cooked."

Elliot sat on the kitchen counter on the opposite side of the room. "I don't know how you're expecting it to taste good. Do you even remember the last time food touched your lips? I don't." He stared at the floor and tapped his fingers on the countertop as if he was nervous about something. Probably Carmela's presence in the living room.

"It'll be fine. How hard can it be? If it doesn't turn out well, I'll go get takeout." But I didn't want to mess this up for her. Not after what she'd been through. Part of me wanted to tell Elliot what happened while I was out—both tracking her scent and the encounter with Prescott—but I didn't feel comfortable revealing what I knew with Carmela in the next room.

Surely her attacker couldn't have been a relative. It had to be someone else. Someone who visited the house, a stranger. But from what I understood in my study of werewolf pack structure that didn't make sense. She wouldn't live with extended family unless something had happened to her parents, but the younger woman with the same colored hair resembled a sister. No, she'd spoken of her cousin before, which meant it had to be her family's home.

I put the steak on the skillet and then sprinkled it with seasoned salt before turning the heat on the stove. From where I stood in the kitchen, I couldn't see Carmela.

What if she tried to run again? No, she knew she was safe here, didn't she?

If only I'd been thinking straight. I should've given her some soap and water to bathe with. Werewolves had an acute sense of smell. She had to be miserable.

"Elliot." I glanced over at my friend. He warily looked up at me from his spot on the counter. "Would you mind keeping an eye on this real quick?"

Elliot raised his eyebrows, giving me an 'are you serious' look. "Okay..." He slid off the counter, and the soles of his shoes softly smacked the hardwood floor.

I filled the washing basin with warm water in the spare bedroom, so Carmela could clean up in the privacy of her own room. However, my hearing was sensitive enough that I could help if she had any difficulty. Not that I expected her to ask.

She watched me as I walked down the stairs.

"There's soap and water waiting for you in the spare room while my friend watches over your food. Would you like me to escort you?" I asked.

She took the last sip of water. "No, I'm okay."

I wouldn't impose on her. She needed time and space. I couldn't begrudge her that or take it personally.

Carmela tried to stand, but her knees gave out, spilling her back onto the couch. Her eyes were wolf amber instead of the sensual caramel color I'd grown to love.

I remained still, not wanting to startle her. At our first

and second meetings she'd had a fire and determination. I hated seeing her this fragile.

She squeezed her eyes shut. "You don't have to help. I can stand on my own." She looked up at me. "Sorry—"

"Don't worry." I helped her up, making sure she was stable before I let go. "Let's get you upstairs." I followed her to the second floor, even though she'd asked me not to escort her. If she tumbled down the steps and I could've avoided it, that would be on me. I might be undead, but my instincts as a doctor kicked in around her. Although, I suspected it was much more than that.

She opened the door to the bedroom and paused in the doorway, glancing back at me. "Thank you for taking me in twice now."

I opened my mouth to reply, but a loud knock sounded at the front door. Who could that be?

I glanced over the balcony to see Elliot come out of the kitchen, carrying the steak on a plate with a fork and knife. He glanced from me to the front door. The banging continued, just as loudly and impatiently.

I motioned for Elliot to put the food down. If it was someone unsavory, I should be here to protect Carmela. Elliot was a centuries-old vampire. He'd be almost as capable of protecting himself as me. The bedroom door creaked a little, and Carmela peeked at me from behind it. Memories of the last time she'd been here came back to me. She'd been so adamant to leave. Now I wished she hadn't.

Downstairs, Elliot opened the front door. "Hello?" Confusion clouded his voice. Not much flustered him. Something wasn't right.

I leaned over the railing overlooking the living room to get a better line of sight to the door. No one answered Elliot. I strained my ears to hear what was going on. I didn't want to get closer. If it was a werewolf and they smelled Carmela on me...we could be in a lot of trouble. Prescott wouldn't do anything at the moment, but that might change if he was forced to act.

A loud *pop* cracked through the peaceful evening, followed by Elliot's soft groan and the sound of his body hitting the floor. Grinding my teeth, I leapt over the rail, wishing I'd answered the door instead of him. Who cared if the werewolves found me? Carmela could go to her future mate. She'd be fine with Brendan.

Reaching the front door, I jerked to a halt. A trickle of blood streamed across the floor, but Elliot was nowhere to be found. I balled my hands into fists and ran down the front steps to examine the street. No blood lined the sidewalk, and I couldn't see anyone walking down the road with a blond vampire over their shoulder.

I sucked in a deep breath, trying to sniff out whoever had taken my friend. The necromancer's faint scent told me he was back, and he'd brought someone else with him. Possibly another nocturne, but I couldn't place them. Anger burned in my veins. I walked back inside, slamming the front door shut behind me.

How could this have happened? I shoved my hands through my hair as I knelt down to further inspect the blood and scuff marks on the floor. I took another deep breath and closed my eyes, trying to focus on the still-fresh scents in the room.

Soft footsteps and the delicate smell of floral soap heralded Carmela's presence.

I shot to a standing position. After what happened, part of me wanted to be her protector, but I couldn't guarantee her safety. Maybe I should take her to Brendan's home. He could care for her while she recovered from this.

But I didn't want that. I wanted her to be mine. She'd chosen me. *You can't have her. You need to help Elliot.* A grimace pulled at my lips. This was the second attack meant for me. Carmela was injured. If Elliot hadn't been able to protect himself from his kidnapper, how could she?

Carmela looked at the floor behind me. "I'm sorry, Derek." She wrapped her free arm over her stomach.

"It'll be fine. I'll get him back." Even as I said it, I knew I couldn't be certain. But I did know a necromancer, not a vampire, had targeted me. This couldn't be related to Tom's death and the High Council position. Necromancers were rare. It had been a very long time since I'd clashed with one, and he hadn't survived the incident so I doubted this was revenge.

"This is your home. We both know who he was after." She took another step closer. "I want to help you."

I couldn't fathom why she would want to help me. Her stomach rumbled, and I grabbed her plate from the coffee table, walking back into the kitchen with her following. "Here's your food." I placed it on the table and held my hand over it to see if it was even remotely warm anymore. It was...barely. "Do you want it reheated?"

She shook her head, gaze stuck on the plate in my hands. "It's fine as is. I didn't realize how hungry I was. I last ate yesterday evening with Brendan." She grabbed the knife and awkwardly carved the meat into manageable pieces with one hand, her shoulder splint restricting her movement.

I wished I'd thought to cut it up for her, but it was too late now. "If there's anything else I can get you, let me know." Crossing my arms over my chest, I stared around the kitchen, remembering the time I'd just spent in here with Elliot. The faint sound of Carmela eating filled my ears as I tidied up. While I wanted to chase down Elliot's kidnapper right this second, I couldn't leave Carmela alone.

She chewed the meat very little before swallowing each

piece. She paused as I watched her, and her gaze rose to meet mine.

I turned away, not wanting her to feel uneasy. Werewolves were known to be protective of what was theirs. They also needed to shapeshift, especially to heal themselves when injured. Her injury couldn't be the sole reason for her not having changed yet. She might be weakening herself further by not shifting.

"May I look at your shoulder after you finish eating?" I said, returning my gaze to her. Surprisingly enough—or maybe not—she was already done.

She leaned back in the chair, her face scrunching up a little from pain. "Yes." She put her free hand over the sling.

"Let's go upstairs for that. It's more comfortable and private." I put her plate in the sink as she climbed to her feet.

"Why haven't you shifted since I first looked at your shoulder?" I asked as we reached the spare bedroom. I removed her shoulder splint and watched her face carefully to note her reaction. I needed to know what kind of pain she was in, since I was sure there was more than just the shoulder. I wanted to help her, but I didn't want to push her too hard.

"The doctor said I shouldn't shift for a few days afterward, and with everything that's happened, there hasn't been a convenient time." She grimaced as I lifted off the bandage. The skin underneath was still not healed. It had a strange grey tint and was possibly infected.

Perhaps it was silver poisoning. Brendan had mentioned it could be the reason why her foot wasn't healing properly.

I ran my fingertip near the wound. If only I'd kept some of the fragments, I might've been able to discern more. This did appear different from a normal silver-bullet wound, but then again, I'd only seen what they did to vampires. I hadn't been up close and personal with any werewolf injuries.

157

"What's wrong?" she asked, looking up at me. Her eyebrows drew together.

"Don't worry. Do you think you could shift? That might be for the best, love." Although it would likely be painful as hell, especially with the multitude of wounds she had.

She nodded. Her hand went to the button on her pants, but she stopped, her gaze meeting mine.

"I'll be right outside if you need me."

8

CARMELA

*G*etting undressed by myself was harder than dressing had been, but I finally managed. I was glad that Derek had offered to step into the hallway. Having him in the same room when I was naked and helpless...so soon after...

My hands shook, and I clenched them into fists. *Stop!* How could I concentrate on shifting my body with those thoughts plaguing me?

I knelt on the floor. My injured arm hung freely. At this point, I should've gained more control over it, which concerned me. Maybe Derek was right about this.

Closing my eyes, I concentrated on changing my form, pouring each drop of lunar power into what I needed. My bones broke and reformed. My muscles stretched until I thought they'd rip apart. I dropped to my stomach on the hardwood floor as torment burned within every inch of me. Every injury, from being shot, to the broken glass, to the wounds I'd suffered at my father's hands, clawed at me. If my concentration broke, I could become stuck between forms forever.

My body lengthened into my wolf form, and fur pierced my skin, making me incredibly itchy for a few moments. When it was over, I leapt on the bed and curled up, placing my chin against one paw. Pain still weakened me, but at least it had generally lessened. My shoulder still bothered me. I'd have to keep most of my weight away from my front left leg.

Derek tapped on the door. I barked, and he opened it slowly. His eyes widened a little before he returned to his calm demeanor. Maybe it had been a while since he'd seen my kind in wolf form, or perhaps he'd never been this close to one of us.

I wasn't sure, but Derek had been around for a long time. Smelling him as my wolf confirmed that. His scent wasn't horrible, but the power cloaking him was awe-inspiring. How had I not been aware of this sooner? I had no clue, but now I finally had a better idea of his ability.

I stretched the muscles of my new form. My shoulder ached, and I sat down, keeping my weight off the paw.

Derek took a few steps toward me, and the hair on the back of my neck shot up. A slow growl trickled from my lips. He held out his palms. "It's me. I'm sorry. I just want to help." He took a small, slow step forward.

I continued to growl, but I scanned the room, seeing it with new eyes. My attention returned to Derek. He stood next to me now.

His hand stroked the fur on my head and neck, scratching gently behind my ears. I'd never had anyone *pet* me. My kind didn't interact with one another this way. But it did feel good, as if he knew where to find every itch.

He slid his hand down slowly until he reached my shoulder, where he parted the fur. I recoiled a little, but somehow I knew he wouldn't hurt me. He was just looking at the wound, so I let him continue his examination. His other hand returned to scratch my neck and the back of my ears. My eyes drifted closed at the soothing pleasure. He'd found a hidden sweet spot. How could I resist? He knew how to make me feel *so* amazing, and I had nowhere else to go anyway.

Part of me wondered about Brendan, but I highly doubted his father would want me to mate with his son now, especially when I was unclean and broken. I barely felt acceptable to Derek, although something about the way he cared for me proved he didn't feel like I was tainted.

"The wound seems slightly better. Slightly being the operative word. It's as if the lycanthropy in this area died. The shifting helped some. I'd guess that more shapeshifting —and time—will be required for it to fully heal. I don't claim to be an expert on lycanthropy, for obvious reasons, but I have read extensively." He trailed his hand along my spine.

I whirled around and clenched his hand in my teeth. My prickly wolf didn't like to be touched so thoroughly and that far down our body, especially after what happened. But Derek had no part in that. He hadn't been the one to nearly violate me.

I turned away and hopped off the bed, landing clumsily as I kept most of my weight on three paws. What he said made sense, and might be why the shift had been so painful in my shoulder.

I limped to the stairs but stopped as Derek blocked my path. My wolf saw him move, and she wasn't awed by his super speed. "Where are you going?" he asked with a frown on his lips. "I hope you're not planning on leaving. You shouldn't go anywhere looking like that."

I drew my lips away from my teeth and snarled up at him. If I could have, I would've rolled my eyes. I didn't plan on running off in my wolf form, but I needed food. After shifting, werewolves needed to hunt and rip their prey apart...or at least eat. Shifting took a massive amount of energy to pull off, and I didn't have much to spare at the moment.

Sighing, he shook his head. "Of course, telepathy would be a godsend right now. You can't talk. Are you trying to leave?"

I swung my head left to right, doing my best to communicate with him. Werewolves relied on instincts and body language in our other form to talk. It was easier than playing fifty questions.

"Do you need something? Is that why you're walking around?" He crouched, keeping a little distance.

I bobbed my head, hoping he'd let me show him instead of answering him like this.

"What do you need?" He cursed himself and stood. "Never mind. Show me. Can you do that?"

Growling, I brushed past him. Silly vampire.

I padded down the steps, putting minimal pressure on my injured leg. Taking a deep breath, I paused in my tracks as scents assaulted my nose. Elliot's smell came to me, as well as that of a magical nocturne. But why would a nocturne be coming to Derek's place and kidnapping his friend?

I walked closer toward the scents, sniffing the ground. I noticed where Elliot and Derek had been, then I followed my nose as I scouted around for more information on what had happened, especially now that I was in the perfect form to investigate it.

Footsteps encroached from behind, but I ignored them, focusing on my senses. A faint chemical odor drew me in as I searched for the source. I leaned closer to the door, but pulled back as the chemicals burned my nostrils. Lightheadedness rocked me for a moment, but I shook it off.

Glancing over my shoulder at Derek, I tilted my head

toward my finding. Whoever had taken Elliot hadn't done so with brute force. They must've knocked him out or weakened him with a potent drug in order to grab him and go.

The discovery made me fear for Derek.

9

DEREK

*J*glanced at the spot Carmela nodded to, noticing a small drop of clear liquid on the floor. I crouched on my hands and knees to take a breath, and recoiled from the scent. No wonder Elliot hadn't put up a fight. They'd drugged him. Not many drugs worked on a vampire, and not many people knew which ones did.

Anger flowed through my veins. Pushing to my feet, I smoothed my hands over the wrinkles in my pants. If only I had an idea of what happened and where my friend could be. I needed more. "Thanks for showing me that."

She nodded again, then limped toward the kitchen. Ah, that's what she wanted. Food. Made sense. "Do you want the steak raw, rare, or thoroughly cooked?"

She cocked her head to the side and stared at me. Right, of course she couldn't answer me in that form.

Digging into the freezer, I pulled out a cold piece of raw meat. She wouldn't want it like this. I cut open the package, then tossed the steak onto the skillet. Staring down at her, I wondered what it would be like with her in my life instead of living the way I did now. I wanted her, mind and body. For better or worse, she brought this out in me. I didn't mind these simple moments together, even cooking.

I slid the warm meat onto a plate and took the knife from earlier to start cutting it for her. A low rumbling growl warned me to stop. I stared down at her as she circled around, her nails tapping the kitchen floor. The wolf in her was growing increasingly impatient. "Okay, I'll put it down and let you have it, love."

She carefully sat, but her gaze remained glued to me.

I placed the plate on the floor, letting her eat while I went into the den and sat in my worn leather chair. Prescott needed to know about Elliot's disappearance. Who would want to come after me? The *Cazador* hadn't been around for a few days, so I didn't think it was them, especially with the necromancer being involved.

Could a High Council member be entangled in this? But why would someone work against Prescott's orders for unity so openly? Sometimes hunters went rogue. That possibility made more sense than vampires, but how would they get their hands on this?

I picked up the phone to dial Prescott, but the clicking of nails on the hardwood floor drew my attention.

Carmela bobbed her head around the corner. She padded across the room, putting only a little weight on her injured leg, which probably made walking difficult, to say the least. Licking her wolfish lips, she sat in front of my chair, simply staring at me.

I set the phone back down. "What is it?" What did she want now? Maybe if she shifted back into human form we could communicate again.

She padded away and headed upstairs. Did I follow her or go ahead and call Prescott? I sorely needed to speak with him. Her soft whine brought me to my feet, and I strode after her. Maybe she needed my assistance with something. Or she might just need sleep or to change her shape again.

I waited outside of the guest room for a moment as loud snapping, ripping and popping echoed from inside. When I glanced into the room, she was crouched on the bed in the throes of the change. Her body rippled and stretched with the grotesque restructuring of her limbs.

When she was finally done, Carmela lay face-down on the bed, naked and fragile. I hesitated to move, not wanting to draw her attention and make her feel vulnerable, but she didn't get up. Perhaps she'd injured herself during the shift. That thought had me sprinting to the edge of the bed.

Her long, even breathing sounded restful. I placed my fingers gently to her neck and felt her steady pulse. She was merely asleep.

I ran a hand through my hair and blew out a calming breath. Maybe when werewolves changed back into their human forms, they passed out from the energy spent, and when they shifted to wolf form, they needed to hunt.

I grabbed a warm blanket from the foot of the bed, then tucked her in. She gifted me with a small smile in her slumber.

10

CARMELA

I opened my eyes and twisted onto my back. With the shift back into human form, I must have fallen asleep. It was common for werewolves to pass out after shifting too soon, especially into human form. My arm and body still hurt, but I was able to move my fingers instead of the limb being completely useless.

Yawning, I looked around. Soft warmth covered me, and I glanced down at my naked torso. While the bruises were gone, not all of the pain had left me, especially the mental anguish. I jerked the blanket over my chest, but I was alone. I released a breath, comforted by the space.

Rolling to my feet, I spotted my clothes on the floor. I needed to pull them on before seeing Derek again.

The soft creak of the hardwood floor alerted me, and I jerked the blanket around me before glancing at Derek in the doorway. He stood there, wearing an unbuttoned shirt as he had when I first met him, looking utterly relaxed. "You're awake," he said. "You slept for a quite a while. It's just after nightfall."

Blinking, I sat on the edge of the bed, his words sinking

in. Normally when I crashed after the shift, I didn't sleep this much. I'd been out of commission for almost a day. "Really?" It was a silly question. It couldn't be daytime, since he'd be asleep. I shook my head and glanced back up at him.

"Yes, you did." He turned around, facing the hallway instead of the bedroom. "I'm sorry for startling you. I heard movement and wanted to make sure you were okay. I was worried." He leaned against the doorframe and ran a hand through his hair.

The muscles in his shoulder and arm flexed, and I tore my gaze from him. Pulling on my pants and shirt with one hand was hard, but I managed it with very limited use of my other hand. At least it was starting to get better, even if it hurt to use it. I dropped the blanket and rubbed my eyes as I sat on the side of the bed.

"You can turn around again," I said.

"Are you feeling well enough to be up and about, after earlier?" Concern tightened the corners of his eyes, creating faint lines.

I couldn't help but smile. "When werewolves change shapes, our bodies expend so much energy that if we shift within a short period of time, we pass out. Nothing more than that, Doc."

He raised an eyebrow at me, and the concern shifted to amusement. "Ah, okay. I wasn't sure if that was natural or not, but you appeared to be sleeping. Should I look at your shoulder now that you've shifted twice?" He shoved his hands in his jean pockets, and I watched his abs ripple.

Stop it, Carmela. Why would he want you?

I squeezed my eyes shut, trying to push those thoughts away. "Okay."

He slid my shirt's collar aside for better access to my shoulder. "This seems to be doing a little better now. The lycanthropy seems to slowly be recovering. After a few more shifts, you should gain more mobility in your arm. For now, I recommend you keep the sling on to prevent further injury. Can you move it around?"

Wriggling my fingers, I glanced up at him. "Still hurts though."

He watched my hand, then drew his gaze up to meet mine. The soft emotion in his eyes seemed foreign to me. "Yeah, I figured it would, but I'm pleased you have more mobility now." He brought his hand up as if to caress my cheek, but reluctantly dropped it. "Sorry. How is the rest of you doing?"

Thankfully, some of the pain my father inflicted had vanished with the two shifts last night. However, the emotional trauma remained. Tears bit at my eyelids, but I refused to cry in front of him. I would remain strong, at least until I was alone.

But I did need to decide what to do with my life. While Derek said he wanted me, I couldn't expect to stay here with him forever. Someone would find me eventually, and I didn't want to bring the Pack's wrath down on Derek. Not when he'd been so kind to me.

But I couldn't run forever. My father needed to be punished for the hurt he'd caused. Where did that leave me?

"The shift helped."

He sat beside me but kept a little space between us. He seemed to be tiptoeing around me now, and while I appreciated it, I didn't exactly like it. "I'm sorry you went through that. Please let me help you."

I wouldn't mind his help, but maybe it was better I do this on my own. But what good had my training done? I'd tried to fight, but he'd made me feel so weak and helpless...like I was nothing better than what my father said I was. *Don't focus on those thoughts.*

What about Brendan? I'd been so caught up in myself that

169

I hadn't considered he might be thinking about me. But I doubted he'd want me after he found out what my father had done. Heaviness settled into my heart.

"Thank you. I appreciate it. I'm just not sure what to do, really." I sighed. "If I go after my fa...my attacker, then I could get in trouble with the werewolves. They might come after us if I were to seek vengeance without consulting them. And they'd really hunt me if they knew I was with you." I laughed at the absurdity of my life. "It seems I've gotten myself into a world of trouble."

He gently placed his hand on my shoulder. "It'll be okay. We'll get everything taken care of." Warmth darkened his eyes as he smiled.

For better or for worse, I trusted him.

11

BRENDAN

*T*he more time that passed without talking to Carmela, the more worried I became. Maybe I hadn't done enough, but my hands were tied. Did she not know that? Was she avoiding me? I balled my hand into a fist over the handset as I dialed the phone again, but I made sure not to break it. Old human devices could be fragile, and Neal would be furious if anything happened to it.

I'd tried calling a few more times after the first attempt, but William kept making excuses. She was sleeping, she was with Dr. Matthews, she was bathing. Each time he said she'd talk with me soon, but that phone call never came.

I hated feeling this way. Guilt ate at me until I couldn't take it anymore. Sooner or later, I needed to act, instead of standing by while her father was holding power over her. I didn't trust him, and he wasn't helping things.

The phone rang, and her father answered with a pleasant 'hello.'

"William, put her on the phone. Now." My voice was a throaty growl. As each moment passed my control unraveled.

"What a surprise, Brendan. You really should have patience. Besides, your parents must not have taught you many manners to harass one of your elders. Just as I'd thought." He chuckled, sounding every bit the cocky asshole that I knew he was.

I opened my mouth to respond, but the phone was jerked from my grasp. My surprise nearly made me lose my balance, but I caught myself.

My father glowered at me. "Don't talk to my son like that, William. Let him talk to Carmela. He has every right as her future mate."

I hadn't talked with Neal about Carmela or what happened with her father. While I didn't particularly want to get into it with him, I'd known it needed to be discussed sooner or later. Guess it was sooner.

"Neal." William hissed out the name. "My apologies, Alpha, but maybe we should rethink mating them. I'm sure you agree that they could both find a better match. Perhaps it's best if your son doesn't call my house again." This was the first time I'd heard him sound submissive to my father, but that couldn't be allowed to happen.

"No, I don't want anyone but her." My voice was loud enough for both my father and William to hear, but not so loud that my father would think I was raising my voice at him.

"There's no need for another mate to be chosen. However, our families don't appear to get along. Maybe it would be for the best." Neal looked at me with a stern frown on his face.

I shook my head and walked away. If that bastard wouldn't allow me to speak with her on the phone, then I'd go in person. I slid on my shoes and grabbed my keys.

They exchanged pleasantries, and I heard my father set the handset back on the cradle.

Neal walked into the entryway. He crossed his arms over his chest. "Where do you think you're going, kid?"

I straightened my spine. "Out on a walk."

"You know it's only going to cause more trouble. That man has always been an egotistical nuisance." He sighed and shook his head. "The only reason I agreed to the relationship is because of his standing in the city."

While I agreed with what he said, I was too far gone when it came to wanting Carmela. "Sometimes the easy path isn't the most gratifying one. I'm going to talk with her. Our customs don't require both sets of parents to agree to the mating."

"Sure, if you're not an Alpha—"

I opened the door. "I'm sorry, Dad. But this has to get figured out. William is arrogant, but I don't think he'd act this way to my face. He's a coward who hits women. He needs to be brought down a notch or two."

Neal nodded. "Do what you will. I know your heart is set on her, but don't be too disappointed if it doesn't work out." He turned his back and walked further into the house.

The truth of his words socked me in the jaw, and I closed the door behind me.

Inside, I faintly heard my mom asking where I was going in my condition. The tap of her heels closed in on the door, but my father spoke to her softly, "He'll be fine. He's taking care of something. I'm sure he won't be gone long."

I smiled and headed down the steps, then made the slow trip to Carmela's. It hadn't taken this long when I'd been able to walk properly, but that didn't matter. I had a spring in my step. Whatever the problem, I'd know soon enough what was going on.

I approached her row house. My ears perked up at the sound of yelling coming from inside. Worry clenched my chest. Was I too late? Was he beating her again? Anger had me marching up the steps, and I held my hand over the door about to knock, but a few words stood out.

"First Carmela runs off and now Chandra, those ungrateful little bitches. It's your fault for bringing that wretched niece of yours into our home."

My mouth dropped open, and I turned to lower myself onto the steps. She'd run away from home? Why? When? Where did she go? She didn't come to my house. I'd been there the entire time.

I stopped myself from sitting and knocked on the door after all. I needed some answers, and they were the only people who could possibly know why she'd do such a thing. While William was a bastard, I stood by my thoughts. He wouldn't physically push around the son of his Alpha.

He went quiet, and Carmela's mother stopped crying. There were rapid footsteps going up the stairs, so she was probably scampering away to get space from that monster. When I couldn't hear her anymore, the door opened. William stood in the doorway. His face was red and the vein in his forehead throbbed, but otherwise his demeanor looked neutral.

"I'm genuinely surprised to see you on my doorstep. I guess you didn't hear what I told your father, but I think it's best you stay away from my house and stop calling. You're only hurting her more with this charade." He started to close the door, but I put my crutch in the doorway, blocking him.

"You're lying. I heard what you said to your wife. Where is she?" I placed my hand on the doorframe to keep my balance. I wouldn't let her slip through my fingers. If she'd run away, then she might be in danger.

He lowered his gaze. "Son, if I knew where she was, don't you think she'd be home?"

"Didn't you send out a search party?" Bile rose in my throat, and lightheadedness made my vision swim a little.

"Of course. Her cousin went looking for her, but the selfish snot hasn't come home either." He shook his head. "They're probably out there together somewhere thinking they'll have the last laugh."

"What if they're hurt? Didn't that cross your mind?" Something flashed through his eyes, but it faded too quickly for me to decipher. My hackles rose. He knew more than he was willing to let on.

"Maybe they are. I'll give them time to come home on their own. If they're still missing in a few days, I'll ask your father to send out the official search team." He glared down at my crutch. "Now if you'll excuse me, I have matters of my own to attend to."

Probably finishing that argument with his wife. The thought soured my stomach, but I couldn't do anything about that. However, I had no idea where to search for both Carmela and her cousin. Unless maybe they weren't together...

I stepped away from the door and pulled my crutch back. William slammed the door in my face, and I waited there a moment before leaving. What did I know? Carmela had run away, and her cousin went out searching for her later. Where would Carmela have felt safe, even if that place wasn't mine?

The image of her arms wrapped around Derek's neck while she smiled at him tore through my thoughts. Dread curled in my gut, and I hobbled down the stairs. Did I go back home or confront them? Maybe she'd made her choice, but there had to be more to it than that.

If she didn't want to be with me, she should tell me herself.

12

DEREK

*H*ow could I look her in the eye and promise her safety when my position was just as dangerous? The people who were after me had taken my best friend, and I was going against the nearly millennial Feud by helping and protecting a werewolf. Everything within me said to just forget it, return her to Brendan and help Elliot, but I didn't want to let her down.

"The substance you smelled last night on the floor is a powerful drug developed by vampires." When she'd gone to sleep, I dabbed up what I could of the drug, took it to Prescott, and reported what happened to Elliot. He'd been able to fill me in. "Originally, it was designed to subdue our younger kind who are prone to insatiable bloodlust. They require training to gain any modicum of sensibility. Unfortunately, someone has amped up the dosage for more powerful vampires, and that was what was used on Elliot last night."

Prescott had ordered me to do whatever it took to get Elliot back. He'd asked if I'd wanted assistance, but I declined since I

176

needed to keep Carmela safe, which meant I couldn't have other vampires around here. I couldn't throw her out on the street, since her attacker might be after her as furiously as the cloaked necromancer and his pals were after me. But I couldn't keep my thoughts from straying to the *Cazador*. They had to be involved. They were the only ones with labs sophisticated enough to do this—but how did they get the drug?

I slid the shoulder brace back on Carmela and led her downstairs. When I was out, I'd picked up something for her to eat, and prepared it upon my waking. "I have steak and crisps in the kitchen for you. Feel free to it."

"Thank you." She headed off toward the kitchen, and the crinkling of the crisps bag followed her.

Perhaps after Carmela finished eating, we would—

Something dark moved behind the curtained window on my front door. A thunderous knock banged at the solid oak, causing my hackles to rise.

Cautiously, I went to the door. The last person to come here unannounced had taken Elliot. I slid aside the curtain to see Brendan standing on my doorstep with a crutch under his arm. His gaze turned to meet mine. He clearly wasn't afraid of me controlling his mind, but I wouldn't because of her.

Not happy with the idea, I opened the door.

Rage filled Brendan's face. "Where is she?" His voice was nearly a growl. He glanced over my shoulder, and his face softened slightly. "Carmela. I was so worried about you. Are you okay?" He flashed hostile eyes back at me.

I slammed my hand against the doorframe to prevent him from entering my home. "Did you lead others of your kind here?"

Brendan shook his head. "No, but I should have. You kidnapped her, didn't you? Why else would she leave her home like this...?" His face paled, and he looked back at Carmela.

I turned my head slightly to look at her. She bowed hers, staring down at the floor. "He didn't kidnap me, Brendan. I left because..."

Silence stretched between them, and I wanted to wrap my arms around her, to keep her safe.

"Babe, you really worried me. I tried calling your house so many times." A low snarl rumbled from Brendan's chest, drawing my attention back to him. "Let me in, *vampire*." His hissed word was low enough so those on the street couldn't hear.

"Why should I?" I asked.

"Let me talk with her." Pain weighted Brendan's gaze. "I *need* to talk with her." It was *almost* hard to say no.

"No—"

"He's fine, Derek. Please." Carmela lightly touched my arm before pulling it away.

"Fine, but you can't stay long. I'm trying to protect her, and someone might have tracked you here." I let Brendan in, then quickly shut the door.

13

CHANDRA

I blinked my eyes open, annoyed with myself for falling asleep. They could've killed me while I was unconscious. Pain stiffened my shoulders and wrists from dangling in shackles. Still, I couldn't get my feet under me no matter how hard I tried. Whatever drug they'd given me was strong and effective. I was aware of what went on, but in a stupor.

Maybe passing out was a better choice, then I wouldn't have to endure consciousness. If they maimed or murdered me while I slept, that'd be better than living in this dark dungeon waiting for whatever they were going to do. The sleep would be a welcome release. My eyes had begun to feel like they were going to bleed from wakefulness, yet sleep would not come now.

Beside me, something moved. I would've jumped if I hadn't been paralyzed. A male groan filled my ears, and I glanced at him out of the corner of my eye. I didn't see him before, so he had to be new here. He wore a dark suit and appeared to be in rough shape, but then again, I probably looked worse.

He turned his head to look at me. It seemed he had more control over his limbs than I did. Maybe the drug wore off quicker for him. The shackles on his wrists clanged softly.

"Who are you?" he asked. His voice was scratchy, with a hint of an English accent.

I tried to talk, but I couldn't force any words out.

Grimacing, he tried to stand, but his legs gave out beneath him. "Guess there's no way we're getting out of this mess." Sighing, he leaned his head back against the solid brick wall. "In any case, I'm Elliot. Perhaps I'll get your name eventually. You do bear a resemblance to someone I know..."

Again, I tried to speak, but I only whimpered.

"Hush now. It's okay. We'll find a way." He gave me a kind smile.

A man walked by the large dark room where we were kept. He glared at us like we were pests before continuing past us. Movement in my peripheral vision signified even more people beyond the man next to me. I'd seen some of them when I was first brought in, but there were more here now. Who were our captors? What did they want?

Cross-species relations are forbidden...

Could that be why we were all here? But the Feud...why would anyone go against that? Some of the other nocturnes in the dungeon looked like faeries or other shifters, not those in the actual vampire-werewolf conflict.

Speaking of which, the man beside me certainly smelled like a vampire. However, he was nice, totally unlike what I'd learned about them in the Militia.

Whatever.

At least I was away from Uncle William, though this wasn't really a better alternative. Memories of his perverted abuse flickered through my mind like a twisted photo album. Anger and frustration bubbled up from my chest. Ever so slowly, I clenched my hands into fists.

Maybe if I built up enough adrenaline, I could burn off the drugs they'd pumped into me.

I thought back to my parents and Uncle William. My parents couldn't have cared less about me. Uncle William just wanted to abuse me, and I finally saw what I'd missed all along. He didn't want me to have any kind of future. I was older than Carmela, yet he'd never looked for a mate for me, regardless of his excuses. He wanted me to be his little playtoy. Someone to sate the twisted desires my aunt couldn't.

Nausea settled into my stomach, and I felt close to vomiting out of sheer despair.

Carmela had an excellent opportunity to be an Alpha Queen, and yet she complained about wanting love in her life instead of enduring her power and position. Didn't she know that some werewolves craved that sacred title?

Some of my strength returned to me as my heart raced and my body pumped adrenaline through my veins.

The man next to me and the girl on the other side of him stared. "What do you think you're doing?" he whispered. "You're pushing a lot of power around. Stop it. Don't draw unwanted attention to us. Our captors could come over and do something to all of us because you're trying to break free."

The girl huddled back, pulling her tattered leather jacket around her as if it would keep her safe from whoever had brought us here. But who would come looking for me...or any of these people? We looked like a bunch of rejects, except for Mr. English. Uncle William would think of my disappearance as one less hassle for him, that much I knew for sure.

I put my feet under me, allowing my aching shoulders and bloody wrists slight relief. I didn't have enough strength to look at them. It was hard enough to not appear too suspicious as I held myself up.

What had I been drawn into?

14

CARMELA

*S*ighing, I ran my gaze over Brendan. He looked a little ragged, like he hadn't slept since we last saw one another. Of course he'd been able to find me here. The day I'd met Brendan, we'd walked past Derek's house while he was outside. I'd been stupid for coming here. Silently cursing, I walked into the living room and sat on the couch.

"He beat you more, didn't he? I should have handled him when I had the chance. I am *so* sorry I couldn't protect you." Brendan sat beside me, almost close enough to brush his thigh against mine. His utter masculinity overpowered me, and panic surged through my veins.

"I don't think fighting him would've been good for you, especially in your condition." I glanced over at Derek, who looked grim. I didn't want to tell Brendan what my father had almost done. Partly from shame, and partly because I still cared for him. What would he think?

"So you ran away to here? Here?" he asked, beginning to sound a little incredulous. He placed his hand on my knee, and the warmth of his touch soaked into my leg.

I scooted away a little, uncomfortable at the closeness.

"How did you know to search for me?" Had he talked to my father? What did he say? Were others looking for me? *Damn it.* I needed to move on soon, even if it meant the Outskirts.

"Like I said, I called your house a few times. William kept giving excuses when I asked to speak with you, so I knew something was up. When Neal commandeered the last conversation, your father said he'd changed his mind about us mating and that I shouldn't call the house again." He placed his hand back into his lap. "Needless to say, that didn't sit well with me. I went there in person, and William said you'd run away. That struck me as odd, since you hadn't come to my parents' place, so I thought maybe you came here." He ran a hand through his blond hair. "I wasn't positive, but after the other day, I figured it wouldn't hurt to check. Here you are. My only question is, why didn't you come to me? I could've helped. I'm one of your kind. It's dangerous for you to be here. Our people will kill you, and him." He jabbed his thumb in Derek's direction.

Why did I come here? To protect myself from my father. If he found me, I doubted I'd escape fate twice. I leaned back into the couch and rubbed a hand over my face. How could I tell him? Did I want to? If I didn't, then he'd never understand.

"My father attacked me. He...did more than just beat me. He tried to rape me. I knew he'd find me at your place, and I didn't want to risk being returned to him." The words hurt, but maybe they needed to be said so Brendan would understand why I acted the way I did.

His face twisted in confusion, before slow horror filled his eyes. He froze, and pain created lines around the corners of his mouth. "Your father did that to you? Your own father?" He balled his fists and lowered his head. Energy pulsed around him, pushing in hot waves against my skin, as if he was fighting for control. When he'd gotten himself more or less stable, he glanced up at me.

I nodded, not wanting to verbalize my feelings, as if that would make them real.

Brendan pulled me to him. "God. I should've helped you whether you wanted it or not. I'm so sorry. I should've objected when your mother suggested you go home. You were under my protection, and I've failed you." He rested his cheek on my uninjured shoulder.

My body froze under the onslaught of touch, and I gently pushed away from him once I regained my composure. "You couldn't have stopped him. Besides, I doubt your father likes me much, especially after what mine said to him. I didn't feel comfortable showing up on your doorstep with his *scent* on me."

He ran his hand through his hair again. "My father does like you, but he didn't appreciate the way William acted. My father isn't used to disrespect, especially from someone who should know better. But I guess you're right about one thing. I would've lost control and ripped William's head off— regardless of the consequences. I'm sorry."

"That doesn't matter now. What matters is that we keep her safe." Derek leaned against the wall near a window. He looked serious and solemn.

"What do you suggest?" Brendan asked.

"Take her to a safe place. Not your house, but somewhere you think she'd be protected. My friend was abducted from my home—the vampire who saved you the other night. I have to find him." His face was grim, and he shifted his weight as if unable to relax.

"Chandra's also missing," Brendan said, glancing back at me. "Your father said he sent her to look for you, but she never came home. He suggested that you two were off somewhere together, but as we can see, that's not true."

My mouth dropped open. Guilt clenched my gut. She'd protected me from my father, and I'd left her and my mother to his violence. What had I subjected them to? I should've done something sooner to return the favor, and now I might be too late. Tears stung my eyes.

Elliot was taken from Derek's home, and now I knew Chandra was missing. What if the kidnappers had both Elliot and Chandra? It might explain why she'd never gone home. Of course, she could also be tired of the abuse, but with her horrible childhood, she'd told me a few times how she never wanted to go back to being homeless. Ever.

I didn't want to think of the third option. Maybe my father killed her. *No, he's a monster, but there has to be limits. There has to be.*

"I don't want to go to a safe house. What if my cousin was captured too? I know her, and I don't think she'd run away. She saved me. She doesn't deserve to be taken, and I want to help you find Elliot, Derek. He was good to both of us." I turned to Brendan. "Please..."

Brendan worked his jaw, tightening and loosening the muscles. "Yes, he was. If it weren't for you two, we might not be here after the incident with the *Cazador.* I wish there was something I could do to help." He was such a good guy, but part of that was probably for my sake. I wished I could repay him for his kindness. "I promise I won't tell my father about you being here, Carmela." He looked at me then Derek. Sadness crept into his gaze. "I'd like to talk with you alone."

Derek pushed away from the wall and moved as if to separate Brendan from me. "You should be leaving. She wants to stay here."

"Derek, don't. Please go upstairs and don't listen in." I didn't want to hurt him. He'd been there for me, but I also couldn't help melting at the pain in Brendan's eyes. He'd suffered because of me, and I hated that. "Please."

He glanced between us and narrowed his eyes at Brendan. "Call my name if you need me."

"I will." I turned on the couch to face Brendan better, but I didn't close the space between us. I didn't feel that comfortable around him yet, even though I knew he wouldn't hurt me.

Derek's quiet footsteps faded as he headed up the stairs.

Brendan returned his gaze to my face. "I know there's something going on between you and him. While I'm not sure why you're interested in him, I know you felt something for me, just as I do for you." He put his forearms on his knees and leaned a little closer. "You're more to me than an arranged relationship. I worried so much when I couldn't reach you. Did I say something wrong? I knew I shouldn't have let you leave. I should have stopped you, but..." He lowered his gaze, his face twisting with emotion. "But I had no idea William was the kind of man to do something like that. I'm sorry, babe. I let you down, but I can't let you slip away from me. That would be my biggest regret."

The tears in my eyes slid down my cheeks. I'd been wrong about him.

His eyes watered too, but he kept the moisture from falling. "Say something. Please."

I scooted closer to him and wrapped my arms around his torso. He held me lightly, as if unsure what to do. "I care about you too."

"If you mate with me, I can protect you. He won't be able to hurt you again." He hugged me a little tighter. The warmth of his affection relaxed me a little, even if the words stirred up panic.

Movement on the balcony overlooking the living room caught my attention. Derek slipped back into the shadows, but I'd seen his stoic expression.

I cared for both men. What was I supposed to do?

PART IV

1

BRENDAN

I couldn't suppress my relief that Carmela hadn't fled to Derek because she hated me. But I still seethed with anger that her father had almost raped her. If I'd known things would get so bad, I could've done something to prevent her pain... Maybe I should've pressed to visit her sooner, or talked my father into bumping up the mating ritual. No, I couldn't second-guess myself. What William did wasn't normal. You didn't expect your future mate's father to do something like that.

"M-mate? S-so soon?" Carmela met my gaze with slivers of panic in her eyes.

Damn. The last thing I wanted to do was scare her. My words had just slipped out in my desperation to draw her close, although I meant them from the bottom of my heart. What if they drove her away from me? I'd been unable to protect her before due to our customs, but now I could change that. My father was the Alpha of Alphas. He could ensure her safety and bring William to justice once we were mated.

The only other thing that bothered me was how she looked at Derek.

"The sooner the better, babe." Glancing up at the balcony, I caught Derek watching us from the shadows. He wasn't trying very hard to conceal himself. Emotions warred within me. She was *my* future mate, but the two of them seemed to have feelings for one another. I was grateful that Derek watched over her while I was injured and at home, but I couldn't let him take her from me. I was falling in love with her.

She chewed on her lower lip. Memories of our kiss shoved all other thoughts aside. The only thing that kept me from leaning in to claim her mouth again was the worry in her eyes. I brushed a strand of hair from her cheek, tucking it behind her ear. She leaned into my palm.

"I—"

"You don't have to make that decision right now, love." Derek walked toward us, stopping mere feet away, and much closer than I'd have preferred.

Every muscle in my body tensed. "She was going to say something. Let her speak." The hair on the back of my neck rose, and a low growl trickled up from my chest. I must've been so caught up in being close to Carmela that I hadn't remained aware of our surroundings. Vampires were stealthy, but I was the Alpha of Alphas' son. My keen senses were sharpened from an early age. He shouldn't have been able to sneak up on me.

She placed a small hand against my chest. "It's okay, Brendan." She leaned up and brushed her soft lips against mine.

I gently cupped her cheeks, not wanting just a chaste peck. After everything that had happened, I needed more than that. I needed her. Her hands covered mine, and she softly moaned as I swiped my tongue over her lower lip.

Derek cleared his throat. "As I said before, you should be going." His power surged toward us in a hot wave.

Carmela tried to turn to look at him, but I kept her gaze on me. "I can protect you. Just say yes." My wolf wanted to rip the vampire's throat out, regardless of the help he and his friend had provided us. That would resolve some of my problems, but it went against the kind of man I was. Besides, he'd taken care of Carmela when I could not. Regret twisted my stomach in knots.

Derek took a couple steps closer. "You had your chance to talk with her. Leave us."

I grabbed the crutch from beside me and stood. Our eyes met, and I felt the soft tug of his power as he tried to mess with my mind. Even though I was injured, I wouldn't put up with this. He might have feelings for her, but she was a werewolf, and my destined mate.

"Guys, please." Carmela looked between us and sighed. "I need to talk with you both."

2

CARMELA

I waved to the couch on either side of me, but the men's eyes were locked on one another. It was as if I didn't exist. I rubbed my hands over my face, but the familiar caress of power wafting off Derek caught my attention.

Brendan swayed on his feet for half a second, then he jerked forward as if he were a puppet on strings. He tackled Derek to the ground, and I leapt to my feet, stunned at what was happening. While I didn't doubt Brendan was swift and agile, he'd moved very fast considering his current condition. He straddled Derek and cocked back his fist.

I leapt over the coffee table and grabbed Brendan's arm. He started to turn his head, but suddenly we were both flying. I groaned as my body hit the soft couch cushions. A loud thud caught my attention as Brendan slammed into the opposite wall.

Derek looked between us before glaring at Brendan. He rushed to my side. "Love, lay back. Let me check you out." He lowered his voice a little, as if Brendan couldn't hear us.

I clenched both of my hands into fists, even though it hurt my right arm. "I'm fine." I pushed into a sitting position. "If you two are done trying to kill each other, I really need to talk with you both." While I cared about Brendan, I also felt deeply for Derek. I couldn't push one away for the other. After everything that had happened recently, I knew without a doubt that I was safest with both of them. I just hoped they'd understand, and not push me away because of my feelings.

Pain tightened Brendan's eyes. He pushed up on his elbows, but didn't make any move to join us on the sofa. His leg. I couldn't just watch him lay there in discomfort.

"Derek, help me get him to the couch." I knelt by Brendan's side and looked up to see Derek lingering a few feet away from us. I shook my head. "You two need to understand something. I care about you both." I sat beside Brendan. "I'm still trying to regain my strength, and we need to search for Chandra and Elliot. They could be dead for all we know. Now I have to sit here and watch you guys fight over me."

Derek closed the distance between us and sat beside me. "What do you expect us to do? Share you?" He looked tired and exasperated.

"Yes." I winced as they both objected at the same time, nearly shouting each other down. I could barely hear either of them. This was exactly the kind of reaction I figured I'd get.

"Come on," I said, but my voice was lost in their arguing. I jerked to my feet and glared down at them both, my frustration overwhelming my desire to avoid conflict. "Stop it!"

They quieted down but stared at me with such an intensity that the hackles on the back of my neck rose. My wolf pushed to the surface, and my teeth lengthened into fangs as fur lined my skin. If I didn't get ahold of myself, I'd shift.

Suddenly having their attention didn't feel so good anymore, but they boxed me in: Brendan on the floor in front of me and Derek at my side, with the wall at my back.

Closing my eyes, I took a few deep breaths, trying to regain control. When I opened them, they were still watching me.

"While that—" Derek spoke as Brendan said, "The wolves—" They shifted their glares to one another. Maybe this was a preview of what being in a relationship with both of them might be like—entirely frustrating.

"Brendan, go ahead since you started talking first, then Derek will speak." I toyed with the fabric on my splint. *Think of the positive. They're not killing each other.* I chewed on my lower lip as I saw the openly hostile look Derek gave Brendan. Hopefully that good luck would last.

"I don't think you've thought this through. The wolves would never agree to something like that. I couldn't agree to that either. It'd be putting both of us in danger." He looked at Derek. "All of us."

"My kindred wouldn't accept that either, and I wouldn't be able to coexist with another man in your bed, let alone in your life." Annoyance marred his pale face.

Butterflies fluttered in my stomach. I'd hoped Derek would be agreeable, but I was wrong. Of course, they had valid points. No one said this would be easy, just as being with Derek alone would require sacrifice. But if we wanted each other badly enough, we could figure out a way, couldn't we?

Disgusted with the conversation, I stepped over Brendan, needing some distance. *Ugh.*

"Carmela?" Brendan said. When I didn't respond, Derek called my name as well, but I ignored them both, heading upstairs. "Wait. Come back here." *No way.* I took a few more steps. "Fine. Maybe we should talk about this." I stopped halfway up and turned to them. Brendan cleared his throat. "Right, Derek?"

I glanced Derek's way.

He still looked grumpy, but his face was more stoic than Brendan's, and harder to read. "Yes, we'll talk about the relationship." He paused. "Still, it's not wise for Brendan to be here for an extended period of time. I'm sure there will be those out looking for him."

Brendan nodded. "Unfortunately he's right. My dad might send out a search party if I'm gone too long. They wouldn't have to go far from your house to find me. Maybe you should come with me to a werewolf safe house."

My father was well connected. The idea of being around a lot of werewolves nauseated me. "I can't. My father knows where a lot of them are, and even if he doesn't, other werewolves might talk."

Wincing, he pushed into a sitting position. "There are a couple only my family knows about. They're meant to house my father if there's ever an emergency where he isn't safe."

I closed the distance between us as Brendan slowly climbed to his feet. "I...I'm sorry," I said, looking into his eyes, then glancing back at Derek. "I just don't feel comfortable with that idea."

"I won't force you to go." Brendan gave me a quick kiss on the top of my head, surprising me. He looked like he wanted to say more but was afraid of how I'd react. "Take care of her, Derek."

"I will. When you return tomorrow, use the back door. It's less conspicuous." At my surprise, Derek shrugged. "I'm not awake during the day, and I'd like to know you're protected while I sleep." He walked with us into the den. "When he comes back, we'll talk this over. Your wolf is right that mating with him will keep you safe. You two should consummate the relationship." His lip curled a little in disgust, but he opened the door.

I widened my eyes at him, then turned my stunned gaze to Brendan. I couldn't believe Derek had said that. Without another word, I retreated upstairs to my room.

3

DEREK

rendan stared between me and Carmela's retreating back, looking almost as stunned as she did. Then he dipped his head and limped out the door.

Maybe that had been the wrong thing to say, but I didn't understand their surprised reactions. It wasn't as if I liked the idea of them being intimate, but I couldn't hold her back from who she was, though. I'd been here to help her heal and rest while she was injured, but now there were problems beyond any of us. We needed to keep her safe from her father and to find Elliot and her cousin.

I closed the door behind me and leaned on it. A blast of wild power and the grotesque sound of Carmela's transformation drew me up the stairs, but I didn't dare get too close before she completed her change. I'd seen her near-shift earlier, and I regretted the pain and stress she was going through. This wasn't easy on any of us, least of all her.

When things quieted down, I took a few more steps toward the door. The soft thump of her hopping off the bed prompted me to knock. I needed to make sure she was all right. It was good for her wound that she'd shifted, but I worried about her.

"Carmela?" A warning growl answered me as I opened the door after tapping on it with my knuckles. I couldn't see her anywhere.

The only sign of her presence was the low rumbling of an angry wolf. She looked over the side of the bed at me, a stunning vision of amber eyes and honey-brown fur.

Through the noise, I heard her stomach gurgle. "Do you need anything, love? Any food?" I couldn't let myself get so distracted by her current form that I didn't provide for her as I should.

She shook her head and vanished again. I walked around the side of the bed to see her curled up on the rug, propping her muzzle on her paws. Her eyes were closed.

I knelt beside her, sliding my fingers through her fur. What had I done? I couldn't lose her. She meant too much to me. I scratched the spot behind her ear that she'd enjoyed before. She tilted her head into my palm a little, but she still didn't look at me.

"I'm sorry for my behavior downstairs. Until recently, the only constant in my centuries on this Earth was Elliot. That's not the same as having someone to care for, someone who cares for me. Before I met you, I'd become disillusioned with life." I pulled my hand away, and she looked up at me. "I didn't know if I could continue on. That changed when I met you." Grimacing, I pushed into a standing position. "I'm not a fool. I know life won't be simple for us. But I hate to think I could lose you forever and return to the bleak existence I had before you."

She perked her head up and gave a soft whimper. I wished she hadn't shifted to her wolf form, but maybe it was for the best.

4

CHANDRA

*W*hile I'd regained some use of my legs, I was still weak. The problem with pumping adrenaline through my body to restore it was the incredible fatigue I felt now. Part of me didn't know whether it was a good or bad thing that I wasn't on the concrete floor with some of the others. If I was, I could fall asleep, but maybe I wouldn't have the strength to fight. Maybe I'd be like the fae girl in the jacket and lose myself.

I wasn't like them. I'd never been weak. If I'd dropped into that frame of mind, I would've been dead a long time ago. Between my parents, life on the street, and Uncle William, I sometimes wondered what it'd be like to be free from all the pain. However, I caught myself when I started to think like that, and continued to push on in hopes that one day I'd wake up and find myself living the life I'd dreamed of for so long.

I didn't know if that day would ever become a reality, but I couldn't give up on the dream.

I was so caught up in thoughts of my past and future that

at first I didn't notice the three men walking through the door. When I did, I subtly lowered myself so all of my weight was on my wrists and shoulders. I couldn't hold back my grimace of pain, but I had to play along. If I didn't, they'd know I was faking.

I recognized the man on the right side. He wore the same skull mask as before, although this time his hoodie was down. He had thick brown hair that was slicked back. I looked away before he could catch me staring. My legs trembled.

That left me looking at the other men. The one on the left had a mask as well, but his was matte black metal with a blue inlaid scrollwork design. While the man in the skull mask had a bulkier, muscled physique, this guy had a leaner build. Power radiated from him, but it didn't feel like death. I couldn't quite put my finger on it. It almost reminded me of the calm before a storm.

The man in the middle, though, looked to be in charge of everything.

"Tom..." Elliot sounded dumfounded. He knew the guy who'd taken us. How?

Small points peeked from beneath Tom's lips. Vampire fangs. But then why would he take vampires, too? This was the doing of the *Cazador*, and yes, there were people with magical powers involved, but a vampire? Vampires hated the hunters as much as anyone else.

"Elliot. I heard that you were my replacement on the High Council. It's a shame you're wrapped up in all of this. However, I know you and your friend Mr. Ashmore helped a couple of werewolves." He crouched in front of Elliot. "You shouldn't have meddled in their business. Now all of you will become an example of why the species should observe the Feud."

My gaze slid in front of me to see the necromancer staring at me with his blue-green eyes, as if he was looking into my soul. It took all my strength not to cry out or recoil. Something about him unnerved me, although I wasn't as afraid of him as I should've been.

The vampire rose to his feet and stepped in front of me, forcing the necromancer to take a couple steps back. He didn't look like he was happy about it. Tom grabbed my hair and stretched my neck out to the side. He licked his lips. "Werewolves are a delicacy. I'll enjoy draining you." He drew his head back.

"She's not the one," Elliot yelled, then cursed under his breath.

My breath came out in pants, and I saw that the necromancer's hands were balled into fists. I wished I could see more of his face, but it might be for the better. If I did, he'd have to kill me, right? What was I saying? I'd been watching way too many movies. Just by being here we were as good as dead.

Tom let my head flop forward. "Excuse me? What do you mean 'she's not the one'? Have you looked at her? She fits the description."

My heart clenched in my chest. What were they talking about?

Elliot stared up at me and then turned his gaze to Tom, but he didn't say anything further. Could he have been talking about Carmela? Was that why she'd gotten hurt again while on her date with Brendan? From what I'd heard, he hadn't been in any condition to outrun them and rescue her, as they'd claimed.

But no one dared to question them. The *Cazador* were humans: of course werewolves had the upper hand when faced with them. If only they knew...

"Silent now? I see." Tom grabbed my hair again, stretching my neck to the side. I screamed as he sank his teeth into my throat.

Right now, I didn't care who knew that I was free from the paralytic as I kicked and flailed. I was well aware that the movement was causing him to rip my neck, but I just wanted Tom's fangs out of me. I felt each pull of his lips draining more and more blood, and my limbs grew numb and cold. If I wasn't chained and tired already, I could fight him, but as the minutes passed...I had a harder time figuring out why I should even try.

"Sir," the man in the skull mask said after a moment. "She might be related to our target. I suggest we keep her alive." He kept his steady gaze on me, and I couldn't look away from his soothing eyes even as I felt my life slowly slipping away.

Tom took one last drink, then slid his tongue over the wounds. He pulled back with some of my blood dripping down his chin. "You might be right, Gareth. Administer another dose to relax her again. We need to find our true target. Jim, let's leave your brother to handle her. Gather the hunters upstairs for a new briefing."

Gareth turned a little to watch them go before looking back at me. He closed the gap between us, then reached out and brushed a strand of hair from my cheek.

"Leave her alone," Elliot said. "You people have done enough."

He held out his hand toward the vampire. Death radiated from him, and Elliot made a choking noise.

"Stop it," I whispered, my voice hoarse. Maybe I could get through to him. Granted, if it wasn't for Elliot I might not have had Tom sinking his fangs into me and nearly killing me, but we were all in this together. If we could break free from this prison, then afterward we could resume all the political bullshit our peoples thrived on.

"I don't take orders from either of you," he said, but he stopped focusing his necromantic power on Elliot. The vampire groaned and rattled his shackles a little. "If you don't want to die again, you'll remember that." His voice was gruff and slightly raspy. He reached into his hoodie and pulled out a rag and small vial from his pocket. The familiar smell of chemicals burned my sensitive nose again the moment he opened it.

"No, please."

"Relax, girl. At least you're not a dry husk." There was the slightest bit of venom in his tone, and I wondered if he wasn't blindly following Tom after all. But why would a necromancer unwillingly go along with a vampire? He took another step forward, and I pushed my last remaining strength into kicking him. The impact knocked him backward, though not as far as I'd hoped. I must've been weaker than I realized from all the blood loss. He dropped the vial, and it broke on the ground. The slightest bit of victory rang through me, until I saw the look in his eyes. It was worse than anything I'd witnessed before. His pupils went white, and he lunged at me, his fist cocked back.

I glared at him, not willing to show any more weakness. There wasn't much else I could do.

The hard blow landed on my jaw and my head snapped back, hitting the wall behind me. Stars swirled around in my vision, and I worked at blinking them away.

He towered over me from inches away and shook his head. His eyes were almost back to normal. "Very stupid thing to do. But I'm always prepared." He pushed the rag over my nose and mouth, pinning me to the wall with his bulky hand on my shoulder.

I tried to hold my breath, but he stayed there, hovering over me. The chemicals still seeped inside, and my limbs turned to jelly. He tilted my head back, maybe not wanting me to get neck strain, or maybe just wanting to see what he'd accomplished before he left.

My mind raced, and I vowed that I'd get revenge for all of this.

5

BRENDAN

*D*erek's words kept rolling through my head. I'd only managed a few hours of sleep. Morning rays of sun shone through the cracked blinds, and I covered my eyes with the back of my hand.

It was bad enough she wanted me to share her, with a vampire of all people, but being told to become intimate with her? My wolf was equal parts pleased and angry. I wasn't sure which one I was yet. All I knew was that our first priority was to keep her safe, regardless of whom she chose.

"Brendan," Neal called out from downstairs. "I need to speak with you."

Any hopes of getting more rest drifted away.

This was the worst possible time for me to talk with him. My emotions were all over the place, and he'd sense that. If my father knew what I was doing, my future would be in shambles. I was next in line to be the next Alpha of Alphas. I couldn't screw that up by being caught associating with a vampire, but I refused to let Carmela slip through my fingers.

"I'll be right down, Dad." I didn't raise my voice, but he'd hear me regardless.

I pushed out of bed, washed up, then slid into a pair of jeans and a red t-shirt, all the while taking deep breaths to center myself. I should've known I wouldn't be able to escape questioning so easily.

Last night, my parents had been in the den talking and laughing as they assembled one of those massive puzzles my mom enjoyed doing. Usually my father found a way to get out of it—either with Pack business or his construction business—but last night he hadn't. They'd called me in and asked if I found Carmela, but what could I say? 'Yes, in the arms of a vampire'? Instead, I gave a noncommittal response and took off to my room, where I tossed and turned.

They'd have both Carmela and Derek killed. I didn't want that. She'd had a good reason for fleeing to him over coming here. Pack law didn't allow much to be done for her until we mated. She'd been scared she would be shipped back to her brutal father.

Once Neal went off to work, I'd return to see her. My mother knew I hated being cooped up in the house, so hopefully she wouldn't ask a lot of questions. As long as my father didn't know, then we could make this work. It'd be a lot better if Carmela changed her mind and went to one of the werewolf safe houses—I could be with her with fewer questions asked. But Derek would be the one sneaking then.

Part of me wondered if I could sweep her away to somewhere she wouldn't think about him, but more than ever I had my doubts. Still, she needed my help. She and her family were in danger. Her cousin was out there, likely kidnapped, and I'd seen the emotion in her eyes when she'd talked about her.

Taking one last deep breath, I steeled my resolve and

went downstairs to see my father at the kitchen table. He should be leaving after breakfast.

"Good morning, son. You didn't really say much when you got in last night." He looked me over, and I remembered the fight with Derek. I hoped I didn't have any visible bruises. I hadn't been thinking about that at all last night. "Did everything go well when you talked with William?" The tone of his voice was fatherly, but there was a hint of authority to it that clearly said he expected me to tell him exactly what I knew. Anyone else might succumb to it, but I was his son after all. When are children ever fully honest and obedient to their parents?

I also knew how far I could push the limits of his patience, though. "No, it didn't. Carmela ran away from her parents' home." I had to say something, but I couldn't tell him everything. "Her cousin went to look for her, and now she's missing."

"They're both missing, you mean?" He leaned back in his chair and crossed his arms.

"No, I..." I cleared my throat and poured a cup of water from the pitcher on the table. "Carmela told me about this place she sometimes goes to get away. I found her there." I took a sip of water, buying myself a little more time. Should I tell him about what her father did? I hated holding back pertinent information from him, but I wanted Carmela to be here to explain.

Neal's eyes narrowed at me. "Why did she run?" He knew something was up.

Maybe I wouldn't be getting out of this so easily.

"She...has her reasons. I'm supposed to meet her in a bit, so I'll be heading out." My pulse sped up a little, and I was on the verge of losing my calm. I glanced up at the clock. "Sorry, Dad." Grabbing my crutch, I pushed up from my chair.

"If she ran, you might not be safe with her, especially with your injuries." He locked his gaze with mine in a show of dominance. "Someone should tag along with you when you meet her."

No, he couldn't do that. If he did, I wouldn't be able to see her. She was at a vampire's house. It would incriminate us all. I kept my gaze connected with his, refusing to bow down. While I didn't hold his position yet, I wouldn't be pushed around unless he pulled the Alpha card—then I'd be forced to. Fortunately, he didn't do that very often with me.

"That's not a good idea. I need to go alone. I can talk with her, and maybe I can bring her to one of our safe houses." Sighing, I lowered my gaze and returned to the chair. "If it's okay and if she's agreeable. She's concerned about her safety. She knows her cousin is missing and she's afraid of being next." I clenched my hand into a fist. "I'm going to mate with her, so we can help her."

Neal watched me for a long moment in silence. My hands trembled. What would he say? He unfolded his arms and placed his hands on the table. "Fine. Consider it done. I'll have a few wolves search for the cousin. Take Carmela to the safe house on Salem Street. I'll have someone set it up." He leaned forward a little. "You call me when you get there. If I haven't heard from you by dinner time, then I'll rip this town apart to find you."

"Yes, sir. I will." The fiery strength in his eyes threw me back to my rebellious teenage years. Very seldom had he ever gotten this way, but this was one time when I wouldn't be pressing his buttons. He meant every word he said.

"Once you have her safe, I expect both of you to tell me everything." Without another word, he rose from the chair and left the kitchen.

I took another gulp of water as the front door slammed shut with a tone of finality.

6

CARMELA

a soft banging sound woke me. *What was that?* I cocked my wolfish head to the side, but it had stopped.

The last thing I remembered before falling asleep was the gentle brush of Derek's fingers in my fur. I sniffed the room, but the faintness of his peppermint smell signaled that he'd left some time ago. Disappointment stung me. I still didn't know where he slept, and I'd never fully investigated the house.

Maybe I could find out. I stood up from the plush rug. My injured arm still ached, but not as badly as I'd feared it would. I drew in a breath and lowered my nose to the ground, sniffing out Derek's trail. I made it into the hallway overlooking the living room when the knocking returned. I hadn't imagined it.

It sounded as if it was coming from the back door, which made sense. Brendan was set to visit today. My wolf pranced with excitement at the thought of seeing him, but the human part of me wondered how he was feeling after what Derek said last night.

Butterflies danced in my stomach, and it was all I could do to put one paw in front of the other on the steps. I limped to the back door and stared up at it. Why hadn't I remembered that I'd need to unlock it and turn the knob? I couldn't really do that in wolf form, could I? But I'd try anyway. It would take time to shift, and Brendan couldn't just be hanging around outside. If something happened to him...

I reared back on my hind legs and clawed at the lock, scraping the paint off the door a few times in the process. To my surprise, it opened.

Brendan peeked around the door, a frown creasing his lips. "Are you okay?"

I bobbed my head. With him inside, I needed to shift. We had things to talk about, even if I'd rather avoid the subject for now. After being in wolf form all this time, my stomach grumbled like crazy. I sniffed the air to find Brendan had brought some hot burgers and fries in the paper bag he carried.

Indecision nipped at me. Eat first or shift first? The thought of wolfing down my food in front of Brendan made me a little uncomfortable. My mother had ingrained good manners into me from a young age, and besides, he was my future mate.

Brendan shut the door behind him. He headed for the kitchen, but I jogged up the stairs to my room and nudged the door shut with my muzzle. I caught the faint scent of peppermint I'd been tracking before, and my heart dropped in my chest. Could I really have both men in my life?

I forced all of my frustration into the shift. Pain arced through every part of my body as it restructured into my human form, pushing a gasp from my lips, but when I was done I felt better than before. More of my wounds were healing. I tested my shoulder in human form, and I could actually move it. The smart choice would be to put it back in the sling and let it continue healing instead of trying to use it again, though, so that's what I'd do.

I dressed in a fresh change of clothes and slid the sling on, then headed downstairs, taking the steps two at a time. My stomach growled constantly as if it had a mind of its own, and I swayed on my feet when I reached the bottom of the staircase.

Slow down. The food's still there.

Brendan sat at the kitchen table facing the doorway. He grabbed his crutch and stood when he saw me. "Hey, babe." It seemed silly for him to do that in his current condition, but he had manners and I truly liked that about him.

"Hi." I smiled. "Smells absolutely delicious."

He nodded to my stomach. "Seems like your belly agrees. Have you had anything to eat since your shift? I didn't see much food in the cupboards." He shrugged a shoulder. "I don't want to be nosy, just making sure you're taken care of."

I opened my mouth and closed it a few times, then shook my head. "It's fine. I'm eating now. Thank you for bringing something. Although I'm surprised you managed to find burgers and fries this early in the morning."

He grinned, and it brightened his blue eyes. "I have my ways. Or more specifically, my father knows a werewolf who runs a restaurant not far from here. I swung by on the way, and I know you mentioned burgers. I wasn't sure what breakfast food you like, so I went with a safe bet." His smile became a little sheepish.

I placed a hand over his. "Thank you. That's very generous."

He covered my hand with his own before pulling away and unwrapping one of his burgers. "We really need to talk."

Wincing, I leaned back, ready to hear what he had to say about the conversation with Derek last night, but he didn't say anything more. I wasn't sure how to take that. Did he not want to have sex with me? I grabbed a few fries from where he laid them out on the bag in the middle of the table.

Silence stretched between us as we ate. I reached for my second burger, but stopped. We couldn't just sit here and simmer. I needed to get some things off my chest.

"I'm sorry I didn't turn to you. After what happened, I wasn't really thinking. But I...I do want to mate with you. Like you said, it will be the best way to protect me and my family while trying to find the missing nocturnes and seeking justice against William." I leaned back in the chair, realizing just how sterile that sounded. No declarations of love. No heartfelt emotions. Just mating for safety and to have an advantage over my father. My stomach revolted at the idea of eating the second burger. The situation I'd been running from all my life now appeared to be exactly what I'd get.

Yes, I cared for him, but I couldn't help the shiver of fear chasing down my spine. Not fear of him, but fear that my future was spinning out of my control.

Brendan's lips stretched into a thin pink line, and pain flickered in his eyes before he stomped it down. "It's fine. I understand why you did what you did. But I'd feel more comfortable mating at a werewolf safe house. We can't stay here." He wiped his hands on a napkin and cleaned up the table, leaving the burger in front of me. "Eat up," he said as he dumped the garbage in the trash. "You need the protein after shifting."

Pangs of nausea swept through my belly, but I did as he said. "We can't just leave. I told you my thoughts on going to a safe house." I swiveled in my chair to look at him.

He grimaced and opened his mouth to reply, but then shook his head. He leaned against the kitchen counter and tapped his fingers on it. Agitation wafted off him, and I could definitely relate. We'd both been put on the spot last night.

"Do you want to... I mean, shall we..." I took a deep breath. "Will we be mating today?"

He nodded slowly. Heat darkened his eyes. "That's the plan, it seems." He closed the distance between us in a few hobbling steps and carefully knelt before me. "This isn't easy for me. I *want* to be with you. I care about you, Carmela. If that means Derek is involved, then I guess *c'est la vie*. But my father knows something is up. We should go to the safe house."

My heart leapt into my throat. "What do you mean? How much does he know?" Did he know I was here? My stomach churned in rebellion, and I pressed my hand against it.

"Not a lot, but he's suspicious. I told him you're safe but that your cousin is missing. He has a few wolves searching for her. Hopefully they'll find out where she was taken." He caressed my cheek, and I leaned into his touch. It was the only thing holding me together right now. "He told me to bring you to one of our family's safe houses. If he doesn't hear from me by this evening, he'll come find me."

"After Derek wakes up, we'll mate and head to the safe house." My heart broke, but it was inevitable. At least someone was out looking for Chandra, although it should've been me. "Until then, I guess we should rest."

7

CHANDRA

*I*t was hard keeping track of the time down here. I could only judge by how sore my shoulders were becoming. I'd tried standing a second time earlier, only to have one of my captors dose me with the paralytic again. But Gareth never returned. I didn't know whether to feel relieved or disappointed by that.

My head bobbed as I struggled to gain more control of my movements. My metabolism was beginning to burn through the drug more quickly, but I'd learned my lesson: I'd bide my time before trying to fight back again.

I looked over at the vampire and other nocturnes as they sat on the floor of this horrible place. A couple of them whimpered occasionally, but no one spoke. Some leaned back against the wall, almost lifelessly, while others rocked themselves or stared, frozen in horror and fear.

Only two others were strung up as I was, and they seemed somewhat familiar. I felt like I should know them. Maybe they were werewolves too. I tried to suck in a deep breath to scent the air, but I choked. My body refused to do much more than breathe shallowly, especially now that the vampire had nearly drained me of blood.

What had my life come to? I didn't even have enough energy to get angry. I had only been fed once since I'd been here. They just kept sedating us all. I hated this. If we were puppets for their experimentation, they needed to get it over with already. Being imprisoned was worse to me than the idea of being tortured. I'd been trained to withstand torture, but this...this sucked.

My wrists and shoulders ached from bearing my full weight for so long. I would give anything to be in my bed. Anything to see the night sky. To breathe fresh air again.

Snap out of it. Survive, and get revenge.

One of the human guards made his rounds again. This time, I watched him as he passed through the room. Maybe if I could get angry again, I could get out of here. Not that there was much likelihood of that happening, but I could dream.

Slowing his pace before me, he stared me down. He was definitely *Cazador*. "You watching me, bitch? Thinking about escaping?" He gripped me by the throat and hefted me into the air, so I was eye-to-eye with him. As horrible as it was to have his dirty hand around my throat, at least it took pressure off my aching shoulders and wrists. The fact that was even a consideration was sad.

As much as I wanted to make a saucy comeback, I couldn't speak, let alone kick him in the balls. I reached within me, trying to call upon my wolf, but I was too weak to draw my beast to the surface to help with the attack. I doubted I'd be able to shapeshift out of the sturdy iron shackles pinning my wrists to the wall, either—not with the strength of my wolf gone due to the drugs and blood loss.

Chains rattled nearby, and Elliot glared at the guard with a venomous black shadow behind his eyes. "Leave her alone."

The guard pressed closer to me, not bothered by the

vampire's threat. "What's it to you? What would you do, huh? Nothing. There's nothing you can do to me." He grinned, showing brown stains on his yellowed teeth. His foul breath brushed my face, reminding me of my father's. He'd enjoyed fear and pain, too. Uncle William was a walk in the park by comparison.

Rage cascaded through me in a torrent, and the wolf within me rose up and up until I could move. I thrust my knee into the guard's groin, making him release my throat, and then dropped to my tiptoes, but my knees buckled. I screamed as the strain against my sore shoulders returned. Desperately I tried to push back to my feet, but my energy was spent.

"Are you okay?" Elliot asked.

I turned and stared at him. His eyes were still slightly glowing. I nodded, then noticed his gaze dart to my side.

"Watch out," he hissed. Fury gave his voice a gravelly tone, almost as if he were a werewolf too.

The guard's fist snapped my head back into the wall. A second blow struck my stomach. He hit my torso again, and a loud crack reverberated through the room. Pain exploded within me. It felt like he'd broken my rib—I knew how that felt from experience—but he didn't stop.

"Leave me alone, asshole," I whispered.

He paused to grab my chin and yanked my face toward him. "What did you say, bitch? Who gave you the right to talk here?" He slapped me, and the coppery tang of blood filled my mouth.

I spit my blood at him, hitting him on the chin.

His eyes widened and he reeled back. He seemed terrified that I might have infected him with lycanthropy. If only the jerk knew how it was done: either you were born into it, or you were scratched or bitten. There were the occasional special cases, but they were few and far between. I doubted he'd get it through having a little bit of my blood and spit on him.

He swiped at his chin carefully with the sleeve of his shirt, trying to get my blood away from his mouth. Maybe if I was lucky he'd run off and leave me alone. Instead, when he was satisfied his face was clean, he pulled his arm back and slammed his fist into my side. The impact took my breath away and caused another loud cracking sound.

I gasped, trying to catch my breath, but it seemed like I couldn't get the air into my lungs. A large rumbling growl came from behind the guard, startling us both.

Gareth towered over my attacker. I couldn't see his face, but his eyes blazed with hatred. This was the first time I'd seen him since our fight. He stared at me and then returned his gaze to the guard. "Don't mess with the prisoners. They're not here to be your punching bags. Report to Jim and tell him what you've done. If you don't, I'll make sure you pay for it." He took a threatening step toward the guard.

The guard didn't move, but the smell of urine seeped into my nostrils, and I spotted a growing wet stain on the man's pants.

"You pathetic piece of human trash. Go." Gareth grabbed the guard by the upper arm and shoved him toward the entrance of the dank holding chamber. When he was gone, Gareth slowly turned to face me. "You just can't stay out of trouble, can you?" He gripped my chin in his big hands and tilted my head from one side to the other as he inspected my face. "Fuck. Tom doesn't want weak and damaged nocturnes." He ran his other hand over the front of my body —not as if he were groping me, but as though he was checking for more wounds. His hand connected with the area where the guard had punched me, and something inside me moved.

I bit my tongue, unwilling to show my pain. Gareth

scared me, and I wouldn't show any more weakness to him than I had to. It sounded like the injuries the guard had inflicted made me unfit to live in these people's eyes. Great. I raised my chin, hoping he didn't take the gesture as arrogance that needed knocked down a notch.

But he didn't pay attention to me, just to my body. He jerked my shirt up, showing off my lean, muscular torso. He placed his hands under my breasts, then slid his palms down again as if trying to find something. Midway down, he stopped as more pain shot through me.

Grimacing, I tried to move away before I realized what I was doing.

"Great. Broken ribs. What the hell was he thinking?" He shifted his gaze up my torso, briefly checking out my breasts before meeting my gaze. "Things don't look good for you. As I said, the people I work for don't want damaged goods. You're damaged now." His gaze descended again. "What should I do with you?"

I just stared at him. Maybe if I pretended I couldn't talk, he'd leave me alone. Maybe if I wasn't slightly turned on by his touch, I'd feel better. Either way I was screwed.

He grabbed my chin again, forcing me to meet his gaze. "I know you can talk. I heard what you said. Give me a good reason to not kill you, or so help me, you'll be one less nocturne for me to worry about." He leaned in until we were almost nose-to-nose. Menace lurked in his eyes. His hand brushed the underside of my breast, but this time it wasn't on purpose.

"If you help me, I'll satisfy whatever needs you have." I pushed my hips toward his. I hated to offer myself up for him, but I'd do what I needed to survive.

Gareth grabbed my waist, thrusting me back against the wall. His pupils narrowed. "You shouldn't make claims like that. How do you know you'd be up to the task?" He trailed his thumb along my jaw line, and pain followed his touch from where the guard had beaten me.

"I know what I'm capable of." Namely, I could outmuscle him and run. It wasn't as if I were a vampire or zombie. His necromantic magic couldn't affect me like them. If I couldn't overpower him, I'd kill him and then run, because I couldn't remain in these shackles. If he was like any other man, I might gain sway over him. He clearly possessed some authority here.

Gareth's breath caressed my cheek as he leaned in closer. "You might live to regret that boast." He pulled back so he could stare into my eyes. "But for now, you're less of a threat than you were." He jerked my shirt down, then grabbed the manacle that held my left wrist and opened it. I groaned as my arm collapsed down, leaving me to dangle by one pinned wrist. He wrapped his arm around my waist while he freed my other wrist.

"Thanks," I whispered, holding his gaze. I'd never felt fear like this—he promised death with one wrong move. I glanced back at the manacles still fastened to the wall.

"You shouldn't thank me yet. The night is still young. If you try to run, or if you help the others, you will die. Do you understand me?"

I nodded weakly. "Yes, I understand. I promise."

"Good. But for security purposes..." He pulled a cloth from his back pocket and shoved it over my nose and mouth. The thought of fighting made my side hurt, so I didn't. I surrendered to the drugs and went limp, like a sack of skin instead of flesh and bone and muscle. "Sorry, but I can't chance that you'll break that promise." He settled me on the ground, propped against the wall, but I kept listing to the side, nearly toppling into Elliot.

I stared at Gareth, wishing I could shoot daggers with my

eyes, but unfortunately, my power wasn't mind control. I had to settle for lycanthropy.

"Damn." He finally laid me on the ground.

I tried to whimper, but the sound wouldn't come. The floors were disgusting. If I ever made it out of here, I'd soak in a tub of hot water for a whole day, regardless of the high cost. I felt so, so dirty. Not that being chained to the walls was any better.

"I'll be back later to check what new trouble you're getting into." Chuckling, he shook his head. I watched as he turned his back and walked out the door.

Elliot touched my ankle. I could only breathe in response. "We'll all get out of this." Even though his words were optimistic, every time he tried to be reassuring he sounded more and more pessimistic.

A few other people in the room whimpered. One of the werewolves looked ready to gnaw his arm off if it would provide relief.

"Does anyone have telepathy?" Elliot asked, "We need to get a message out."

A young female, probably the fae girl with the jacket, spoke up from close by. "I do." Her voice was shaky, as if she hadn't talked in days. "I've tried calling out to my people for help, but I can't get anything through. It's as if someone's psychically blocking me." She sighed.

"Try one more time for us. The target is Carmela, a werewolf."

My eyes widened. It seemed my suspicions were right: my cousin was involved in something dangerous and beyond my knowledge. Why hadn't she told me? Her actions had caused me to be drawn into this.

"Sent." A moment after the word left her mouth, a guard marched into the room and hauled her away. The fae's shrieks echoed through the room and up the hallway. Her screams lingered in my head long after they stopped.

8

CARMELA

I surged up into a sitting position on the bed. Sweat dripped down my chest, and my heart raced as I sucked air into my lungs. The words echoed over and over in my head: *'Danger. Help us. Warehouse. Danger. Need you.'* Up until then, the dream had been relatively neutral, nothing involving danger or warehouses. The urgency in the words was what startled me the most.

Brendan pushed onto his elbows and rubbed his eyes. "What's wrong? Bad dream?"

"It was more than that." Derek stood in the doorway with only a pair of pajama pants on. I hadn't heard him approach, and his smooth alabaster chest almost distracted me from the message. "Someone communicated with you."

"How do you know?" Brendan rubbed his hand over my back, and while it was soothing, I knew it had another meaning too—he was showing his possession. They'd have to learn to live with sharing me, though, especially if I was going to be mating soon.

Derek remained silent, but the look on his face was grim, almost as if there was something he didn't want to share.

He'd never been closed off like this before. Did he know more than we did about the voice?

"Derek, tell us what you know." I patted the covers next to me and scooted into the center of the bed.

He looked from me to Brendan and back again, but he plopped down on the bed beside me. "When you were here that first night I aided you as best I could with medicine, but you were bleeding too heavily." He went silent for a moment, staring away from us. "I licked the wound closed. It was the best chance for your survival. We're...connected in a way. I can sense when you're afraid, or when someone's in your head..."

Brendan glared at Derek's back, but he didn't say anything. I wished Derek had told me this sooner, but there wasn't much to be done about it now. All we could do was move forward.

"It wasn't just a dream, then?" I asked.

"No, it was a message from a fae. They're obviously taking a wide variety of nocturnes. I wonder if the other races know that some of their kind are missing." He turned to face us. "Once you're mated, we should split up. If I go to my people and you to yours, we might stand a greater chance of helping our friends."

"Until one of our people does find them," Brendan spoke up, and I turned to him. "Then the others will be killed."

"The three of us stand no chance of finding them by ourselves. There are hundreds of warehouses all over the city." I wrapped my arm around my waist. "If the Feud didn't exist..." I sighed and shook my head.

"Where there's a will, there's a way, love." Derek smiled at me, then rose from the bed. "Speaking of which, I believe you two have unfinished business."

Before I knew what I was doing, I grabbed his hand. "Wait." I looked between him and Brendan. "Stay with us."

He watched Brendan's carefully neutral expression, neither man saying anything. It frightened me that they weren't speaking, but I did my best to remain calm.

Finally, Derek pulled me into him, pressing his chest against my back. I looked up at him, but he bent forward, placing kisses on my neck. The sensation warmed me in a way I'd never quite felt before. It was different from what I'd felt when I kissed Brendan for the first time. Was it some kind of vampire trick he was using?

Brendan moved in closer to us, but grimaced as his injured leg bumped the other one.

"He should be in the center. Due to his injuries, you can mount him more easily than he can you." Derek's breath caressed my shoulder, but his words made my stomach clench in unease. Maybe it hadn't been a great idea to have him here too.

"Unfortunately, you're right." Brendan looked me over as if he were undressing me with his eyes. "Help support her so she won't hurt her shoulder."

I opened my mouth to say something, but Derek spoke up first. "I will." He reached around me, offering one hand to Brendan while cupping the underside of his uninjured leg with the other. "This might hurt a little." He tugged him toward the center of the bed.

Brendan groaned, squeezing his eyes shut. His knuckles were white on the hand holding Derek's, who was looking more than a little uncomfortable. If I didn't do something soon, I worried Brendan would break Derek's hand.

I carefully straddled Brendan's waist. "You can't remain in your human form like this. If you shift, you'll get better. Trust me," I said, leaning down into him and supporting myself with my good arm. My lips brushed against his, and he slowly opened his eyes.

"I trust you. I just need to be here to protect you." He

wrapped his arms around me, sliding his arms down my waist to my backside.

"You'd be able to protect me better if you were healed." I pushed back into his hands, enjoying the feeling of them on me. Suddenly the clothes between us were too constricting.

Brendan pushed me back from him for a moment. "My wolf isn't as well-mannered as yours." He gave me a sideways grin. "When this is over, I'll change. Your doctor," he said, nodding over my shoulder to where Derek stood beside the bed, "hasn't led you astray. Maybe he's not so bad, for a vampire."

Derek laughed, and the bed squeaked a little as he rejoined us. "Good to hear, wolf. But you're both stalling. Brendan will heal with time, just as you are." He turned my head toward him, beckoning me to look into his eyes. "You need to remain focused." His voice took on a sultry quality that struck renewed fire in my belly. He glanced at Brendan, meeting his eyes as well. "Make her your mate."

I wobbled a little. My head felt like it was stuffed with cotton balls, but the drive to mate with Brendan overrode that.

Desire darkened Brendan's eyes, turning them impossibly blue, like an ocean ready to swallow me whole. He reached for the hem of my shirt and tugged it up, but my shoulder splint prevented it from going any further.

Derek took the shirt and lowered it. He removed the shoulder splint, and then carefully lifted my shirt over my head.

Brendan splayed his hands over my stomach before sliding them up toward my breasts. I'd been in such a hurry to eat that I hadn't put my bra on after I shifted. Now I was glad I hadn't. The feeling of his hands on me chased away any dark, creeping thoughts.

Derek unfastened the button on my jeans, then unzipped

them. I moved my hips to help him remove them, which placed my breasts nearer to Brendan's face. He pulled me closer, curving his tongue over one nipple and then the other. His mouth sucked and teased each peak until they were both incredibly hard. He smirked, as if pleased with his achievement.

I moaned, unable to stop myself. The sensations burning within me were like a fire that could never be quenched. Suddenly the romance novels began to make more sense. If this was how it felt...

Brendan stroked his hand down my torso, and I gasped as his fingers dipped between my naked thighs. I didn't remember Derek taking everything off. "You're beautiful, Carmela," Brendan whispered, slowly sliding one finger inside of me and curving it to hit a particularly sensitive spot over and over.

I cried out, savoring the feeling and yet wanting more of him. My thighs trembled as desire pushed me toward the edge.

He smiled, a hint of male arrogance in the curve of his lips. My body trembled with need, but he pulled his finger from me. Only then did I notice the incredible bulge in his jeans.

I blinked down at it, watching him carefully unbuckle his belt, unbutton, and unzip. He pushed his pants down to his thighs just enough to unleashed his large cock. My jaw dropped open. How was I supposed to fit that inside me?

Derek held my waist and rubbed his thumbs over the small of my back in strong, circular strokes. My body relaxed a little, and I let out a breath I hadn't realized I'd been holding.

Brendan drew me toward him and kissed me with such raw passion that it overwhelmed my senses. I opened my mouth to him, letting him ravish me. For the moment, only he and I existed—only his lips and mine.

My hips angled toward his, and he nudged his cock against my entrance. Any fear I'd felt before vanished. I knew I was protected. This wasn't a horrible experience: there was no violence, no anger, no pain.

Inch by inch, Brendan sank into me, waiting for me to accommodate him before lowering me further, until he was all the way inside. I ground into him, feeling confident in my position over him.

He gave me a sideways grin. "Don't get too cocky. I can still flip you to the bed and take you, pain or not." He blinked slowly, and his eyes changed from blue to wolf-amber.

My breath caught in my throat. Seeing the sudden change surprised me. Perhaps he was right about his wolf not being as well-mannered. Mine rolled around below the surface of my skin, pressing every once in a while for me to change, but more than anything she wanted to become mated to him.

"That wouldn't be a good idea for either of you," Derek said from behind me.

I sat up to feel the cool press of Derek's chest against my back and his legs trapping mine against Brendan's. He held my hips and pulled me up a little before guiding me back down Brendan's shaft. I bit my lip at the pleasure coursing through me.

Brendan stared up at us, but his gaze returned strictly to meet mine. "You're right. I wouldn't want to hurt Carmela." He rocked his hips up to meet my strokes. Our bodies met, in a leisurely rhythm at first, as if we had all the time in the world to enjoy ourselves, but that didn't last long. Soon we were writhing against one another.

Brendan held me in his arms, supporting me as best he could. He nuzzled my neck as his body drove into mine with an intensity that I craved. I arched my back a little, feeling my wolf push harder against my skin. It would be so easy to give in and let her take over, but I refused to. Not when we were so close to the edge of climax.

Brendan sank his teeth into my neck, claiming me as his mate, a second before my body exploded with pleasure. I dug my nails into his arms, and he grunted, though I wasn't sure if it was in pain or pleasure. I should've cared, but wave after wave of ecstasy shook me as his hot seed poured into me.

My body was weak with release, but the soft caress of Derek's cool hand on my lower back rekindled the flames in my lower belly. Brendan's sweat mingled with mine, between our bodies. I could barely move. How would I be able to mate with Derek too?

Brendan gave me a lingering kiss before lifting me back into Derek's arms. He tucked his hands behind his head, and I noticed the blood sliding down his arms from where I'd scratched him, but the heat still burning in his eyes reassured me.

9

DEREK

I'd done many things in my centuries, but sharing a werewolf with her wolf mate wasn't one of them. The scent of their blood taunted and teased me, drawing me back to the fact I hadn't eaten yet tonight. It was still fairly early, but now I needed to sate my desires, whether those were for blood, sex, or both.

I caressed my hand over Carmela's breast, toying with the hard tip of her nipple. My lips descended to the spot right above her shoulder where Brendan had bit her. The desire to lick her wound nearly won, but I switched to the opposite side of her neck instead.

She shivered and pressed her bottom against me. I looked down at Brendan, who merely watched us. He looked particularly comfortable, except for the subtle tightness at the corners of his eyes and mouth, and he inclined his head slightly.

I slid down my pajama pants. I wanted to take my time with her, make love to her as I'd hoped to, but her body thrummed with an urgent desire, and her blood sang a siren's song.

I leaned her forward and thrust into her warm, wet center, filling her completely. She yelped and glanced over at me, surprise widening her eyes. I pulled out a little, then slammed back into place, angling my hips for maximum pleasure. While I might not have Brendan's size, I did have many, many years of experience.

As I fell into a steady pace, I pulled her back up against me so I could fondle her breasts and kiss her neck. Her legs wobbled like jelly. Brendan moved below us to hold her hips and help keep her upright.

"Derek," she gasped, her voice husky with desire. Her walls clenched around me, and I could smell her arousal thicken once more. She was close again.

I lengthened my strokes, trying to bide my time with her, but she wreaked havoc on my sensibilities. My fangs lengthened, and I sank them into the juncture of her neck and shoulder. Her blood poured into my throat, and I rocked into her, faster and more desperate than before.

She screamed, and her body squeezed around my cock. She thrust back against me again almost as if she were as needy as I was. My body tightened a moment before I came, filling her with my semen. I swiped my tongue over the two perfectly round holes I'd made in her skin—a memento of this beautiful moment.

With a groan, I pulled her to me and lowered us beside Brendan, who carefully positioned himself more toward the right side of the bed. The only sound penetrating the silence was her panting breath. I wrapped my leg between hers as she rested her head against Brendan's chest.

They drifted off to sleep again, but I lay awake. My kind only 'slept' during the day.

Thoughts of our time together shifted to what had called me to the bedroom in the first place. The connection between Carmela and I was no longer shaky and weak, but solid now that I'd bitten her. I reached for our bond to glimpse in her mind the words the fae had spoken, when something in the atmosphere changed.

I untangled myself from Carmela and crossed the room to the window that faced the road. Two figures crouched on the roof opposite us. Vampires. Dread filled my gut. There would be no help for any of us anymore. They darted off, presumably to tell Lord Prescott.

We had very little time to get out of here.

"Both of you, get up." The bed squeaked behind me a little, but neither made much effort to move. Brendan blinked at me, and Carmela cuddled closer to him. "Now." I put a command into the word, and that finally got them going. "We've been spotted by vampires."

Carmela froze. Her eyes widened, and she looked between Brendan and me. "No. This can't be happening."

"It is. We need to get you two to safety. Hurry." I darted to my room and dressed. By the time I came back, they were mostly decent. Brendan was grabbing his crutch as Carmela pulled on her sling. "Let's go."

10

CARMELA

*T*he three of us froze in place at the bottom of the stairs as the sound of shattering wood came from the front of the row house.

"We need to go. Quickly," Derek whispered, grabbing my hand.

I pulled away. "Help Brendan. He has a crutch."

Brendan handed the crutch to me, and Derek tossed him over his shoulder. "Great. Here we go again," Brendan grumbled under his breath.

We darted for the back door. We were running as fast as we could toward it when it burst open. We turned again, this time jogging up the stairs. I had no idea where to go if both of the doors were blocked, but Derek knew his house better than I did. Hopefully he had a backup plan. Our lives were in his hands.

The familiar scent of a musky forest flooded my nose a moment before a werewolf's strong arms pulled me backward down the stairs. I screamed as the hand brushed my injured shoulder, and the crutch fell from my grip. But this didn't make sense—Derek said we were running from vampires, not werewolves.

Derek stopped at the sound, and Brendan raised his gaze to meet mine. His eyes widened.

"Go! Don't let them take you." I struggled against the man holding me, but my body was weak from sex and feeding Derek.

"Brendan Kelly. I should've known you were up to something. You tried to be secretive about your girlie's location, but I'm not an idiot. I told you I'd find you, pup. Don't even think about leaving this house with that vampire." Neal Kelly's commanding voice came from behind me, and I looked up to see him standing over me.

I averted my gaze, cowering slightly before I could stop myself. Brendan had said his father didn't dislike me, but I doubted that was still true. I'd involved his son in things a future Alpha shouldn't be part of. Still, I didn't want this to be the end of us. He had to see reason.

Instinctually, I twisted and broke away from his strong grip. He reached for me again, but I jumped a few steps away. My Militia training took hold of me again. Granted, it didn't have great timing. "You don't understand, sir." I looked at the four guards flanking our Alpha. They closed in on the staircase as if I were some kind of threat.

"I don't understand?" Neal chuckled, looking between the stone-faced guards and us. "No, I don't, because no one is telling me anything."

Derek set Brendan on his feet on the steps.

"What are you doing?" I asked, incredulous that they weren't fleeing for safety.

"I don't think they're here to harm us," Brendan said, using the bannister to hobble toward me. "Dad, as I said before, Carmela ran away out of fear for her safety. You saw what her father did to her in our house. You didn't—couldn't

—do anything to him, but her father is a bad man. He nearly raped her." Brendan's jaw clenched, and he wrapped his arm around my waist. "She's—"

"Is this true, girl?" Neal stared me down with regret in his eyes.

I winced and lowered my gaze. I hated that what my father did to me was becoming known to more and more people, like juicy gossip.

"You chose a vampire for protection because you didn't think your kind would take you in?" Neal knelt in front of me, meeting my gaze again.

I nodded.

"I'm sorry you went through that abuse. You would've been cared for. I'm just sad the Feud requires punishment to be brought upon you all. You've already been through so much. It breaks my heart that you'll have to go through more because you didn't make the right decision." Neal paused, heaviness in his tone. "Take them."

"What?" Brendan yelled. "No, don't do this to her." The man beside Neal dragged him away from me. "Leave her alone." He struggled, but he looked as hopeless as I felt.

A hand closed over my arm, pulling me down the stairs to stand beside Brendan and Neal. "Let's go." The woman gripping me had burgundy hair that flowed around her face. She frowned at me sorrowfully, but nudged me on my way. Derek walked before me with two werewolves on either side of him. He glanced at me, his eyebrows drawn together. He could've escaped. I'd seen how fast he could move.

My chest ached at the pain I was causing those I cared for, and I lowered my gaze. Why was this happening?

The wolves stopped short as vampires appeared, blocking both exits. Their faces were neutral, but power radiated from them like angry stinging bees.

One young-looking male stood out amongst them. He

held himself with exquisite grace and power. He seemed to float into the room. His platinum blond hair flowed around his shoulders, and his grey eyes sparkled.

"It seems we arrived a moment too late to the party. We'll just have to extend it. Seems you've found trouble among your new friends...or should I say lovers, Derek?" He walked up to me and ripped my collar, leaving my neck and the bite marks from both Brendan and Derek bare to the room.

The female werewolf at my back snarled. It seemed more directed at the vampire than at me, but I couldn't be sure. Her grip on me tightened, and I wanted so badly to be away from her at that moment.

"Is he right, Brendan?" Neal looked to his son. "Your mate is bound to both you and this vampire?" His face was tomato red. "Damn it, son." His voice boomed, sending chills down my spine. He turned back to the vampire who appeared to be in charge. "Who are you anyway? How did you know this was going on?"

"I'm sorry, how rude of me. I am Lord Prescott, Chairman of the Vampiric High Council. And you are Neal Kelly, Alpha of the Alphas. Little known fact." Smirking, Prescott took a seat on the couch and propped his legs on the coffee table. "I suspected disobedience. Try as I might to overlook it, I received an anonymous tip early this evening about what was going on. I sent a couple of people to investigate, only to have my fears confirmed."

Derek perked up. "Wait. When did you receive the tip?" He pulled against the werewolves on either side of him, and they struggled to remain in place. "Elliot tried to send a message through a fae. They're being held somewhere. Tell them, Carmela."

All eyes turned my way, and I blinked at them as I struggled to remember the exact phrasing. "Uhm..." I chewed on my lower lip. "It was 'Danger. Help us. Warehouse.

Danger. Need you.' We couldn't really determine their location for sure, since there are hundreds of warehouses in the city."

"It's the *Cazador*. They're the biggest danger to all of us." Derek looked from me to Prescott. "The only way we can get Chandra and Elliot back is to work together. The hunters have joined forces with a select group of nocturnes."

"That's impossible," Neal shouted. "They're out to kill us all."

"Yes and no. The hunters sent a necromancer after me, twice." Derek grimaced. "He's powerful, too. If they have him at their disposal, I'm sure they have more."

Prescott looked enthralled by the conversation. "Release them." He waved his hand and power surged outward from him. The werewolves let us go almost in sync, then looked among one another in confusion.

I ran to Brendan as he swayed, letting him lean on me. I couldn't contain my relief that this hadn't turned into a bloody battle between the two species. There was enough fighting between nocturnes already. In times like this, all of us were weakened. Someone had managed to capture each of the different races, proving to us that we weren't at the top of the food chain.

"This is quite concerning," Prescott said, removing his feet from the coffee table. "Let's get down to business. We're looking for a missing Senior High Council member taken from this home only a couple of nights ago, using a powerful drug which very few vampires have access to, much less humans. I'm guessing your son came to find the lovely wolf who is bonded to both him and my vampire.

"As much as the unending Feud amuses me, the time has inevitably come for change, Neal. Necromancers are a bane to my people's kind just as the *Cazador* are to yours. They restrict and kill us. We need to make them disappear, just as you can clear these three of their death sentences. Why the female wolf came here is anyone's guess, but that's not the point, is it? However, she is mated to your son. She shall provide pups to continue your lineage." He looked completely relaxed. "It appears we have a common goal here: missing people, and a threat to both our races. Perhaps we should hang up our differences for a while to get things done, yes?"

Neal Kelly crossed his arms over his chest and sighed. He didn't look happy, but the vampires outnumbered his wolves. It wasn't as if he had much choice. "Regrettably, there are three werewolves missing to my knowledge."

"We're in agreement to work together, then?" Prescott rose to his feet as if he were a puppet on string.

"If we do find your vampire and our werewolves, what then? We both know who holds more influence over the lesser nocturnes, and who has acted openly hostile toward us in days past: vampires. What's to say you won't use what knowledge you find to finish my people off?" Neal's jaw clenched in a similar fashion to Brendan's earlier. It was interesting to see their striking resemblance now.

I glanced at Derek, nibbling my lower lip. He was watching me, taking in the small action, and I averted my gaze back to the Alpha and the chairman.

11

DEREK

I watched Carmela nibble on her lower lip. Fire spread through my body again, and I wanted nothing more than to have her. Slight jealousy stung my flesh as I saw Brendan stare at her the same way, but I pushed it down. It was far too late to have those thoughts.

She might primarily be an Alpha Queen to her mate, but she was also mine.

I returned my gaze to Lord Prescott and Neal Kelly.

"You would have to take my word for it. We could set up a written agreement at some point, if you wanted to," Prescott said.

Neal didn't look convinced about what Prescott was saying, but at least he wasn't disagreeing. And they did have a point. We should start working together. It was in everyone's best interest to fight against the *Cazador* before they took down all nocturnes, and more humans, too. I didn't particularly care about humans when they hunted my kind, but they were a food source. The innocent ones didn't have to be needlessly slaughtered as the *Cazador* did everyone else.

"No," Neal growled. "I'm not going to take your word for

11

it. I want proof that if I back you, you won't backstab me and my people."

Prescott smirked. "Exactly what I wanted to hear." He snapped his fingers, and another vampire came to his side, holding a sheet of paper and a pen, which he placed into Prescott's hand. The vampire stepped away, and Prescott quickly scribbled out a few paragraphs before setting down the pen and spinning the paper toward Neal. "This written agreement shall declare a temporary peace between our races. If you choose not to sign, I will not help you find your werewolves, and if I do find them, I will have them killed."

I didn't like that. I wouldn't stand back and watch Carmela die by Prescott's hand. I would fight to save her. Obviously Brendan felt the same way, because he pulled her closer to him. She was protected, and regardless of what might happen in the end, that was what mattered most.

"I'll sign your document. However, this agreement shall not become null and void unless we both agree to dissolve it. You will not escape through any loopholes." Neal signaled a male werewolf to take the offered paper.

"Agreed. I'll have a copy of our truce made for you."

Neal scribbled his name on the document, then handed it back to the werewolf. "Do you have any other information on where we might find the missing nocturnes?"

"Carmela led me to discover that the kidnappers are using a substance that vampires developed to help their younger kin deal with the hunger following change. There aren't many people who would have access to something like that. Only a few on the High Council." I hoped I was wrong, but there had been a little suspicion with Tom's death. It didn't seem connected to the necromancer attack before, but now I wasn't sure. Could he have faked it? No, I had to be grasping for straws. "There's also the silver bullets both Carmela and your son were shot with. They've kept them from healing at the normal rate for werewolves. Something in them kills the lycanthropy near the bullet wound. The *Cazador* were responsible for that, so I think it's fair to say we might find them at one of the *Cazador* strongholds."

Neal glanced at Carmela before turning away. "Well, it's good we have an idea of who might be behind this. It'd help if things were clearer here." He turned his gaze to Prescott. "What about you? What do you know about what's going on here?"

"I have some of my trackers out searching." Prescott cracked his knuckles. "Mostly, I know what my vampire said. However, I'm certain we won't see the end of these kidnappings until we've done something about it."

I looked at the vampires and werewolves around us, wondering who might be the next target.

CARMELA

I rested my head against Brendan's chest as I toyed with the hem of my shoulder splint. I wanted to seek refuge in the spare bedroom. The proximity of all these other werewolves and vampires made me increasingly uncomfortable. It didn't help that the kidnappings could go on until we somehow managed to stop the *Cazador* and its nocturne allies.

Neal and his people made me feel like a traitor, but he'd been compassionate about what happened. Maybe he would've taken me under his wing if I'd gone to them, but it was too late to second-guess my decisions now.

My attention rested on Derek, who was watching the two leaders go back and forth devising a plan to find and rescue the captives and stop the hunters. Derek's gaze drifted my way, and our eyes connected, sending a shiver of lust through my spine. Now was not the time to become aroused.

My heart pounded in my chest, and I needed to get away. It wasn't as if my presence was necessary to the planning. I retrieved Brendan's crutch and retreated upstairs to the spare room. The sheets still smelled strongly of our lovemaking. If I just closed my eyes, I could pretend I was back in that moment, not trapped here, scared for those I cared about.

I shut the door behind me and rested my back against it. My pulse steadied as I drew in deep breaths, feeling a little more relaxed now that I had some space.

A soft knock sounded behind me. "Are you okay?" Derek asked.

"Please. I just need a moment." If he came in here, I didn't know if I'd be able to behave myself. What I needed most was to recover my composure before the search started for Chandra and the others.

"Are you sure?" He sounded disappointed and more than a little annoyed, but he didn't raise his voice.

"Yes, I'm sure," I said. He remained there for a few moments as if I'd change my mind, before finally retreating. Sighing, I looked up at the window I'd broken on my first night here. I needed air.

I walked to the window and stared down into the alleyway below. A strong scent hit my nose: something familiar, chemical. I leaned closer to the window, but the scent faded. I twirled around, but a cloth slammed over my nose and lips with bruising force. A hooded figure with a skull mask grabbed the back of my thighs, and then, heedless of my sling, tossed me over his shoulder.

I couldn't move. I tried to open my mouth to scream, to get a warning out to Derek and Brendan, but I was paralyzed. I only hoped Derek could feel my terror through our connection, because I had no idea how that worked.

The large man tightened his grip on me and slowly eased us through the window, careful not to make a sound. That was probably how he'd gotten in. He pushed off from the side of the building, hurtling us through the air, but instead of landing in the alley, we were on the roof of the next building.

My head bobbed against his back as he sprinted away from Derek's, and the pain in my shoulder was like a knife sliding into me over and over. My tears splashed onto the roof below. I wanted nothing more than to be back in Derek's home, curled up in bed with him and Brendan.

If only I hadn't pushed him away...

PART V

1

DEREK

*A*fter Carmela told me to go away, I came to the mostly unused bathroom down the hall. What would I say to the others downstairs? I needed to collect my thoughts before I rejoined them. Regardless of my concern for Carmela, Elliot was counting on me to rescue him. I had to get my act together.

Unease trickled along my spine. I scanned the bathroom's tight confines, confirming I was still alone. Suddenly fear exploded in my chest, but the emotion wasn't mine. My mind drew back to the way I'd felt the night Carmela came to my home after her father abused her. I darted through the hallway toward the spare room where I'd left her.

Something wasn't right. I could sense nothing but utter stillness from inside. I tried the doorknob, but it was locked. "Carmela? Open up." I listened, but she didn't reply. "Love? Are you there?" Silence.

What's going on?

The sound of footsteps and a crutch tapped up the stairs. "Everything okay?" Brendan asked from behind me.

"No, I don't think it is." I jerked the doorknob to the right, breaking the lock. My gaze whipped around the room—Carmela was gone. My heart raced in my chest. The curtain billowed in the gentle breeze, bringing my attention to the open window. Had she run again? "Damn it!" I slammed my fist into the wall beside the door.

Brendan stood in the doorway, just inches from the spot I'd struck. His eyes widened, and he stepped away from me as he checked for himself that Carmela wasn't here. A harsh growl rumbled up from deep in his chest. He pushed further into the room, heading toward the bed where we'd made love to her a little less than an hour ago. His shoulders slumped forward as if hit by a wave of emotion.

I looked away. I knew about pain all too well, but time was of the essence if we were to figure out where she'd gone and why before she got into even more trouble. But why had she run? I walked toward the window, and a strong, chemical scent seeped into my nostrils. Something like what I'd smelled before.

No! She hadn't run after all. Someone took her from under my nose, and the noses of the dozen or so vampires and werewolves downstairs. That bastard.

"Carmela was kidnapped." Brendan's gaze rose to meet mine, and he hobbled over. He sucked in a deep breath, only to end up coughing and pinching his nose. "Shit. I can't believe this is happening. Someone should've stayed with her."

"What is it?" I asked, not really sure I wanted to know the answer.

"The chemical has elements of a drug that's been tested on werewolves as a temporary paralytic. The *Cazador* concocted it." Brendan sniffed around the window, then raised his face to an area where the intruder's scent was strongest. His eyes narrowed. "The *Cazador*...but somehow, this guy is different. He exudes death."

The necromancer. It had to be. I scented the air, confirming it for myself.

Several footsteps thumped on the stairs. "What's going on in here?" Neal said from the doorway.

I frowned, searching for the words to tell him.

Neal glanced between me and his son. When neither of us spoke, he examined the room. Confusion creased his forehead for a split second before realization set in. "Damn it! Those bastards." He strolled into the room, sniffing the spots that Brendan and I had discovered moments before. "We should've taken out that lab when we had the chance." He frowned at the burgundy-haired female werewolf standing near the door.

I caught Prescott's eye as he joined us. He nodded toward a corner of the room, furthest from the window where Carmela had been taken.

An unfamiliar handkerchief lay abandoned on the floor. I crossed the room to investigate, then picked it up and sniffed. It had the kidnapper's scent, and only a trace of the chemical. Hell, this whole area carried his scent, as if he'd been hovering here for a while. "Found something," I said, lifting the cloth for the others to see.

Neal snatched it from me, holding the fabric near his nose. He winced, but quickly seemed to brush off any discomfort. "Let's get some trackers on this." He held the handkerchief out to the female werewolf he'd looked to moments ago. "I want you searching the rest of the room, top to bottom. Report anything you find." The Alpha werewolf paused, then turned back to me. His lips tightened. "Thanks."

"Anything to help find Carmela and the others." I retreated to the hallway as the burgundy-haired werewolf began her search of the spare room.

Prescott leaned against the wall beside me, shrugging a shoulder as if to say, *What did you expect?* Two vampires lingered nearby, waiting for instructions. "Timothy and Jane, join the werewolf in investigating the room," Prescott said before slipping back down the stairs.

The look on their faces showed their displeasure before they could censor themselves. Horror came over Jane's, while Timothy wrinkled his nose as if the task was distasteful. I couldn't blame them. They weren't used to being around wolves.

Brendan and Neal talked further along the hallway in harsh whispers. I didn't envy the young werewolf. When this was behind us, I'd probably be getting the same treatment from my leader.

Turning away from them, I followed Prescott downstairs to talk with him. What we needed was to be out scouring the streets for Carmela, not searching my spare room. The house felt more like a circus than a command center with this many people loitering about.

Prescott retreated into the living room and propped his feet on my coffee table...again. I hated how comfortable he acted in my home, with my furniture, but I was in no position to speak out against him. Not this time.

"You've made some poor decisions in your old age. First skipping High Council meetings, and now marking and fornicating with a werewolf. You used to be smarter. Where did you go wrong?" Prescott waved a hand at the couch beside him, but I didn't exactly want to sit, let alone that close to him. I settled in the nearby armchair instead. "Obedience never was your forte, but I've overlooked a lot to give you the chance to reach your full potential."

Here we go again. I kept my expression neutral, but memories of the crushing blow he'd delivered with his mind at the Council meeting came back to me. It was hard to tell sometimes how he felt and whether he'd be lenient or not.

With the werewolves around, I doubted he'd show his true power again, but I couldn't be sure.

"I'm sorry to disappoint you, sir," I said. The sudden banging of tools made me jerk around, to see a couple of werewolves repairing the front door. Tension bunched my shoulders, and I forced my gaze back to Prescott, who stood over me now.

"You will be punished in time. For now, you should think on how charitable I am to let you continue existing." Smiling, he stalked off toward the den at the back of the house.

"At least we're both still breathing, huh?" Brendan said from the bottom of the stairs. His words were light, but they stood in sharp contrast to his agitated expression.

Vampires didn't have to breathe. I smirked at the joke, appreciating the humor. "For now. However, my biggest fear is for Carmela." I rose to my feet, then strode to him. "Allow me to see to your leg. You should probably shift to expedite the healing process. It worked, to a degree, for her."

"My son is following the instructions of his doctor." Neal descended the steps to stand behind Brendan. "What knowledge do you have of my people's healing?" The words came out in a clipped tone. He narrowed his eyes at me, but he also looked genuinely curious. "And what do you mean the healing process was expedited for her? You are referring to Carmela Santiago, I assume?"

"Before I became a vampire, I was a physician. The subject has kept my interest throughout the centuries, so I've kept up my knowledge of medicine. I also feed my curiosity about other species as more information becomes available to me." Having to explain myself to a werewolf set me on edge, but to be fair, I doubted I was the only one feeling that way. "Yes, I did mean Carmela. I've cared for her while she's been in my home. The lycanthropy in her arm and shoulder was severely impacted, but after being given time to heal and change to her wolf form a couple of times, she appeared to be on the mend."

Sighing, Neal shifted his gaze between me and his son. Apprehension pinched his facial features.

"I trust that he won't do me harm, Dad." Brendan took a few hobbling steps my way. "He's not bad for a vampire."

"Fine." Neal nodded, then disappeared back upstairs.

"You're not bad for a werewolf, either," I said, pointing him toward the kitchen. It would afford us the most privacy on this level without going into the cramped bathroom, which hadn't seen use in ages. While I related more to Brendan these days, I didn't want to be stuck in that tight of a space with him.

He sat on a kitchen chair, then carefully rolled up his pant leg. When he'd managed that, he propped his foot onto the chair next to him. Trying to do anything in my home was awkward, especially with vampires and werewolves constantly walking by and sticking their noses into our business. Their eyes judged us, but I couldn't pay them any attention. We had more pressing concerns.

"Do you regret saving us?" Brendan's question startled me. Even with all we were facing right now, the thought that I shouldn't have saved Carmela—or even both of them—had never occurred to me.

"No, never." I repositioned his leg to look at the wound better. His healing had progressed a lot quicker than Carmela's, even without shifting. I wondered if it was due to him being the future Alpha of Alphas. It stood to reason that their line would be more resilient than normal wolves, but I'd keep that speculation to myself. My kind couldn't be trusted with such knowledge. They might see it as a weapon.

"How does it look?" he prompted, sounding a little concerned. Maybe I'd mused over it for too long.

"Better." I smoothed the pant leg back in place. "I'd still

advise the crutch for now, but..." I lowered my voice and leaned in a little. "If you shift, that should put you back to about eighty percent wellness." I returned to my normal voice for the next part. "From my limited experience, of course. Regardless, we need to track Carmela, and I trust you the most to help me find her."

Brendan winced as he pulled himself into a standing position. "I'll shift." He met my gaze for one of the first times since I'd attempted to take his mind. "We'll find her."

2

CARMELA

*F*rom the corners of my eyes, I watched the darkened hallway go past as the large man carrying me slowed. We passed thick metal doors every so often, and my stomach churned at the muffled cries that carried through them. This had to be a *Cazador* experimentation facility. I'd heard of them, but this was my first time seeing one. Probably my last time, too.

I wanted nothing more than to go home. No! I wanted to be back at Derek's, snuggled up between him and Brendan, their limbs entwined with mine. Where was my home these days, anyway? Would Derek and Brendan think I ran away from all the chaos? No, they'd figure out I was taken and rescue me.

If not, I was doomed. Heaviness settled into my chest. I didn't want to consider that possibility. Not when the pain in my shoulder was squeezing me like a werebear. More than anything, I wanted to be put out of my misery. If my kidnapper didn't set me down soon, I would pass out. There was only so much I could take.

I tried to scream or even take a deep breath, but I couldn't do either. Nothing I did shook me from the paralysis. I hoped it would wear off eventually, but with how I felt right now, I wasn't so sure. If I couldn't even control my breathing, then I highly doubted I could do much more than lay here like a vegetable.

The man shifted his hold on me, gripping my legs tighter.

"Good to see you're back with the female wolf," a deep, masculine voice said from behind me. "She's the correct one this time?"

"She is. I'll take care of her, Jim. There are several nocturnes at the vampire's house—bring back the male werewolf. The Alpha's son. I'll go back in a few for the vampire." He spit the word. "We need to get them before the final targets are taken into protective custody."

My captor clamped my hips, and I was maneuvered until he cradled me in his arms instead of hauling me around like a sack of potatoes. It helped a little with my shoulder, but not much. My head hung back, and I stared at the wall until he supported my neck. I glanced at him for a moment before looking away. He was a really muscular guy.

The man he spoke with wore a black mask with a blue scrollwork design on it. Whereas the man holding me was thickly muscled, the other one had a lean, athletic build.

"I'm the least of your concerns. Just a thought," he said to me. At the end of the hallway, I noticed a large steel door. My heart beat faster. "Don't do anything stupid. I don't want to kill you." His words brought my gaze back to him. The cold expression in his eyes sent a chill down the entire length of my body. At least he didn't look enticed by the idea.

I blinked at him.

"Good. I'll take that as your word." He shifted me in his arms and pushed open the door. "Here we are. Your new home for a while."

I turned my gaze to the room, only able to see part of it.

From what I could see, Elliot sat on the floor, with a few other nocturnes I couldn't place. Two werewolves were chained to the wall, and a woman lay very still before us, on her side. Chandra. *Is she alive? Oh, God...*

The man rested me next to her. "What's wrong with your arm?"

It was a stupid question, since I couldn't talk. Maybe he hoped I'd give some indication with my eyes.

"She was shot in the shoulder by the *Cazador* with one of the new enhanced silver bullets." Elliot's formerly crisp voice sounded rough, if not downright feral.

"Hmm. Even though you violated the Feud, I can't see why they'd want a weakened nocturne like you for their experiments." The masked man narrowed his eyes at me. "Why not finish the job when they had a chance?" He appeared genuinely intrigued, which frightened me the most.

If only I knew.

He knelt and laid me on my back. It wasn't the most comfortable position, but I was a lot happier he'd done this instead of shackling my arms.

I stared at the brick wall, not wanting to look at him any further. He moved to Chandra next. Was he going to hurt her? I strained my eyes to see what he was doing, but he'd moved out of my line of sight.

"Still here and not making any trouble. Good." His leather boots creaked. "Maybe I'll consider what you promised."

My eyes widened a little. What had Chandra done?

3

CHANDRA

*M*y pulse sped as I stared up at Gareth. I wouldn't mind getting out of here with him, but I doubted he'd ever let me escape. *Remember your vow. Revenge, then freedom.* The slight attraction I felt for him warred with my need to eliminate a threat. This was crazy. He wasn't a werewolf, and I didn't want to go outside of my species.

I glanced toward my cousin. Why had they brought her here? No, I remembered. She'd escaped from the *Cazador* before with Brendan and the vampires. I'd only been a mistake, perhaps held as bait. My cousin was the more important captive. Hell, maybe when the vampires raided this place, they'd kill us all except her and Elliot.

Anger boiled beneath my skin, but I quickly suppressed it. *Not now. Not with Gareth so close. He'll know if I break through the stupor.*

He remained crouched over me. His hood was up, covering his hair again. More than ever, I wanted to see his face, but maybe it was better this way. Maybe he'd been scarred in battle and horribly disfigured. It wasn't my business. All I knew was that danger lurked below the humor in his eyes, as if he were so used to darkness that he emitted it like a musky cologne. Gareth trailed his warm hand across my hip and slid it along my thigh to the knee.

Stop toying with me. Arousal formed between my legs, because clearly my body didn't care how messed up I truly was.

The door squeaked behind him, and Gareth sighed. He straightened and turned away from me.

The guard from earlier stood in the doorway, his pants still smelling like urine. Then the scent of blood hit me like a wave, overpowering the piss. But I couldn't get a good look at him. "I'm sorry if I'm disturbing you, sir." He bowed his head, seeming completely unlike the man who'd broken my ribs.

"What is it?" Gareth crossed his arms over his chest. Deathly power radiated from him, crawling over my skin like thousands of bugs.

"Jim had me reprimanded, sir. He instructed me to see you for my next assignment." The guard's voice trembled, and he looked ready to jump out of his skin at a moment's notice.

"Fine. Get yourself new clothes and a shower. After that, grab a bucket and mop the test chamber. I heard the experimental injections with the female faerie went very wrong." He turned to stare at me again. His pupils were white, and he fidgeted with his mask as if it had become uncomfortable.

"Yes, sir." The guard turned to leave, and my eyes widened. The source of the blood smell was clear now—the man's back looked like raw hamburger meat. My wolf stretched toward the surface. *Food.* We were ravenous. I shook my hunger aside. It was a wonder the guard was still standing, particularly as he was human. He paused in the doorway and twisted back toward Gareth. "Sir?"

"What?" Tension tightened his shoulders, and he tore his unearthly gaze away from me.

"I think I need to..." The guard collapsed to the ground in a heap, either unconscious or dead. From this distance, I couldn't be sure.

"Ah, fucking fainters." Gareth hauled the guard up, but kept him at arm's length. He paused in the doorway to look me over from head to toe one last time, then slammed the steel door behind them.

What exactly was he going to do with the man who broke my ribs? Dispose of him? Take him to get medical care? The thought of him killing the guard didn't disturb me. Not after all the pain he'd caused.

4

DEREK

I walked into the living room while Brendan stripped. It wasn't out of respect for his modesty. We'd passed that point earlier, in the bedroom. From what I'd read, and what I'd experienced with Carmela, werewolves were vulnerable during the change. They wouldn't want a vampire stalking about within arm's reach. Still...it was more than that. I'd grown to respect him, both as the mate to my lover and maybe even as a friend.

Upstairs, I heard a few loud bangs, the sound of glass breaking, and Jane cursing in French about werewolves. The sound drew me toward the stairs. *When did the chaos ever end?* Once Elliot was safe, I would be moving, especially now that the werewolves knew where I lived. I needed to have my solitude back, my quiet sanctuary away from danger.

A subtle shift of magical power disturbed the atmosphere behind me. It didn't feel like Brendan. I spun around to see a werewolf lying in the entryway, his head at an awkward angle, and a lithe figure in a mask creeping toward the kitchen. He sprinted back outside the open front door when he realized I'd spotted him, but it was too late.

I lunged forward, ready to kill, but stopped short as Prescott appeared in front of me. His eyes were almost black with power. "Trail him. See where he goes. Don't initiate combat just yet."

With a nod, I darted after the person in black. Disappointment stung me when I drew in his scent—this wasn't the one who had taken Carmela. Regardless, he couldn't get away. I *needed* to find her before anything worse happened. She'd been through so much already that I'd been unable to save her from. The thought of finding her dead warmed my cool blood with rage.

On the opposite side of the street, a few rough-and-tumble *Cazador* staggered drunkenly along the sidewalk, laughing and pushing one another. I couldn't move very fast with them around. It would draw too much attention. If I went to the rooftops, I could stay out of sight.

The hunters turned into a pub at the corner, and I blew out an unnecessary breath. *Good. Maybe they'll drink themselves into a stupor.*

Running into the nearby alleyway, I jumped high. Gripping the rusty fire escape, I propelled myself to the roof. Carmela's faint scent threw me off-guard, and I scanned my surroundings before following it.

Maybe the person who grabbed her hadn't gone through the streets. If she was limp and unable to walk, they might have used the rooftops. I leapt over a gap between two buildings, my mind strictly focused on following Carmela's trail. I paused a few times to suck in deep breaths and made sure I was still on the right path.

A powerful wave of fear and unease crashed through me again, nearly knocking me off-balance. I crouched by the edge of a roof overlooking a massive warehouse. Carmela had to be close. There were no other warehouses around. This had to be the one the faerie told her about. A couple of men milled around a side door, talking and smoking. They appeared to be *Cazador*. I pulled the shadows around myself, not willing to let anyone see me. Something like that could get Carmela killed.

I'd do everything in my power to prevent that. I wanted her safe and in my arms. I would give anything—even my own life—to see her face again.

Noise drew my attention away. Glancing back, I saw two wolves bounding over the rooftops as if they were hounds on a fox hunt. *Damn it...* I jerked my gaze back to see the two men tossing down their cigarette butts as they walked into the building.

Luckily, the door closed right as the wolves hopped onto the rooftop where I perched. I tossed back the shadows to expose my presence to the clumsy beasts. They skittered to a halt, and one took a couple steps back from me, while the second wolf bared his fangs.

"Stop fooling around. I found the building. We must alert the others so we have a better chance of breaking in and getting our people out alive." I hissed the words, hating that they'd caused so much commotion. What if they'd put Carmela at risk with their over-exuberance? *It's fine*, I told myself, trying to calm down. I couldn't let them get to me, not when so much was on the line.

The werewolves cocked their heads to the side, staring at me.

Sighing, I stared at the warehouse one last time before heading back toward my home. Part of me didn't want to leave, not when I was so near Carmela. While I might be an elder vampire, I couldn't sweep down there and save her and Elliot single-handedly. Not when I didn't know what I was up against.

I couldn't go in without backup.

The wolves trailed behind me as I took off running. Their

claws kicked up gravel on the rooftops. We were a little ways off from my row house when something struck me—I'd forgotten all about the mage I'd been chasing. *Shite.*

The masked, hooded figure crouched on a rooftop, staring down into an alleyway. *My* alleyway. Who could he be after now? I frowned, not knowing what to think. I'd pursued him. He'd had plenty of opportunity to sneak up on me while I was preoccupied. Who was this person? Did they really think they could attack me three times in a row? They'd taken my best friend and my love. Who else was there?

Then again, if it'd just been a ploy to hurt me, why would they take Carmela's cousin? It didn't make sense. Maybe they weren't just hunting me.

Brendan... No!

The hooded figure leapt down, and a savage snarl ripped through the air from within the alleyway. I threw all pretense aside and ran at full speed, sailing over the edge of the building to see Brendan pinning the hooded figure to the ground, his fangs squeezing the man's neck.

Relief washed through me. I should've known he could protect himself. Moonlight glinted off a silver blade in the mage's hand.

"Watch out!" I shouted, throwing myself toward them. I caught the mage's hand just as the knife pressed against Brendan's fur. He turned his head toward me and blinked. "I'll take it from here. We don't want to kill him."

Brendan let out a rumbling growl, but he took a couple slow steps away from the downed mage, who looked dumbstruck by us both. His neck was covered by a black turtleneck, but I still smelled the blood from the puncture wounds Brendan had created.

Neal came out from around back. "What's going on here?"

"Another attack. They were after your son." I nodded in Brendan's direction. "He fought bravely."

Brendan slowly nodded back to me, but he bared his fangs a little. I suspected it was a wolfish smile, but it was hard to be sure.

"Damn it. Get in the house, boy," Neal commanded, then pointed at the female werewolf who'd followed the Alpha outside. "Take the nocturne in and secure him." He glanced up, and I followed Neal's gaze to see the two werewolves staring at us from above. "Shift and get down from there. *Now.*"

I turned toward the back door and ran a hand through my hair. Prescott had been right about not attacking. I needed to tell him what I'd found. Besides, I didn't want to get mixed up in the vagaries of werewolf politics.

"Hey," Neal called out.

I glanced back at the small group of werewolves. Was the Alpha talking to me?

"Thank you for helping out my son, and not just this time. He told me that you looked over his wounds previously, and I knew your scent seemed slightly familiar. I realized it was the strange scent from my doorstep." He didn't look pleased, but his expression remained civil.

I froze, unable to believe I had just received thanks from the Alpha of Alphas, not once, but twice in a single night. The world had ended after all. "You're welcome. I wouldn't have left him to die. No one deserves to be hunted by the sick *Cazador* we share this world with."

"Yes, that's the truth. Anyway, carry on." Neal nodded and strode past me to the door, where a couple of other wolves waited. The burgundy-haired she-wolf knocked out the mage before moving him into the house, and Brendan followed after his father in wolf form, limping just a little but seeming much better than before.

This many people around one home was pretty suspicious, especially with all the snarling and growling, but surprisingly none of my neighbors dared poke their heads out to check on the noise. Perhaps they were too scared. Fairly reasonable, considering all of my neighbors were human.

I leaned against the building, deciding to keep some distance between myself and the wolves for the moment. Prescott sauntered toward me, looking a little amused. Maybe he'd overheard the Alpha thanking me. Regardless, he'd be interested in what I'd found on the rooftops.

Brendan. I should've told him too, since it involved our mate.

"I know where she is." I kept my voice low to make sure I could talk without being overheard. "She's being held in a large warehouse, not far from here. I tracked her scent over the rooftops. We need plenty of people on this. The building will likely be quite secure."

Prescott rubbed his chin. "Of course, we'll need to discuss this with the werewolves."

I nodded. "Right."

"I'll talk to their Alpha." Prescott grimaced as if that didn't sound very enticing, but he'd suffer through it. Just so long as I didn't have to engage in the politics.

We headed in. I shut the back door behind us as best I could, content except for the werewolves loitering in my living room. They watched me as if I were an intruder. While they'd taken care of the front door, the back must've been considered my problem. Granted, it wasn't in view of the street, but still, they'd broken it.

After a few minutes, everyone had gathered around their leaders and the prisoner. I perched on one of the bottom stairs near Brendan, who remained in wolf form. He still smelled like Carmela. My chest hurt thinking about her, but having him by my side steeled my nerves. We'd get her back, together. I rested elbows on my thighs, trying to focus on Prescott as he engaged the room, catching everyone up on what we'd learned since Carmela was taken.

Neal removed the hooded figure's mask. The mage was a male in his mid-twenties. He jerked his head up, and his breathing came out in harsh pants as if he'd just been underwater. He looked wildly around the room, struggling in the confines of a foldable metal chair I didn't remember having in my home. "What's going on? Who are you people?"

It seemed he was suffering from amnesia, which went to show how powerful the werewolves were.

Prescott crouched in front of him, making eye contact. "You're here for your own protection. Could you help us?" Prescott's voice had a strange melody to it that told me he was controlling the mage's mind.

He blinked. "Yeah, I guess I could. What do you need my help with?" His tone had a slightly dreamy quality to it, as if he weren't all there.

Frowning, Neal ran a hand through his hair. The Alpha obviously disliked the blatant display of power.

"What is your name, boy?" Prescott asked, leaning in closer.

"Jim."

"Good, Jim. Who do you work for?"

"T...I'm not supposed to say who he is. He's *Cazador*, but...he's different." Frustration swept across his face, as if he wished he could better accommodate Prescott, but the words wouldn't slide off his tongue.

"How is he different, Jim?" Prescott pushed a little more power into his words.

"He's a v..." Jim opened and closed his mouth again, but the words choked in his throat. His whole body shook violently—nearly tipping the chair over—as if drawn into a seizure, and then he went limp.

I pushed forward to assist him, but it was over before I could do anything. *Damn it.* I checked his pulse, but he was dead. Our one good chance of discovering more information before infiltrating the *Cazador* was gone.

"Whoever took Jim out has to have psychic bonds with their minions, especially if he was able to do this at a distance." Prescott turned away from the body and put a little space between them. He downplayed his feelings, but I could tell by his mannerisms that this death bothered him.

"Hopefully whoever did this doesn't know we've already pinpointed their locale," I said. All eyes in the room turned to me as if I had just appeared.

"Yes. They shut down our contact before he could give us anything. Still, we should be careful when we go in. We don't know what will be in store for us." Prescott turned in a circle, looking at the vampires and werewolves in my living room. "We need to stay united. We can't allow the centuries of distrust we're all struggling against to overcome us. We need to be strong allies to take care of this foe preying on our people."

Neal nodded. "Yes, we have to stand together to battle our greatest enemy. After that, we can figure out what the future of our races will be, but this is important for all of us."

Brendan spun his wolfish gaze to me, wearing an almost accusatory glare. But he was right. I should've taken him aside. We were supposed to work together for Carmela. I trusted him to want her back as badly as I did. Besides, he'd proven he was more than capable of defending himself against the hunters.

"All right then. Let's go before they catch on that we know more than they think." Neal nodded to his son. "You're staying here. You aren't in any shape to do this."

Brendan's hackles raised, and he growled.

"I agree with Brendan. She's his mate...our woman." I looked back at him, and he settled a little. "He should go."

Prescott nodded. "That is true. If you believe he should go, then I'm inclined to agree with you, Derek." He switched his gaze to Neal. "But I think we should head to a more secure location. If you went, your people's attention would be more focused on protecting their Alpha than freeing the captives. You know I'm speaking the truth." His tone was neutral but authoritative.

Neal narrowed his eyes at Prescott, seeming pissed that he'd taken the option from him in front of his people. "I'm more than capable of making that decision for myself. Thanks for the concern." His words came out harsh. He looked at his werewolves. "You two stay with me. The rest of you go with my son." They milled around for a moment, casting glances at one another. "Head out. Listen to my son, protect him, and get our people back alive."

I looked to Prescott for the final word. He waved his hand. "Go. Bring everyone to my safe house."

5

CARMELA

*M*y back ached from pressing into the cold hard floor for so long. Sniffles and hushed whimpers came from the other captives in the room. If only I was able to move around as they could, then I could relieve some pressure on my bones and joints.

Why did these people take me? What experiments were they doing here? This was probably where they designed the highly efficient silver bullets I'd nearly died from. *God.* I'd be set up for target practice for them to unload their guns into. Tears formed in my eyes. *No, don't think of that.*

Footsteps sounded from the other side of the massive steel door leading to the hallway. I watched as it creaked open, my heart hammering in my chest. The man with the skull mask lingered in the doorway. His whole demeanor had changed from when he'd come in earlier. He seemed almost like a pained animal now. Taking a deep breath, he peeked into the hallway again before closing the door behind him.

Chandra's breath hitched, and I heard her move just a little.

I focused my attention on him again, trying to get a better look as he approached my cousin. More than ever, I wished I knew what was going on between them.

He mumbled something under his breath. I tried to make out the words, but he spoke in a guttural language I didn't recognize.

A current of dark magic spread through the room, and I heard the rattling of chains as the other captives moved around.

"What did you do, Gareth?" Chandra asked, her voice sounding breathy.

"Don't say a word until I figure out what I'm doing." His voice was gruff and no-nonsense. He moved into my line of sight, and I heard the same low murmuring of words again. His large palm rested against my forehead, pitching me into darkness for a moment before I emerged from my paralysis.

I wiggled my toes and carefully pushed into a sitting position, scooting a little away from him and my cousin, who was cradling her bloody wrists to her chest. Why had he released us? I didn't know whether to thank him or be very afraid. Granted, I doubted he'd take all of us to the experimentation rooms at the same time.

"I'm the least of everyone's concerns." He massaged the back of his neck as he looked over the other prisoners, as if considering them. Surely he'd unbind them too? My cousin and I shouldn't be the only ones freed. Shaking his head, he knelt at Elliot's side to work on his bindings. "Don't just sit there, ladies," he said, nearly snarling at us. "If you want out, do the work."

Chandra climbed to her feet, a little unsteadily, and glanced my way. She reached out her hand to me, keeping the other pressed to her side. "Let's get out of here, cousin," she said. Something obviously troubled her, but now wasn't the best time to ask about it.

I accepted her hand and she carefully pulled me to my feet. My legs wobbled, and I steadied myself against the wall, then set off to help free the dozen other nocturnes here, trying to rip away ropes and pry off the thick manacles with my limited mobility. As more people were freed, more were able to help. I didn't see the fae girl who'd touched my mind, and I wasn't sure if I wanted to know what they'd meant about the experimentation room. What had happened to her? Could they have known she'd helped me?

The door creaked open behind us, and a few cries of panic reverberated throughout the room. Those who were free huddled together in a group, regardless of the differences in species.

Gareth stood between us and the door, standing tall with his hands balled into fists and his shoulders bunched up. He looked fierce, ready to attack at a moment's notice. "Tom."

The other man blocked the doorway. He didn't seem like just another guard. He looked older, with salt and pepper hair, and held an air of authority. His gaze swept the room, taking us all in. "What's going on in here? Are you helping my prisoners escape? Such a shame, my angry little necromancer. I would've thought you smarter, especially after I killed your brother Jim when he merely talked. I know you felt his pain as he died. You brothers had such a special bond. If you don't obey me now, I will kill your precious sister and these weak nocturnes. All that hard work to free her will have been in vain." He held out his hand, and a powerful gust of energy shot from his palm.

Gareth flung his arms open as he began muttering again. He wavered on his feet, but didn't go down. No one else seemed affected. It was as if he'd taken the full force of the attack into himself. "Asshole. Don't hurt her. I'll hunt you down." He continued in the dark language under his breath.

271

His fists clenched at his sides, and the muscles in his arms flexed with the effort.

"You won't be able to hurt me with your black magic. I'm much older than you, Gareth. I've dealt with your kind before." Tom jerked his head toward the door as an alarm rang out from deeper in the building. "No, this isn't how things should be." He looked back at Gareth and hissed, showing his yellowed fangs. "My experiments must continue. The *Cazador* mandates it." Concern drew his brows together for a brief moment. "Looks like I don't have time to deal with you after all. The explosion will have to do. Perhaps I'll keep your enchantress sister around as my blood doll." Without another word, Tom sprinted through the door, and it clanked shut with a heavy finality.

Gareth lunged for the door, but it was no use. He pounded his fist against it.

Shivering, I wrapped my arms around me. Explosion? We were going to die. There was no way we would get past that thick steel door. Tears brushed my lashes. While I was a werewolf, I knew my limits, especially in my current condition, with an unknown amount of time remaining.

A hand descended on my shoulder, and I looked up at Elliot. "This isn't over. We'll figure out something."

I took a deep breath. He was right. We didn't have the luxury of wallowing in self-pity right now. We needed to stay focused. I had two reasons to live: Brendan and Derek.

Gareth dropped his head forward and resumed his muttering. Power swirled around him like a tornado as the stale air thickened, making it harder to breathe. Everyone in the group took a step away as if we all expected him to snap. He exhaled in a rush and thrust his fists at the steel door. It slammed off the hinges, hitting the hallway wall as if smacked by some hulking giant. He staggered against the ragged doorframe.

I blinked, unable to believe he'd been capable of doing that. There was more to him than we knew. Chandra had to be careful. Something was going on between them, some sort of...agreement, or even relationship. Besides, he paid more attention to her than he did anyone else. I didn't want her to get hurt, or worse.

I watched my cousin, who remained focused on Gareth. Complete shock slackened her jaw. She still held her hand against her side, and pain was etched in her face.

Gareth pushed away from the frame and took Chandra by the elbow. "Let's go, everyone. Keep up or be left behind. We're not out of this yet."

6

BRENDAN

*a*ny of the werewolves who had been in wolf form, including myself, had shifted. We were less conspicuous and more in control as humans, although right now my control was shaky in both forms. Derek had kept the information of Carmela's whereabouts to himself, but he'd agreed that I should be here. While I was pissed, we'd both been busy when he'd arrived back. I doubted he'd intentionally held her location from me. *Put it aside. What matters is finding and freeing her.*

We walked down the road, keeping to three small groups of four since the *Cazador* were always suspicious of crowds, and usually dispersed them. Mine consisted of me, Derek, a telepathic vampire, and another werewolf.

"She's in that building. I feel her fear so strongly." Derek nodded to the large warehouse ahead of us. He pinched the bridge of his nose as if wrestling with her emotions.

A twinge of envy swept through me that he could sense her, but it quickly passed. Did I really want to feel her fear? What would that do to me?

I cleared my throat. "We have to remain split up. If we

don't, we might not find the captives in time. Once we're spotted, they'll be in danger. We have to get in and out quickly."

Derek nodded. "You're right. We should probably separate, with six people going to each entrance. Once we're in, they might start killing the captives. We can't allow that to happen."

The telepathic vampire bowed her head to Derek. "*Oui, monsieur.* Message sent."

"Thanks, Jane."

"I'll take a team around back." I looked at Jane, then Derek. "You lead the other through the front."

Derek grimaced. "I don't like that idea. Jane should stay here as a lookout. If anyone else goes in or comes out the front, she can let me know telepathically. We'll go through the back of the warehouse together." He lowered his voice and pointed out, "You're still injured."

My jaw clenched painfully. I didn't like being questioned, and it was better to have a person of authority with each team. But the longer we stood here arguing, the more we risked Carmela's safety. "Fine. Tell everyone to get in position now."

Jane bowed again and blended into the shadows before me to the point that I couldn't see her anymore. Only my sense of smell informed me that she was still there. The other group formed and headed toward the side door. I watched them until they disappeared from sight.

We jogged around to the back. As we closed in on the entrance, the door burst open and a large cluster of people ran toward us. My nose twitched and I let out a harsh breath. They had to be the captives, because they smelled as if they'd been stomping around in filth.

"It's them," I said to Derek, pointing at the people. A couple of familiar faces appeared in the group. Elliot had his hand on Carmela's wrist as they jogged towards us. I also saw two male werewolves who'd lived down the street from me before my father became Alpha. Elliot shifted his gaze in our direction.

Just then, loud explosions boomed through the still night air, toppling most of the group.

A wave of heat passed over me, and fire and debris rained down all around us. I threw my arms over my head to protect myself. Did the other group survive the blast? I'd seen them go inside before we turned the corner. If only they'd waited a little longer... But how did the nocturnes manage to get free in time? Cries rang out around me, but all noise was muffled now.

Carmela. I crawled around the others to where I'd last seen her, desperate to make sure she was okay. Her honey-brown hair—now covered in dirt and debris—stood out from the crowd, and I headed straight for her.

She looked up, and her eyes widened. "Brendan. I'm so happy to see you." She pressed a frantic kiss to my lips. "Where's Derek?"

"He's here." I pushed to my feet and scooped her into my arms. "It's okay. We'll get you to safety." The others were slowly starting to stand now as well, but I didn't see Derek. I scanned the crowd again, worry gnawing on me, until I spotted him.

A tall, muscled man in a skull mask stood in front of Derek. "Where's the man your people captured earlier?" the man asked. Rage and dark energy spread out from him. Had he been one of those taken? Something didn't seem right about him. The other masked guy had been working for the enemy... "He's my brother, and I want his body." The thick muscles in his arms flexed.

"Who is that?" I asked Carmela, keeping my voice low.

"His name is Gareth. All I know is that he was working

for the *Cazador*, but he rescued us. His superior killed his brother for talking, and is holding his sister hostage." She frowned and leaned her head against my chest. "I don't really know."

Derek kept his face completely neutral, as if he were a statue, but I saw his eyes dart over the small crowd. When he saw us, his posture relaxed a little, and he returned his attention to the masked man. "Fine. But you'll have to wait. We need to get everyone off the streets first."

Gareth crossed his arms over his chest, but he didn't push.

Derek closed the distance between us with a few long strides. He leaned in and pressed a firm kiss to Carmela's lips. "I'm so glad you're safe, love." His gaze rose to meet mine. Pain ached within it, and I knew why. "Jane contacted me. The other team hasn't come out yet."

"Damn. We can't waste time second-guessing ourselves, though. We need to move out for the safe house." I looked around at what remained of our team. Several of them were helping up the captured nocturnes.

Jane appeared beside us from the shadows. Blood streamed from her eyes down her face, and even for a vampire she looked entirely too pale. "They're...gone." It took me a moment to recognize what was happening: she was crying.

The building was in ruins. There was no way the other team could have survived the blast.

Elliot grasped Derek by the shoulders and gave him a hug. "It's good to see you. I knew you'd come, to save your lover if nothing else." He nodded toward Carmela.

"Don't be cheeky. I came for you too. I'm glad you're well." Derek ran a hand through his hair. "We need to get everyone to Lord Prescott's safe house, as he requested."

"Aye, let's go." Elliot looked at the crowded alley of

people. "We'll need to split up, though. If we stay in this group, we're just begging for trouble from the *Cazador* patrols."

Gareth walked closer again. "Where does this lord of yours want to meet? I can lead a few people there."

Derek told him, although I could tell he wasn't comfortable giving the stranger that information.

A few nocturnes went up to him with their heads bowed, thanking him for the rescue. Gareth's lips thinned, but he gave a sharp nod of his head. He looked increasingly uncomfortable with the attention. Regardless, I was happy he'd saved the captives. If not for him, we would've been too late for Carmela, her cousin, Elliot, and the others.

7

CHANDRA

I touched a hand to my broken ribs, holding them lightly. It hurt to touch them or even to breathe. I needed to see Dr. Matthews, sooner rather than later. My gaze landed on Gareth, and I sighed, only to end up wincing. What would I do now?

It wasn't like me to feel an attraction for someone like him, especially with the fear he'd caused. *Wrong.* But we didn't have a thing going on—I hadn't even seen his face. Would he even hold me to my pledge? Probably not. I was free now.

I turned toward home, not bothering with the safe house, as the others spread out in their small groups. No one could save me from what I'd face with Uncle William.

A hand gripped my arm, and I glanced up to see who it was. Gareth. My gaze rose to take in his unmasked face. He was more handsome than I could've guessed, without any deformities or the horrid scars I'd imagined.

"Leaving so soon?" His lips tilted in a half-smile. "Don't think I won't find you. Promises aren't made to be broken."

Energy quivered through me from his touch, and I couldn't stop myself from rising to meet his kiss. His lips were soft but aggressive, just as I thought they'd be.

My blood warmed, but I pulled away from him, not willing to open my heart only to be hurt. "That's a small taste of what's to come," I said.

Gareth stood there unmoving, watching me with passion darkening his blue eyes. He took half a step toward me, but stopped himself. "Can't wait."

Carmela was cradled in Brendan Kelly's arms while a dark-haired vampire talked with her. I couldn't understand why Carmela enjoyed the company of vampires, but maybe it wasn't my place to wonder. Perhaps the Feud was around for a reason. I shook my head. I didn't know what to think anymore.

At least she was safe. I'd done one thing right in my life. I only hoped she wouldn't forget about me in my time of need. I didn't look forward to seeing William again, especially after what he'd done. Should I even return home? Maybe I could ask Gareth for a temporary place to stay. When I looked through the crowd, however, he was nowhere to be found.

My shoulders slumped forward, and I headed toward the home I despised. I'd vowed not to return to the streets, and I wouldn't break that promise now. I'd bide my time and hopefully survive the horror. Money was incredibly tight since Uncle William didn't allow me to work, and mates were a distant vision since I wasn't a virgin. Maybe my dreams just weren't meant to come true.

Stopping near the front door, I glanced back at Carmela as her group passed with a few other nocturnes heading for the safe house. At least one of us had succeeded. I leaned against the cold brick wall behind me, not ready to go inside yet, and frowned.

Carmela looked between the vampire and werewolf

adoringly. She smiled, and they laughed a little as they walked. Carmela's vampire wrapped his arm around her waist and pulled her closer.

Jealousy tickled the hardened heart behind my fractured ribs.

My parents hadn't cared for one another. They were driven to marriage because of me. Having a pup outside of wedlock was punishable. Of course, my father had been a player, while my mother was his ball and chain. But she wasn't much better. Neither seemed capable of any real emotion. At least Carmela was lucky in that regard. Her mother really did love her.

Shaking my head, I pushed away from the wall, my ribs aching horribly. Sudden movement blurred before me, and I was slammed back into the bricks. Uncle William fisted his hands over my shoulders, and I yelped. Fear set my heart racing as I stared into his angry eyes.

"Let go of me," I said, groaning in pain. My shoulders were still agonizingly sore from being chained to the wall and lying on the cement floor.

"You betraying bitch. Where were you? The Alpha sent people out to search for you. Did they find you? You better not have said anything about us." He sneered, but his gaze caught the group across the street. "No, not my daughter." He released me, causing me to stumble back against the wall, and spun around to take off after Carmela.

Shooting pain ripped through my torso as I kicked out at him. I aimed for his kneecap, but my foot skimmed his thigh instead. I wouldn't let him hurt Carmela. My cousin seemed happy for the first time in a while.

William grabbed my foot, twisting until the bones crunched. I started to scream, but he slammed his knee into my stomach, sending the oxygen exploding from my lungs.

Blackness narrowed my vision, and I saw Carmela's

vampire over William's shoulder a moment before all light faded away.

8

CARMELA

a familiar scream shrilled in my ears, and I snapped my head in that direction. We were close to the house I'd escaped from a few days ago, but I was so swept up in being back with Brendan and Derek that I hadn't thought much of it.

Fear spiked within me as I saw Chandra crumple to the ground beneath my father, after he jammed his knee into her stomach. I raced toward them, only to be passed by Brendan and Derek. The latter grabbed Father by the back of the neck and slammed him into the brick wall, face-first.

Behind me came gasps and soft cries from the small group I'd come out of the dungeon with. I grabbed Chandra's hand and dragged her away from the fight. What did I want to happen? Should I look away and let them beat him? While William Santiago was a horrible man, he was still my father.

A savage growl resonated through the quiet night, and Father looked between his two attackers, drawing himself to his full height. He threw a heavy punch at Derek, but it seemed like Brendan had been expecting that, because he tossed his own, catching William in the side of the head.

Derek stumbled backward to where Chandra had lain moments before. He lunged forward and slammed his fist into my father's stomach as William turned to assault Brendan. Air surged from my father's lungs, and he staggered back.

If I didn't move Chandra farther away, we were going to be stepped on, or worse, used as leverage during the fight.

Chandra opened her eyes, her breath wheezing. "Ah, please. I don't want to move. Hurts too badly." Pain drenched her face. There was obviously more to her condition than what I could see.

"Allow me," Elliot said, kneeling beside me. He scooped Chandra up carefully, then dodged as Derek smacked into the wall near us after a hard right hook. Pieces of brick exploded outward from the impact.

Derek brushed it off. He bared his fangs and leapt for Father's throat.

Brendan knocked William out with a swift punch to the back of the head, then clamped his fist tight over Father's throat. "No. He might be a monster, but he's a werewolf too. He'll be judged and punished by my Alpha."

Worry tightened my throat. What if my father schmoozed his way out of trouble and didn't face any consequences? What if Derek's desire to kill him was my only chance for true freedom? I wrapped my arm around my stomach, suddenly feeling vulnerable and cold in the warm evening air.

Derek hissed. He turned his gaze toward me, and his fierce expression softened. "Fine. He can be tried by your father, Brendan. Let's just hope he makes the right decision, or this fight might not be over yet."

"Believe me," Brendan said, and his voice was almost a growl, "I wouldn't stand idly by and let that happen." He looked at me with a red-hot stare, one that mixed with passion and possession.

My body heated up, and any chill I'd had evaporated. I believed them both. They'd thrown themselves headlong into danger to rescue and protect me. My fear dissipated.

The thudding of heavy footsteps caught my attention, tearing me away from my freeing realization. Before I could do or say anything, a loud gunshot rang through the air. "We have to get out of here. The *Cazador* are coming." I looked to Derek, then Brendan. "Everyone should go. You should be fairly safe, for now. Just stick to the alleys and the shadows."

The other prisoners from the dungeon all rushed off in different directions. Some darted down alleys, and others took to flight like birds. If only...

Derek lifted me into his arms, and we ran.

9

BRENDAN

I could hardly stand upright by the time we finally got to Lord Prescott's safe house. I'd run with Carmela's father over my shoulder, which on a good day wouldn't have been so bad, but my leg was still trying to heal. The glimpses of concern I kept getting from Carmela unnerved me, so I kept my attention on the room.

I leaned heavily against a wall near my dad while Prescott perched on his massive chair, his arms crossed over his chest. Impatience creased the corners of his eyes. "Where is everyone else?" Prescott asked.

Derek met my gaze. Frustration and sadness tightened his expression, and he looked back to Prescott. "Some ran home. Others... They didn't make it. We split up, thinking if we went into the warehouse's two entrances we'd have a better chance of finding the captive nocturnes alive. However, the building exploded shortly after the other team went inside."

A sniffle sounded nearby, and I glanced up to see Jane hanging her head. She turned away, wiping at the scarlet teardrop sliding along her cheeks.

"We must find out who this enemy is and take him down.

If only we knew more." Prescott fixed his attention on Elliot. "Do you know anything about your captor?"

"Tom. It was Tom." He said the name as if it should mean something.

From the look of disgrace and horror on the vampires' faces, I was almost afraid to ask. "Who's Tom?"

"He was a vampire with a seat on the High Council." Elliot turned his attention back to Prescott. "He came into the room where we were being held and spoke with Gareth, the necromancer guard who helped us escape. He told us about an explosion, and said that this wasn't the way it was supposed to end. I'm not sure what he meant by that, only that he uses the *Cazador* to police the races and ensure the Feud continues."

"I see." Neal rubbed a hand over his stubbly chin. "What else do you know about this guard?"

"He helped us because Tom killed his brother, Jim." Elliot cast a glance at Carmela's cousin, half passed-out in his arms. "He was quite interested in this one. Said he'd be finding her in the future."

Chandra opened her eyes, and a low growl rumbled in her throat. Other than that, she didn't react to his words.

"Enough, pup!" Neal snapped. She went silent and turned her gaze to her Alpha. "If you come in contact with this man, you will report to me about it." He gave her a long, assessing stare. "I'm reactivating you in the Militia once you're healed." He pointed at two werewolf guards who'd stayed with him. "The girls need to be seen by Dr. Matthews. Escort them home."

Elliot handed her over to one of the werewolves and sat in a chair heavily, as if he'd spent all of his energy on just holding her.

I pushed away from the wall to go with the werewolves. No way would I sit back and let my mate walk away with them. She'd been captured once, and I didn't want to repeat that experience. Not with the enemy still out there.

Derek piped up again. "Wait. The necromancer did ask me about retrieving Jim's body."

Neal and Prescott both turned toward him, no longer interested in the female werewolves. "What did you say to him?" Neal asked.

"I told him I was busy at the moment, but I'd let him have his brother." Derek stomped his foot. "Damn it. We're probably too late."

Prescott nodded at the vampire near him. "Go. Try to intercept this necromancer and bring him back here. We should talk with him."

"Good idea," Neal said, signaling one of his wolves to tag along. "If we find him, we can learn more about our enemy."

Carmela laced her fingers with mine. Concern weighted her gaze, and I detected a trace of something else as well. Apprehension, maybe? Then again, going back to the home were she'd almost been raped by her father had to be terrifying. I moved to go with her, but Dad gripped my wrist and shook his head.

She frowned and let me go, then brushed her hand along Derek's arm before walking out of the room with the second werewolf guard.

Prescott waited until the girls were out of the room before speaking again. "We still have business to attend to."

Neal nodded. He pointed at his remaining people in the room. "Go. Take William to the cage to await judgment. I'll let you know if there's anything else."

The vampires stayed firmly in position. "Away with you," Prescott said, flicking his wrist.

Jane helped Elliot to the door, and they joined everyone else in the smaller antechamber outside.

The room went silent for a few minutes. No one said a

word. I stood there, keeping my expression pleasantly neutral. Why had they kept me and Derek here when the others were told to leave? This had to be about Carmela. I should've known judgement would come for us...

"You both have shown incredible initiative to bridge the gap between our species. If we are to remain at peace, then certain questions must be asked and answered." Prescott flicked his gaze to Neal. "We've come to the conclusion that intermediaries should be in place to continue good relations. You are both experienced, strong, and everyone listened to you when you sought to rescue the missing."

A feeling of foreboding churned in my chest. It all sounded a little too good to be true. I shifted my gaze to my dad.

Neal nodded. "With both of you claiming Carmela, you've tied our hands. We would each be out a high-ranking member of our respective societies if the proper punishment —death—were meted out. Don't think that either of us is happy with your subterfuge, but it can be overlooked—once, and at a cost." He shot me a seething glare before turning his gaze on Derek. "Your interest in my son's mate is beyond my comprehension, but Prescott assured me that you...being with her won't negatively affect my lineage, as your kind cannot produce children."

Derek frowned at him but inclined his head. "Yes, that's true." He met my gaze, not looking particularly happy with all of this.

"We're all in agreement then." Prescott clapped his hands and rose to his feet. "I shall be seeing you at the next High Council meeting, Derek."

Derek turned on his heel and walked toward the door. I followed after him, ready to be out of this suffocating room.

Neal grabbed me by the wrist and leveled his gaze at me. "Once Carmela has been seen by the physician, you *will* take her to one of our safe houses. We have a lot to talk about." His stare slid past my face, and I turned slightly to see Derek watching us. Neal's jaw ticked a couple times as he ground his teeth. "You can join them. However, you'll stay out of Pack business, and figure out your own sleeping arrangements." He released his hold on me and turned away.

Even as they placed new responsibility on us, I could only wonder if this was the real punishment. But nocturnes did desperately need a champion to step up and unite us so we could defend ourselves. Besides, if the vampires and werewolves remained out of the Feud, our lives with Carmela would be much better.

10

CARMELA

I sat on the edge of Chandra's bed while Mother stood on the opposite side, next to Dr. Matthews. Several bruises marred my mother's face. This was the first time I'd seen her since the incident with Father. Memories crashed back through me, but I shoved them away. I would *not* focus on that anymore. My life had changed for the better now.

The werewolf guard leaned against the wall in the far corner, looking a little uncomfortable, as if he were intruding on us. No one else really paid him any attention.

Dr. Matthews pulled Chandra's shirt up just under her breasts, and lightly pressed on her torso. "Seems like quite a number was done on you. Whether by William or the kidnappers, I'm not sure. The best way to heal your ribs is with rest. The broken bones will heal on their own, but I'll give you medication to help with the pain." He glanced to my mother. "Katarina, if you wouldn't mind getting some for her from my bag..."

My mother smiled at him, but she paused. "Chandra, I know you'll be heading back to the Militia. I'm sorry you went through all that torment too, but thank you for protecting Carmela. Eventually, I'll be putting the house on the market. We'll talk about you moving your things from here once you're in better shape."

Chandra clenched my hand tightly. Pain scrunched up her face, but she nodded, simply fixing her gaze on the ceiling. My heart went out to her. Everyone else had a place to go now. Granted, I wasn't sure where mine was, but I knew my mates were looking out for me. She didn't have that.

"How are you going to make it on your own, Mom? Father used to provide for us." I didn't blame her for letting this place go. This house had too many bad memories.

Mother looked at Dr. Matthews and smiled softly. "Dr. Matthews is allowing me to become his nurse. It's something he's mentioned a few times before, but your father never would have allowed it. Thank you once again, Doctor. I appreciate it."

His cheeks turned rosy and he chuckled. He lowered his lashes, a hint of embarrassment fluttering in his eyes. I had a sneaking suspicion that he'd like her as more than his nurse, but my father was still alive. Until his death, she wouldn't be able to fully move on. "You're talented and well-educated. It does me, and our patients, a great service to have you." He glanced back down at Chandra. "Now then..."

"I'm sorry, but I think I'm going to lie down," I said. Chandra released her hold on my hand as I stood. "Get better, cousin."

"Thanks." She squeezed her eyes shut.

Mother looked between us before the doctor piped up, "Yes, that's a good idea. Rest for a while. It'll do you good." He grinned. "Doctor's orders." He always found a way to say that phrase.

Smiling, I walked down the hall to my bedroom. The

other werewolf guard sat on the stairs, blocking anyone from coming up or going down. He turned to look at me and then glanced away.

My hand hovered over the doorknob of my room, and I grimaced, not wanting to go inside. The last time I'd been here, I was desperate to get away from this place. To be here voluntarily startled me a little. Maybe I could nap downstairs… I glanced at the guard's back again. The last thing I wanted was to show weakness, so I shoved the door open. Taking a deep breath, I looked around the room. Flashes of my father's angry face flickered in my mind's eye.

He's not here. He can't hurt me anymore.

I took a deep breath, letting it out slowly before heading to the bed. It was neatly made with fresh bed linens that smelled clean and cottony. I eased onto the bed and closed my eyes.

Being here reminded me of how much my life had changed. Where were the men in my life who mattered most to me? What was Prescott and Neal doing with them? I wished we were together again.

11

CARMELA

linking my eyes open in the twilight of my bedroom, I heard a low male voice downstairs talking with my mother. It didn't sound like Dr. Matthews at all. My heart seized in my chest, but I forced myself to listen in until I identified the speaker—Brendan.

I breathed a sigh of relief and climbed out of bed. Walking to the top of the stairs, which was no longer blocked by the werewolf guard, I saw Derek and Brendan standing near the door. My breath caught in my throat.

Brendan turned his gaze my way, and it burned hot when he saw me standing there in my nightgown. He took a step toward the bottom of the stairs while Derek drank me in. His eyes ran over my body as if he were undressing me in his mind.

My mother came into view at Derek's side, and she frowned, likely at my lack of proper clothes. But Brendan and Derek had seen much more than my nightgown. "You should get dressed, dear. Our Alpha requests that you accompany Brendan to a safe house. He needs to speak with you, and you're a mated woman now." She smiled sadly. "It's time for you to find your place out in the world, with them." She looked to Brendan. "Once you have a home, she can move her things."

Brendan nodded and returned his warm gaze to me. His muscles were tense, as if he was forcing himself to remain in place.

Derek's smile scorched my insides, but he seemed almost intrigued by the way Brendan and I were reacting to one another. He looked like he was filing the information away for the future.

My pulse spiked, and I went back to my room. I pulled out several outfits from my closet, trying to figure out the right one to wear for a meeting with the Alpha. While I knew we were going to see Brendan's father and likely answer a ton of questions about whatever he needed to know, all I could think of was the immense pleasure I'd experienced being between Brendan's and Derek's bodies.

I settled on a black skirt that brushed my knees, with a red blouse and strappy sandals. Dr. Matthews had examined me shortly before leaving, and said that with another shift, I wouldn't even need the sling anymore. I couldn't wait.

I walked downstairs to meet them. Brendan and Derek were in my father's former office, sitting by the lit fireplace and talking low enough for privacy. Negative memories of my last experience in that room washed over me, but I shook them off. "Hi," I said, drawing their attention.

Derek stood and offered me his hand. I took it, then walked into his arms and hugged him instead. He gently held me to his chest, then guided me toward Brendan, who wrapped his arms around me and pulled me close. "We should go," Derek said. "Your father is expecting you two to arrive any time now."

My mother walked into the study from the kitchen. "Be

safe, sweetheart. You've been through so much recently." She didn't know the half of it. "I hope I'll see you again soon."

"You will, Mom." I smiled and gave her a goodbye hug before leaving with Derek and Brendan.

We walked for a while in comfortable silence. The warm breeze on my face was amazing after being in the dungeon. After the madness of having our lives on the line and then me being kidnapped, just being in their presence was so sweet. But questions plagued me about the last time I'd seen them. They'd both seemed a lot more somber.

Derek beat me to it, though. "How are you doing?" he asked. He slid his hand over my back, and it soothed me like a cooling balm.

I drew in a deep breath, calming myself. "I'm doing well. I was worried I might not see you guys again. When they kept you two there, yet sent everyone else away..." My throat tightened.

"It's okay." Brendan lowered his voice. "They made us liaisons for our species, to help keep us united and prevent us from falling back into the Feud." He held her hand and brushed his thumb over her knuckles. "I stocked the safe house with some groceries, if you're hungry. I bought a little bit of everything: steak, burgers, chicken, pasta. We could have anything you'd like. But we don't have time to hit a restaurant, since we have to meet with my dad."

"I'm okay, but I might take you up on the steaks later." I paused a moment, then glanced up at him. "What does Neal need to talk with us about?" We stopped at a nondescript, if not cozy-looking, building.

Grimacing, Brendan looked over his shoulder. "Not sure. We'll find out soon, though."

"Your father is already waiting inside." A werewolf guard frowned at Derek, giving him a skeptical look. "Follow me."

We walked into the house's tight hallway, passing a few

closed doors before it opened into a large living room with shabby-chic furniture. Neal leaned back in a chair that faced a couch big enough for three people.

"Take a seat. All of you." He nodded to our guard, who walked back outside. "Carmela, I want you to tell me everything." Neal leaned forward in his seat. "Everything your father did to you, your cousin, and your mother. Everything you did with Derek and Brendan. Be completely honest with me. I'll know if you're not being truthful."

I bit my lower lip and shifted in my seat. This felt more like an interrogation than a talk with my father-in-law, but I started at the beginning, telling him about my parents' relationship when I was born and how it shifted over time to become what it is...was. I related everything my cousin had told me, and how she'd sacrificed herself for me when my father almost raped me. "The night the *Cazador* raided the *Teatro de la Noche*, my cousin and I were staying to watch both movies there. We managed to escape the building, but we split up to get away from the hunters that caught sight of us. She made it home, but I wasn't so lucky. They shot me, but Derek..." I placed my hand on his leg just above the knee. "He saved me."

"That's noble, but why would you do such a thing considering we are—were—enemies?" Neal shifted his thoughtful look to Derek.

"I've witnessed the *Cazador* chase down many people, but when I saw her, I couldn't help it." He kept his expression calm and neutral. "She's like a breath of fresh air after the many centuries I've lived. Rescuing her was like an uncontrollable instinct."

Neal returned his gaze to me and leaned back. "Continue with your story."

I told him the rest of what had happened: how I'd escaped from Derek because I was worried about Chandra, how my father had treated me when I'd gotten home, meeting Brendan and going on our date, even about asking Brendan not to tell on Derek.

Brendan wrapped his arm carefully around my shoulders and pulled me a little closer. "I didn't know things were that bad. If I had, we could've talked with my dad."

"That's true, but maybe things worked out in the long run." Neal looked between the three of us. "You'll all have to handle the path you've chosen together." He rose from his chair. "Thank you for telling me what happened to you, Carmela. Your father will be banished from the city for his crimes against you and your family. Death would be too kind for him. He'll live with the consequences of his actions in the Outskirts."

My heart skipped a beat. Part of me was pleased with the sentence. Banishment was like a second death for werewolves. My father would be dead to the Pack and therefore give up his claim on my mother. She'd finally be free from him. I sighed in relief.

"Thank you, Alpha." I bowed my head to him.

"Call me Neal." Neal smiled. "But in the future, don't keep secrets like that. It helps no one and puts your life in danger." He looked to Brendan. "I do forgive you. You did what you could to keep the one you care for safe, even if you made a few poor decisions. Get some rest. I'll be around. The guards will keep you all safe, and you know how to contact me if you need me."

"Thanks, Dad," Brendan said, and walked him to the door. It was hard to believe that we'd made it. Everything would be okay after all.

CARMELA

*S*everal days had passed since Brendan and Derek had rescued me. It was a little strange at first, living with the two of them at the werewolf safe house day in and day out, but we'd fallen into a nice routine, aside from a few notable events: the Pack accepting my mating with Brendan, no longer needing my shoulder splint, and witnessing my father's banishment, with my mother and Chandra.

I squeezed my eyes shut as the memory came back.

My family and I stood with Neal as a few brawny werewolves supervised my father. He raged at us, spewing curses and threats. Each time Father jerked against the men holding him, I jumped, wondering if next time they might not be able to restrain him. One of the many gates to the city opened, and he was shoved out into the Outskirts. My chest clenched at seeing that place again. I'd only seen it once before, passing through during my Militia training.

"You are hereby banished from this city. If you're ever spotted inside these walls, you won't be escorted back out—you will be killed. Good bye, William." Neal nodded to his man operating the gate, and he closed it again.

My father-in-law had many more connections than I'd

ever imagined. He'd talked us through what would happen beforehand. If William tried to reenter, Neal's informants would alert him.

Sighing, I brushed it all aside. Something was mentally wrong with my father. I knew that now. He wasn't a typical male werewolf, as I'd wrongly assumed.

During the day, Brendan and I had become close. We searched for a new home fit for the three of us, while Derek slept in the master bedroom's closet. He'd reinforced the door and installed locks for added peace of mind, almost creating a panic room out of it. When the sun set, the three of us enjoyed the nightlife together and explored our sensual side in the bedroom.

While we were free to live our lives, I knew there was an expectation for me to get pregnant now that Brendan and I were officially mated. He didn't say anything about it one way or the other, though. He was just there when I needed him, kind and caring.

I walked into the bedroom, knowing it was nearly time for Derek to wake up. Taking a deep breath, I caught the fresh scent of peppermint and smiled. I slid off my clothes and folded them, laying them on a chair in the corner. The doorknob squeaked a little as it turned, and I glanced back at Derek.

He looked a little sleepy until his gaze landed on me. I slid my tongue over my dry lips, and he lowered his gaze to take in the small action. My naked flesh lit a dark fire within his eyes. His gaze dipped ever lower, warming my body just from the feeling of it on my skin. He stalked toward me, but looked at the door. "Where's Brendan?"

"Just finished preparing dinner." Brendan slipped off his shirt and threw it to the floor. His muscular abs flexed from the swift movement, making my mouth water. "It'll be in the oven for just about an hour. We have some time to kill."

Grinning, I perched on the side of the bed, spreading my legs a little for effect. "Going to make me work up an appetite?"

"I know I will." Derek crawled onto the bed behind me. He ran his hands over my shoulders and down my arms before sliding his palms up to caress my breasts. I leaned into him, savoring the sensation of his cool chest against my back, and then I turned my head and kissed him slowly and sensually.

He slid his thumbs over my nipples, but pulled his mouth from mine. Derek tilted my head to the side, letting his lips tease the flesh over my pulse. His hot breath sent shivers down my spine.

My heart thundered in my chest. I ached to be filled—craved what they would give me.

Brendan pressed between my legs, his hands pushing my knees apart. He tilted my head up and grazed his lips against mine. The electricity between us sparked into pure fire.

Derek pulled back a little, letting Brendan gain more access to my body. They usually alternated who had me first, but Derek knew my concerns over getting pregnant. I think he let Brendan have priority...for now.

Brendan kissed me hard, thrusting his tongue into my mouth and claiming me in the same fierce way I wanted to feel his body in mine. He laid me down on the bed, never breaking from our embrace. His shaky hands slid over me, as if he wanted to memorize my curves.

He ran his tongue over my skin, and I moaned at the pleasure radiating through me. He crept lower, to my stomach, peppering small bites and nibbles across my torso.

I writhed beneath him, aching and anticipating what was to come. He teased me until I was panting and throwing aside any remaining inhibitions I had. I took Derek's hand and closed his fingers around my breast as Brendan's warm breath caressed my thigh. His tongue slid slowly along my entrance, tasting me, and I bit back a yelp.

Derek squeezed my nipple and rolled it between his fingers, just hard enough for pain and pleasure to collide. I arched my back and moaned. "Yes. I need you both."

Brendan brought his mouth up to my clit and sucked, slipping a finger inside me at the same time. My body bucked under his tongue's onslaught. I slid my hand down, massaging my fingers through his hair. Just as I felt ready to tip over the edge, he pulled away. A growl rumbled in my chest. Maybe my beast wasn't as tame as I'd thought. The idea made me grin.

Derek pulled back from kissing me as he drew my nipples to hard peaks. Pain and a bead of moisture welled on my lip. I licked it, tasting the coppery blood. He frowned at the nick on my lip and slid his tongue over it, healing the wound.

"I need to be in you." Brendan's voice was more of a snarl than actual words. The men exchanged glances, and Derek helped roll me to my stomach. While he knew I was better, I think he was a little too cautious of me using my barely healed arm too much. It was sweet.

My gaze descended on the bulge and the spreading bead of moisture on Derek's silken boxers. I licked my lips, pushing down his underwear. Derek locked his lusty gaze with mine.

Brendan pressed his hard length against my entrance, teasing me, then slowly he eased himself inside me, inch by inch. He paused when he was as deep as he could go, giving me time to adjust.

The angle made me cry out in pleasure, and I raked my nails down Derek's thighs, leaving thin red marks behind.

Derek gave a harsh sigh, his hands tangled in my hair as my mouth covered his cock like a warm velvet glove. He moved his hips, rocking himself deeper into my mouth just as Brendan began thrusting into me, gripping my hips for leverage.

Having them both inside me at the same time was beyond anything I could've imagined. Derek and Brendan quickly found a compatible rhythm, moving me back and forth between them. In the midst of my heat and mounting pleasure, I felt safe and at home with them. They showed their love for me in their actions, and that meant more than words could describe.

Perspiration built up on our skin, glistening in the bedroom's dim light.

Each thrust drew me closer to the edge, and I groaned against the pleasurable onslaught. They were in control of my desires, and my body listened to their commands.

My core clenched as ecstasy sent me reeling. I moaned around Derek's length, and he tightened his grip on my hair. His seed spilled down my throat as Brendan climaxed inside me. I panicked a little at the overwhelming sensations all raining down at once, but quickly rebounded, drinking in as much of Derek as I could while Brendan's roars of pleasure slowly subsided.

My body shook, and my bones and muscles all felt like they'd give out at any moment. Derek moved to the side so I could lie down next to him as Brendan collapsed beside us.

Brendan nuzzled against me, pressing his nose into my hair as Derek slid his leg between mine. My eyes drifted closed just as the timer went off, indicating that dinner was ready.

Derek pushed up on his elbows. He smiled at me and trailed his fingertips along my jaw line. "I'll turn off the oven while you two get dressed." He slid off the bed wearing only his boxers. I hated to see him go. "I love you, Carmela."

Brendan tilted my head to the side, pressing a soft kiss to my neck. "I love you as well."

"I love you both," I said, looking between them. "My life is better with you in it."

Life was now far better than I could've ever imagined. I'd searched for love, not a restricted life where I'd have to spit out children and fulfill a role. While I'd still have to do the latter part, it was okay, because I had two mates I deeply cared for and who cared for me. My dreams had come true in a big way.

———

Looking for more sexy shifters? Grab the first book in the bestselling Cry Wolf series *The Witch Who Cried Wolf*...

AUTHOR'S NOTE

Thank you for reading *Beneath the Broken Moon: Season One*. I hope you enjoyed it!

The world building and interesting characters in the first season of *Beneath the Broken Moon* made this such an exciting story to write. There were several firsts for me here. I'd never written a post-apocalyptic dystopian paranormal romance before. Plus, having the Romeo and Juliet type dynamic with Derek and Carmela was a lot of fun since they're from races that hate each other. Throwing in handsome and sweet Brendan, too... He was so delightful. It was a full-on writing by the seat of my pants adventure with these the books, that's for sure.

Please consider leaving a review at the retailer's website or on Goodreads, even if it's a line or two. It truly helps!

Craving more? Get *Hunter's Moon Rising*, a Cry Wolf bonus story about a woman who learns she's dating a werewolf here.

ABOUT THE AUTHOR

Sarah Mäkelä is a New York Times and USA Today Bestselling New Adult Paranormal Romance Author. If shifters, witches, and vampires tangled up in dark, passionate stories are your thing, you're in the right place. Her books deliver romance with a bite, literally.

When she's not writing, Sarah reads sexy books, watches scary movies with her spouse, dives into magical research, or spoils the pets who rule the house. She's also an avid gamer and a night-light enthusiast because you never know what's lurking in the dark. Whenever she can, she loves traveling to new places, finding inspiration and fueling her imagination along the way.

- amazon.com/author/sarahmakela
- bookbub.com/authors/sarah-makela
- instagram.com/authorsarahmakela
- facebook.com/authorsarahmakela
- x.com/sarahmakela
- goodreads.com/sarahmakela
- pinterest.com/authorsarahmakela

ALSO BY SARAH MÄKELÄ

Currently Available for Free *

Cry Wolf Series

(Shifter/Witch Romance)

Book 0.5: Hunter's Moon Rising

Book 1: The Witch Who Cried Wolf *

Book 2: Cold Moon Rising

Book 3: The Wolf Who Played With Fire

Book 4: Highland Moon Rising

Book 5: The Selkie Who Loved A Wolf

Book 6: The Leopard Who Claimed A Wolf

Cry Wolf Series Boxed Set (Books 1-3)

Beneath the Broken Moon Serial

(Shifter/Vampire Why Choose Romance)

Part 1 *

Part 2

Part 3

Part 4

Part 5

Season One (Parts 1-5)

Edge of Oblivion

Book 1: The Assassin's Mark

Book 2: The Thief's Gambit

The Amazon Chronicles Series

(Shifter Romance)

Book 1: Jungle Heat

Book 2: Jungle Fire

Book 3: Jungle Blaze

Book 4: Jungle Burn

The Amazon Chronicles Collection

Hacked Investigations Series

(Futuristic Paranormal Romance)

Book 1: Techno Crazed

Book 2: Savage Bytes

Book 2.5: Internet Dating for Gnomes *

Book 3: Blacklist Rogue

Book 4: Digital Slave

Courts of Light and Dark

(Fantasy Romance)

Book 1: Captivated

Book 2: Surrendered

Standalones

Moonlit Feathers

Captive Moonlight

Vera's Christmas Elf

www.ingramcontent.com/pod-product-compliance
Lightning Source LLC
Chambersburg PA
CBHW061538170626
46811CB00001B/28